THE DYING LIGHT

THE JAKE SAWYER SERIES (BOOK 3)

ANDREW LOWE

GET A FREE JAKE SAWYER NOVELLA

Sign up for the no-spam newsletter and get a FREE copy of the Sawyer prequel novella **THE LONG DARK**.

Check the details at the end of this book.

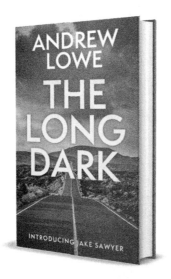

Email: andrew@andrewlowewriter.com
Web: andrewlowewriter.com
Twitter: @andylowe99

First published in 2019 by Redpoint Books
This edition April 2024
Cover photograph © Mat Troke Photography
Cover by Book Cover Shop

ISBN: 978-1-9997290-6-6

For Tom and Josh

Fancy thinking the Beast was something you could hunt and kill!

— WILLIAM GOLDING, *LORD OF THE FLIES*

PROLOGUE

The girl swished through a patch of long grass and dropped to her knees in the shadow of a tall perimeter hedge. She was nine, maybe ten, with long brown hair gathered in the fur-lined hood of a pear-green winter parka.

She dug into the cold earth with chewed-down fingernails and raised a few chunks of soil, petrified by the morning frost. She had been promised snow, but had woken only to a brief swirl of hail as it scattered over the bedroom window.

She looked back at the building: a vast three-storey farmhouse set at the end of a broad driveway. The front lawn was open to the elements, with a high fence and road entrance sealed by a pair of wrought iron gates. But here in the sheltered back garden, the plants craned for their morning flare of filtered sunshine, and sulked in the shade for the rest of the day.

The girl swept the soil from her hands and peeked through the gap in the hedge. She had been working on it for five days now: unpicking the branches, blunting the hawthorn, folding the leaves back into place to retain an illusion of density. She squinted at the empty meadows,

1

crusted white by frozen dew. The ground dipped away to the horizon, swallowed by a grove of evergreens, swaying in the half-light.

The side door opened and shut, and the girl scrabbled backwards, away from the gap. A short, sunken woman appeared at the edge of the garden and pulled on a black woollen hat and a pair of yellow gloves. She smiled and hobbled down a stone staircase, her face misted behind vapours of laboured breath.

'Come on, love. It's a cold one today. Best be inside.'

The girl cast her wide blue eyes up at the woman. 'Can I please stay out for a bit? I don't feel very well. Fresh air is nice.'

The woman tilted her head. She was in her mid-sixties; a little hefty but well preserved, with the hint of a sparkle in her narrowed eyes. 'Okay. But stay close, remember?' She turned and hauled herself back up to the house, glancing behind as she re-entered through the side door.

The girl shuffled back to the gap. She reached down her leg and rolled back the fabric of her jeans. The metal collar was locked tight around her ankle, with only the slightest gap for circulation. She brushed her fingertips over the rough metal and gazed out at the field beyond.

How long to the trees? A few minutes of sprinting?

But what was beyond them? If she could make it, maybe she could stay hidden in the forest, find her way to a road.

Cars, people.

Her breath came in short bursts now. Panting. Her heart beating hard and fast.

A quick look back at the house.

All quiet.

She reached forward and prised open the gap,

shouldering her way through the hedge and into the weeds at the fringe of the field.

She stumbled, rose up and ran, out across the open grass. A lateral blast of wind staggered her, but she leaned into it and kept her aim, charging for the trees.

A jolt of pain, surging up from her feet, ripping through her core, flashing outwards to her fingertips. A vibration, rattling her teeth and bones. A buzzing sound in her ears.

Her whole body stiffened, and her view of the treeline switched to the dirty white sky, as her head was yanked back by some unseen force.

The buzzing and vibration stopped and she tilted, no longer in control of her legs. The ground was cold and brittle, and she dragged her arms forward, trying to push herself back onto her feet.

Another jolt. More vibration. All ambient sound shut out by the buzzing. Her limbs tensed again: joints frozen, suspended. She willed herself on, but her body wouldn't comply.

The sound cut out, and her body relaxed. But she was exhausted now. Face down, flat out.

A shout. The woman, somewhere back near the house.

A male voice in response.

Crunching behind.

The girl twisted her head round and saw the man approach. He adjusted something on a handheld device and slipped it into the inside pocket of a dark-brown leather jacket. He loomed over her: tall and slender, struggling to stay upright in the wind.

He dipped his head and studied her. There was hurt in his eyes. Disappointment.

He scooped up the girl and turned back towards the house.

PART ONE

MADE OF STONE

1

Jake Sawyer stepped out of the main doors of Greater Manchester Police HQ. In a single motion, he spun his jacket around over his head, twisting it and slotting in his arms, then shrugged it over his shoulders and headed for the car parked over the road.

He was a tall man: broad shouldered, long armed, with a lope to his walk that never quite slipped into a swagger. His black hair was cropped tight, and he had trimmed his beard down to a shadow, pruning a couple of years off his thirty-six. His long jacket flapped in the icy wind, and he kept his keen green eyes on the driver as he approached the car. He blew into his hands, opened the door, and flopped into the passenger seat.

In the back, two young children wore wireless headphones and stared into the screen of a seat-mounted iPad. Maggie Spark started the engine but didn't move off. She kept her eyes on Sawyer, as he tilted his head and rested it on the window. Maggie was slight and compact: around Sawyer's age, with shoulder-length rust red hair and enquiring hazel eyes. She was dressed down for the occasion: wash-day jeans, comfort jumper.

At last, Sawyer shifted his eyes to her. 'Thanks.'

She pointed to the cup holder. 'There's a latte. Might be a bit tepid. Sugar's in the glovebox. And a pastry. Chocolate.'

Sawyer squeezed out a lopsided smile, dimpling his right cheek. He switched his gaze to the windscreen and Maggie steered the car onto Northampton Road, away from the bland business park, with its permanent parade of evenly spaced, manicured trees; more North Korean than northern England. She threaded through the back streets of Newton Heath, past the ugly wholesalers and shuttered pubs. Sawyer didn't take the coffee or look for the pastry; he just sat there, eyes front.

Maggie glanced back at Mia and Freddy, lost to *Incredibles 2*. She slowed for a gridlock outside Asda. 'Have you eaten?'

Sawyer shifted in his seat. 'Partially defrosted lasagne.'

'No special treatment for Detective Inspectors, then?'

He shook his head. 'Well. The common lags get Tesco Dinner For One. Pretty sure mine was Waitrose.' His voice was soft, muffled by the strain, but still clear. The vowels were extended: northern, with a twist of London.

Maggie hustled through the late-afternoon traffic, following the signs for the M67: the escape route from the urban squall to the relative peace of the Peak District National Park. It would be a long, tense hour, unless she could draw him out. But after ten years as a counsellor, she had honed her technique with the cold starters. 'Remember when we were at Keele, Jake? Your battered old *Fight Club* VHS? Your housemates hated it, and it was your way of clearing them out when I came round. I hated it, too, at first, but you won me over.'

Another dimpled smile. Warmer, this time.

'Remember that line from the film? "It's only after

we've lost everything that we're free to do anything." It fits with your Stoicism. You can't control what's happened to you, but you can choose how to react, what steps to take to rebuild."

Sawyer let his head drop against the window again. 'Are you okay with it?'

'What's "it"?'

'Your separation. You mentioned it over breakfast.'

'Three days ago, yes.' She sighed. 'It's ran its course. Better to get out while we're still friendly.'

Sawyer took out his phone. 'What's Justin doing now?'

'He's a partner, at his Stockport firm. His mother lives there. He's staying with her while he finds a place.'

He nodded to the back seat. 'Kids know?'

Maggie lowered her voice, despite the headphones. 'Sort of. It'll be hardest for Freddy. I'm just telling him that his dad's very busy at the moment. Mia's a mummy's girl. And she's older, more mature.'

Sawyer scrolled through the stories in his news app. 'Sorry to hear.'

She stopped for a red light and studied him. 'Jake. You do have a way of confounding my expectations. Usually when I start to relax and think that things are going right for a change.'

'You mean the getting arrested for murder thing?'

The car behind honked its horn; the light had changed. She moved off. 'Yes. That certainly raises the bar. Extreme, even by your standards.'

Sawyer opened a local story.

POLICE STEP UP HUNT FOR MISSING GIRL

'I don't know what all the fuss is about. I posed as a journalist to get close to Marcus Klein, the man who was

9

wrongly convicted of murdering my mother thirty years ago. I used him for leverage to get the name of the person I believe actually did it. But then he was killed, probably by the same person. And now I've been framed for his murder.'

Derbyshire police issued a new appeal today in the case of Holly Chilton, the ten-year-old girl reported missing by her family over a week ago.

He held up the phone. 'You seen this?'

Maggie ran a hand across the back of her neck. 'So, what now?'

'Keating handed me over to Manchester police. They questioned me. Not very well. Held me for two days. They must have got an extension on the standard twenty-four hours, so I assume there was a tussle about charging me. CPS demanding more evidence. They don't like to bin off one of their own unless there's a really good chance of getting a result.'

Hundreds of people have been involved in searches to find Holly, who was last seen on Monday near Hartington.

'And you're suspended, right?'

He glanced over. 'Right. I'm out on bail, pending charge. No warrant card. Suspended with pay. They'll have searched my house and, because they haven't charged me already, I assume they didn't find much.'

'And what are your conditions?'

In an emotional video appeal, Holly's parents, James and Sara, pleaded with anyone who might have seen something, or who might have information relating to Holly's whereabouts, to come forward and speak to the police in confidence.

'Surrendered my passport, and I have to stay out of range of Klein's brother's house. Oh, and I'm required to sign in at my own station twice a week.' He pocketed the phone and looked over. 'Awkward.'

2

At Sawyer's cottage on the edge of Edale, Maggie parked in front of the orange-and-black Mini Convertible. Sawyer got out and let himself into the house.

She turned to the children and they lifted their headphones. 'Do you want to stay here or come inside?'

'Stay here!' In unison.

'How long for the film?'

'Ten minutes,' said Mia. She waited for Freddy to replace his headphones. 'Is Uncle Jake okay?'

Maggie patted Mia's wrist. 'He'll be fine. I won't be long. Don't talk to any strange men.' Mia rolled her eyes and replaced her headphones.

Maggie followed Sawyer inside the low-beamed, L-shaped sitting room. It was her first visit, and she was surprised by the tidiness. A bookshelf with a section reserved for neatly packed DVDs, PS4 and games was tucked under the small TV. The galley kitchen was spotless, with an empty dishrack, nested chopping boards, gleaming surfaces. It was a gloomy morning, and Sawyer had switched on the overhead light, revealing a side door leading to an unloved patio and picnic bench. There was a faint tang of cleaning chemical.

She crouched by the DVDs. Mostly blokey, with a couple of sports titles and natural history box sets. 'You still watch these?'

Sawyer looked over from the kettle. 'Yeah. Streaming services are patchy. And things disappear because of rights issues. You don't come home and find one of your DVDs missing. Tea?'

Maggie shook her head. 'Got to go.'

Sawyer opened a cupboard and pulled out an opened packet of biscuits, twisted shut. He approached Maggie, held eye contact for a second, then waved the biscuits at her.

She shook her head, and ran a finger over the dining table. It came up clean. 'Now this *is* special treatment. They wouldn't make it so nice for a civilian.'

Sawyer nodded to the floorboards. 'Sally's team, I'll bet. Hard to tell, but I think they've stuck the Hoover round. Pretty good, considering I don't have one.' He walked back to the kitchen.

Maggie gulped in a breath and winced at the lungful of soapy air. 'I spoke to Shepherd. He fed your cat.'

'Uhuh.' The steam from the kettle drifted over Sawyer. He kept his head down, lost to something.

Maggie perched on a kitchen chair. 'So when you say they didn't question you well, do you mean they missed things?'

'They're meant to keep you in the dark on what they know. But it was pretty obvious. They haven't got much. Keating said they found an "item" of mine at Klein's place. Circumstantial. Didn't feel like they had any supporting evidence. They were mostly trying to put me at the scene. They knew that I knew. Waste of energy all round.' The kettle clicked off and they shared a moment of silence. 'It's a good thing.'

'What is?'

'Klein's death.'

Maggie flinched.

'It means I'm not going crazy. It means I'm right. It means my mum's killer is still out there. Someone was following Klein and didn't like the idea that we were getting close to the truth.'

She squinted at him. 'Will Keating keep you under surveillance?'

'I would, if it were up to me. I'd put Moran on it. Not my biggest fan. Good copper. Bit unreconstructed.' Sawyer turned away and prepared his tea.

Maggie stood. 'So what are you going to do with yourself?'

'Wait until they either charge me or give me my warrant card back.'

'How long could that take?'

'Couple of weeks. Maybe three.' He looked over his shoulder. 'And, yes, I'm still seeing Alex. Appointment on Thursday.'

Maggie smiled. 'That's good. You're going to need her.'

He scoffed, with affection. 'How about you? What are you up to?'

'Jake, you know I can't talk about any family liaison work.' Sawyer nodded, squeezed out the tea bag. 'I have to go. Let's have coffee soon.'

He turned. Maggie moved in for a hug, but he pivoted towards the fridge and opened the door. 'Fresh milk. Definitely Sally.' Sawyer added a splash to his mug and stirred. He toyed with the mug handle and turned again, holding out his arms, forcing a smile. She hugged him hard. He felt rakish, taut. Tightly wound. All edge and sinew.

She stepped back and looked up at him. Was it a trick of the light or were his eyes glassy? 'Self-care, Jake. Keep your head down for a while. Get a lawyer. Keep your appointment with Alex.'

'Thank you, Mags. And let me know if you need my help.'

'In what capacity?'

He shrugged. 'Concerned citizen.'

3

The house was cold, but Sawyer stripped to his underwear and worked out on his Wing Chun kung fu dummy: jabbing and thwacking his forearms against the wooden poles, following the forms, holding a precise centreline. He was slow and sloppy, his normally sharp reflexes deadened by the prison limbo: the burnt coffee, the unstifled smirk of the desk sergeant, the indignity of being bossed around by bobbies.

He showered and scrubbed up. As he padded out of the bathroom, he froze. Scratching sounds. He walked through and opened the back door. His adopted black-and-white cat, Bruce, slunk into the kitchen and wound himself around his ankles.

'Tired of the mice, big man?' He scraped some evil-smelling food into a saucer and scratched Bruce's back as he ate, staring at the claw marks in the paintwork around the door frame.

He dressed and switched on the TV, selecting the original 1979 series of David Attenborough's *Life on Earth* on iPlayer. He started the first episode—*The Infinite Variety*—and sprawled back on the sofa with his laptop.

The IT boys would have had a rummage through his files and browser history, but there was nothing to find.

He opened the *Derbyshire Times* website. Two photographs, side by side. A posed school photo of a young girl with long brown hair, and an older boy, seated at a dinner table, zoomed in to crop out the surroundings. The girl gazed into the camera, looking bored, impatient. The boy grinned: head tilted back, teeth bared. The story confirmed that both were missing: ten-year-old Holly Chilton for seven days; eleven-year-old Joshua Maitland for close to four months. Holly's parents were quoted, urging locals to join their daily searches of the farmland near the family home in Blackwell. She had left to visit a 'friend' after school one afternoon, and never returned. Over the last two days, Sawyer had noted the journalists' tone shifting from urgency to inevitability. Soon, there would be talk of closure, and the enquiry would be scaled back. There were only so many patches of water that could be dredged, outbuildings searched, sections of woodland probed with thermal imaging.

Joshua had simply failed to come home from school one day. His disappearance, back in September, pre-dated Sawyer's transfer from the Met by a few days, and the case had been covered by local police near Joshua's home in Youlgreave. Now, though, with two children missing, Sawyer's MIT unit at Buxton station would have taken over, with Maggie working as liaison to both families.

He glanced at the TV. An impossibly young and dashing Attenborough, crouched in the jungle, enthusing about fossils. Clues: to our microscopic beginnings, our endurance over dizzying timeframes.

He leaned in closer to the laptop screen, studying Holly's imperious expression. According to her parents, she was 'wilful' and always 'pushing boundaries', but also 'big hearted'. Sawyer would have dispatched officers to talk to Holly's friends, tracked her online activity, checked for parental disagreements, trawled CCTV near her home and school. But he had no power to give orders, and nobody obliged to take them. He had been stripped of his role, his status, his dignity.

But not his instinct.

He was sure that Holly Chilton's big heart was still beating.

4

The Rambler Inn, just outside Edale village, was a converted pub-hotel that served as a fuelling station for the casual climbers out to conquer Kinder Scout: the highest point in the Peak District. It sat at the end of a leafy lane, minutes from the start of the Pennine Way: a 268-mile stomp along the backbone of England. Sawyer ducked into the doorway and scanned the room. Eva Gregory had taken a corner seat at the far side, requiring him to sidestep along the edge of the bar scrum.

Eva was reading and, as he arrived at the table, she took off her thick-framed Tom Fords and lifted her eyes, but didn't move her head. 'Hello.' Smile. Mock surprise.

She was laid out and long boned, with glossy black hair pinned to one side. She hadn't removed her coat: a fitted woollen wrap with a waist buckle. As Sawyer took his seat opposite, he stole a look at her toned legs, encased in tight jeans tucked into knee-length boots. A less confident woman might have blended in to the rustic backdrop. But Eva had a way of switching the polarity in a room, fading out the surroundings.

He hung his jacket over the chair. 'Not stopping?'

Eva put down the book: *The Seven Deaths Of Evelyn Hardcastle*. 'You sound like my dad.'

'I'm not a natural father figure.'

She leaned over and kissed him. One cheek. He caught her perfume: subtle, expensive. Not for public consumption. 'Did you drive?'

He shrugged. 'Could have walked, but it's getting late. Dangerous.'

Eva wriggled out of her coat and folded it over the chair beside her. 'You've been quiet. Four days since we agreed to meet. I'd expected a bit of text tease.'

He leaned back. 'You could say silence is the ultimate tease. Would you like a drink? Are we eating?'

'I am, yes. But not here. I've got about an hour. How about dinner later in the week? You said you'd cleaned the place. I could come over. Let you know if I agree.'

They ordered coffee: black for Eva, white for Sawyer.

He lobbed in a lump of brown sugar and watched it sink into the froth. 'How's Luka?'

'Still tricky. Still going on about your promise to show him some of your... underhand skills. Whatever you think of Dale, he's Luka's dad. And when you're ten, and your dad is moving out, it must be hard not to read it as a personal rejection.'

'Might be tough now, but he'll be better off in the future without a petty gangster father.'

She laughed. 'Dale isn't a gangster.'

'Maybe not in the traditional sense.'

'He sells property. Refurbishes old places.'

Sawyer blew on his coffee. 'So he's in construction? Who are you, Carmela Soprano?'

'Never seen it.'

'In denial, I mean. Dale used to get his hands dirty. He's implicated in a few legacy cases. But now he gets his associates to take the risks. He sent a few friends round to see me, you know. About seeing you.'

Eva ran a finger around the rim of her cup. 'And how did that go?'

'We agreed to disagree. You mentioned a going-away party?' Sawyer took a European Health Insurance card out of his wallet. 'I swiped this from one of Dale's goons.' Eva raised her eyebrows. 'Stooges? Henchmen? Associates. He was one of my visitors. If I hadn't strongly objected, he would have chiselled off one of my thumbs.'

She squinted at him. '*What*? Literally?'

'Yeah. Just the one, though. He's not a monster.'

Eva studied him for a second, then looked at the picture on the card. Unevenly shaved head, poking up from a black polo-neck. Irritated expression. 'Shaun Brooks. He used to be one of Dale's bouncers, at his old club in Sheffield. He was at the party the other night.'

'So where is Dale moving to?'

'Manchester. He's opening a new club in Deansgate. They were talking about gaming. Videogames for the kids, pool and snooker for the adults. Two tiers. Different licenses. I think they want to make it a franchise. The main place in the city centre is above a pizza parlour called The Firehouse. Dale will buy that out, probably.'

'Why go there personally, though? Surely it's easier to stay with you. Leave the club to his lackeys.'

Eva took a slug of coffee. 'He doesn't want to actually *divorce*. He's looking for a "break". Says the distance might bring us closer together.'

Sawyer sat back, frowned at her. 'You said you took some photos?'

21

She pulled out her phone and held it screen side up, swiping through a series of images. Burly men in hired-looking suits. Defendant chic. Drinking, laughing, leering. Shaun was there, leaning in, talking to Dale.

Sawyer reached out a hand and stopped Eva's swiping. 'Let me see that one.'

He peered in close to the screen and pointed to a short man in the background, propped against a door frame. 'This guy is Marco. Another one of my visitors.'

Eva shuddered. 'He's very touchy.'

'As in easily angered?'

'As in feely.'

He slurped at his coffee. 'Thank you for this. It's a big help. Can you keep an eye out for me? Comings and goings. I can't do much about it at the moment, but maybe soon.' He flicked his gaze to the table, then back up to Eva. She had raised her eyebrows again, catching his deflection. 'Lots going on.'

'Those missing children?'

'I'm interested in that, yes.'

She squinted. '*Interested* in it?'

'I'm dealing with another case.'

'Must be something big.'

He drew in a deep breath. 'Do you know how many children go missing every year in the UK? Around a hundred and forty thousand. That's one in every two hundred.'

Eva gasped. 'How do you find them?'

'Search the home or last known address. Start close and work out. Try their phone if they have one. Check computers. House to house. Hospitals. CCTV. Land and air search. Use the media. Public appeals. Most of them are found quickly, with nothing suspicious. Have you heard of the golden hour?'

'Yes. In photography. The time before sunset, when the sun is low and the light is redder and softer.'

He nodded. 'We use the term to describe the first hour of an investigation. The critical time when you snap into action and gather evidence, secure scenes, find witnesses, track suspects. It's particularly important in missing person cases, because the earlier you move in—'

'The more restricted the catchment area.'

'And the more likely you are to find the person. It's like you're on a clock. The light fading, dying away. The possibility of a happy outcome vanishing, moment by moment.'

'So, what about these two children? One's been missing for months.'

'Yes. Joshua Maitland. The second, Holly Chilton, has only been gone for a week, but it might as well be a lifetime on the golden hour principle.'

Eva rolled her wedding ring around her finger, then clasped her hands together and rested them on the table. 'And when you say you're "interested" in the case...'

'I mean, I think at least one is still alive. Joshua didn't come home from school, so that's more open-ended. But Holly told her mum she was going out to meet a friend. In my experience, those are the cases that end well. Not always. But there's usually something the parents aren't saying or don't want to say. Some breakdown or estrangement. Maybe an extended family connection. If you probe the right areas, you can shake it out. There's usually someone known to the person. When Luka was taken by Dennis Crawley, our first thought was with Dale and friends. In the end, it turned out to be more colourful than that. Although there was a link with the past.'

Eva sighed. She pushed her hands beneath the table and

leaned forward. 'I want to get away from Dale's past, make better choices.'

Sawyer muted the moment with another gulp of coffee. 'So if you're working on this other case, how are you going to help find these children?'

Sawyer grinned at her. 'Creativity.'

5

Dale Strickland swivelled his desk chair and stared out of the floor-to-ceiling window, down at rain-smeared Deansgate. A yellow-and-white Metrolink tram slowed on its approach to the station, brakes squealing. He winced. 'Is there anyone we can call?'

Two men stood before the desk: one short, in dark suit and yellow tie, with a tidy crop of blond hair. The other: a hulk, with a clean-shaven cannonball head pushed through the collar of a polo-neck sweater.

The short man glanced at the hulk. 'Call?'

Dale didn't turn. 'About this fucking weather.'

The hulk shrugged. 'Manchester.'

'Get me God on the phone.' Dale stood up, and perched on the edge of the desk, facing the two. 'I bet you've got his number, Marco.'

'I'm beyond salvation.' A Scottish lilt.

Dale managed a small smile. He squinted at the pair from behind thin-framed glasses. He was slight but agile; well fitted into a cobalt blue dress shirt. Late forties, with a thatch of greying hair and salt-and-pepper stubble. He massaged the deep double frown lines above his nose and dropped his gaze to the mock Persian rug that covered the space before his desk; he often joked about the potential for a concealed piranha pit below. 'Shaun.'

The hulk raised his head. 'Boss.'

Dale sighed. 'Don't call me "boss".' He skewered Shaun with a clock-stopping stare. 'Makes you sound like a slave.'

'We're all set.' Shaun kept his focus on Dale. 'Down near Buxton.'

Dale raised an eyebrow. 'Set and forget?'

'Couple of things to finalise. But, yeah.'

Dale hopped off his desk and walked over to Shaun. He stood close, just off the edge of the carpet, and stared up, showing no discomfort with the height difference. 'But, no. You're hands *on*. Momentum is important at the start of a business. Pick up enough speed and you can base here as franchise manager. But you're not here yet. You need to find us a home. There. *Storage.*'

'We still going with bath salts?' Shaun sniffed and rubbed at his nostrils. Dale caught Marco's eye.

Marco grinned. 'It's the substance *du jour*. Don't see why Stoke should get all the fun. Plenty to go round.'

Dale ambled back to his desk. 'How's recruitment?'

'Even easier than we thought,' said Shaun. 'Round here and down there. Even better down there.'

Dale dropped back into his chair, keeping his eyes on Marco. 'Limited opportunities for cavern guides and village Balti house dishwashers.' He slapped both palms down on the desk. 'Item Two on the agenda.'

Marco's shoulders rose and sank. 'We're still doing this?'

'We're still doing this.'

'He might come for us first.'

'He's got nothing. Connections. Associations. All circumstantial.'

Marco took a step forward. 'I mean, unofficially.'

Dale nodded. 'I get it. You were humiliated.' He raised his voice a notch, just enough to drop the temperature. 'Maybe you're scared of him. You can't go into jobs like that with fear.'

Marco shook his head. 'He's clever. Hard to read. And he can look after himself.'

Dale sat back in his seat. 'Marco. Look at what you've done here. It's a money-printing machine, in so many ways. Are we getting a taste from the Firehouse?'

Shaun winced. 'It's pizza. Low margins.'

Dale beamed and pointed at Shaun. 'He'll have your job, Marco.'

'I was thinking of putting him on the door. Not on weekends, though.'

'Fuck off.' Shaun glanced at Dale for support, didn't get it.

Marco ignored him. He leaned forward on the desk. 'It's a bad idea. Let it settle. Let him relax first.'

'You're right. He *will* come for us. Which is why we can't afford to have him sniffing round.' Dale narrowed his eyes at Shaun. 'Not while we're setting up. Basic economics. I pitched the work too low. We need to go up a grade. Call in a professional.'

'Dale.' Marco stood upright, away from the desk. 'Fletcher's not a professional. He's a psychopath. Psychopaths don't care about business models or long-term planning.'

'I have a problem. I asked you to solve it. You weren't able to do that.' Dale rubbed at his frown lines again. 'We need a more permanent solution. Fletcher is a handful, but I can handle him. And I don't think Mr Sawyer will have seen anything like him before.'

6

Sawyer hurried along the spotless, spotlit corridor on the fifth floor of Sheffield's Northern General Teaching Hospital. His shoes squeaked against the gleaming linoleum, corrupting the silence at the end of the graveyard shift. The conflicting scents of floor polish and fried food tainted the air. He paused to shake off a flutter of nausea and dredged up a smile as he approached the nurse at the station desk.

She was young, harried, dabbing at the keyboard of an ageing PC. 'Can I help?'

'Morning. I'm here to see Matthew Walker.'

'So sorry, but visiting hours—'

'Police officer. I'm a colleague of Matthew's.'

It was technically true; he was suspended, not active, but still occupied his position. He couldn't just stroll onto a crime scene, but he should be able to fudge it here.

The nurse looked up, nodded. 'Do you have any ID?'

'I do, but not with me.' A note of alarm on the nurse's face. Sawyer leaned forward, lowered his voice. 'I'm not officially meant to be here. Undercover. It's why I can't keep normal visiting hours. I'm sure you're aware that DC

Walker was recently involved in a serious violent assault. And you will have been dealing with extra security around his room, right?'

The nurse nodded, working him out. 'Have you got any other ID?'

'Yes. But it's fake. In case I get searched.'

She frowned, her eyes glancing to the corridor behind, looking for support. 'I can't let you through without—'

'Do you want my number?'

'Sorry?'

'Warrant number. It's unique. Easy to check with my station. Buxton.'

'*Sir*?'

Sawyer and the nurse looked up. A short, twentysomething man in a hospital gown stood in the corridor, by the door of a private room. He was pale, crumpled, struggling to keep his shoulders back.

Sawyer raised a hand. 'DC Walker. Good to see you moving around.'

Walker nodded. 'Heard your voice.'

The nurse sprang up and dashed over to him. 'Mr Walker. You must wait for the doctor.' She urged him back into the room.

Walker spoke to Sawyer over his shoulder. 'They're letting me out today, sir.'

'I hope you're getting changed first.'

Walker shuffled back inside and sat down on the edge of his bed. The nurse turned and glared at Sawyer.

He smiled. 'Ten minutes.'

———

Sawyer filled a plastic cup with tepid water and sat down by Walker's bed. 'I'm not here, by the way.'

'Thought so.' Walker sat up as Sawyer handed him the cup. 'How was Manchester? Shepherd briefed me yesterday.'

'Warned you not to talk to me?'

Walker sipped at his cup. 'Course.'

Sawyer looked up at the ceiling. His eyes were sore and heavy, after another night of fractious sleep. 'I didn't do it.'

'Will they charge?'

Sawyer screwed his eyes shut, opened them again. 'Too bright in here. You'd think hospitals would go in for ambient lighting. More soothing.'

'Maybe a few scented candles, too?'

Sawyer looked at him. 'I'm not sure they have enough to charge.'

'You got help?'

'Not yet. Don't want to talk to lawyers until it's really necessary.'

Walker finished his drink. He waggled the cup; Sawyer shook his head. 'I'd love to see how they interrogate a fellow officer.'

'One of the Manchester DCIs did it. Couple of DIs sat in. I don't need a lawyer to tell me to say, "No comment". If they were fishing or seeding, they were hiding it well.' He nodded to a sign next to the door: loud white text on a red background.

STOP! HAVE YOU CLEANSED YOUR HANDS?

Walker followed his gaze. 'Sounds like good advice. For cops and criminals.'

'I think it's more about purification. Body first. Soul can wait. How come they moved you from Cavendish?'

'Something about specialist care. Red tape.'

Sawyer scoffed. 'Keating shifting the result of a botched

operation away from his domain. He's never been the transparent type.'

'Apparently, there's a news blackout on your arrest.'

Sawyer sniffed. 'The Streisand effect. The blackout will be news in itself. It'll certainly get the vultures circling.'

'Streisand?'

'Google it.'

Walker rolled his head around, cracking his neck muscles, revealing the angry red wound across the base of his Adam's apple. 'Speaking of Keating, have you seen him?'

'He'll be taking fire for bringing me back. He'll point to the Crawley and Ballard cases. They'll paint me as rogue, unstable.' Sawyer laughed. 'I'm not Jason Bourne. I'm just trying to find out who murdered someone I loved.' Walker kept quiet, fiddled with his phone. 'When are you back in work?'

'Tomorrow. They want me to rest. I'm okay, though. I need to get busy with something.'

Sawyer stared down at the smooth floor. 'You're young. You repair quickly. But don't jump straight back in just to show how strong you are. Your denial doesn't count for much. The body keeps score. You keep seeing it happen, yes? The sounds, the sensations.'

Walker bristled. 'I've spoken to the psych, sir. It wasn't personal. It happened fast. I didn't really see that much.'

'You had your throat slit. Ballard missed the carotid by a millimetre. Nicked your windpipe. He successfully stalked and murdered four people. If he could attack you again, in the same way, a hundred times, he would only miss the carotid once.'

'I was lucky, sir. Luck is part of life. You got to me in good time. You're first aid trained. The paramedics were skilled. He didn't kill me, so—'

'Don't go all Nietzschean on me.' Sawyer glared at him. 'The physical wound is healing, but that's the easy bit.'

Walker sat up. 'I wasn't going to say it made me stronger. I was going to say I just have to move on. Keep going. Do my job. Focus harder on stopping the "parasites", as DC Moran calls them.'

Sawyer got up and walked to the window. He tugged at the cord for the blinds. A morning mist hovered over the hills towards Lightwood and the Corbar Cross viewing point. 'If it were up to me, I'd put you on victimology. Keep you off the streets for a while.' He closed the blinds again, turned to Walker. 'There are two missing children to find. Your instincts are good. I'd have you working out where they are, get the others to tackle whoever's taken them.'

'I'll pass on your recommendation, sir.'

Sawyer raised his eyebrows.

'Sorry,' said Walker. 'That sounded sarcastic. I just... I *can't* talk to you. You know that. You're not here, remember?'

Sawyer flashed him a smile. 'Take it easy, Matt. I'm glad you didn't die. And don't worry. I won't dine out on it too hard once I get back. If you're lucky, they'll charge me and you can play down my involvement in saving your life.' He headed for the door, paused. 'The children. We'd have found one by now, if it wasn't going to end well. Don't look for bodies. Look for somewhere they could be kept alive without arousing suspicion.'

7

The hospital lift opened at the ground floor and shed its load: mostly homebound nurses out of uniform. Sawyer jabbed a thumb into the button marked *BASEMENT: PATHOLOGY* and leaned into the corner as the car sank away from the land of the living.

The doors jerked a little before they opened again, as if reluctant to reveal the warren of peeling, off-white walls: joyless, unadorned. Sawyer strode down the corridor, past the chemical storeroom and into a lobby with a suite of refurbished admin offices. He slowed as he approached a large corner office connected to the mortuary and autopsy room. The door—marked *F. DRUMMOND*—was ajar. He touched it open. Empty. The office was austere: desk with one chair, stacked wire document tray, no pictures apart from a few family photos in a corkboard propped against the wall by the desk. The window in the connecting door reflected the blazing white light of the overhead lamps, trained on a central gurney: soon to be occupied. Sawyer's nose twitched at an edging of alcohol; was it chemical, drifting under the door, or evidence of an unseen private supply?

'Are you looking for Mr Drummond?' A lively young woman in sharp business dress trotted through from a small side room, clutching a stack of papers. She set them down on a well-organised desk and stood there, smiling, angling her head. 'I'm Gina.'

Sawyer nodded. 'Detective Inspector Sawyer.'

Gina looked shocked. 'Goodness! I've read about you. In the paper. You're the "hero cop".'

'That's the tabloid version. And it's only one side. You might hear about another soon.'

Gina beamed. 'You teaser.' She slipped the papers into a folder, keeping her wide eyes on him. 'Mr Drummond is in the break room.' She waved. 'Second on the right.'

Sawyer walked through to the pale green door and stepped into a poky converted storage room with a cheap beechwood coffee table in the centre and a couple of mangy chairs pushed against the far wall. A man sat cross-legged in one of the chairs, with a paper cup in one hand and a book —*Unnatural Causes*—in the other. He was too big for the chair; almost too big for the room. Short-sleeved brown shirt, semi-rimless glasses; shiny-bald on top, thick grey beard underneath. As Sawyer entered, the man's head dipped as he disengaged from the book. He took a few seconds to compose himself, then shifted the glasses up over his pale blue eyes, regarding his new companion.

'Frazer.' Sawyer dragged the second chair over and sat down. 'You've never shown me your boudoir before. I was wondering where you retreated to recharge your ebullience.'

Drummond grimaced, and styled it into a smile. 'They used to let you smoke in here.' He nodded upwards at the ceiling, acknowledging scorched patches of grimy yellow. 'But of course, that avenue of pleasure has been closed off. Now it feels like a dirty secret just to sneak five minutes with a shit cup of coffee.' Drummond's Scotch baritone bounced off the walls; the echo held for a few seconds. He set down the book and cup on the table and folded his arms. 'Now. Are you sure you're allowed to be alone in a room with someone?'

Sawyer stretched his legs out, feet together, until he was almost horizontal on the chair. 'Just passing through.'

'Popping in on Walker? A tidy deposit in the redemption bank, Sawyer. You saved a decent copper there. That's your good deed for the decade.'

'Gina seems nice. Looks like an *Apprentice* candidate. Didn't think you were the PA type.'

Drummond waved a hand, picked up his coffee. 'I'm not. But I was told I had to be. We're trying to go paperless.'

'You're a minimalist, though. Could be a useful contrast. The vivacious yin to your—'

'Lugubrious yang?' Drummond slurped at the cup. 'Do me a favour, Sawyer. Get yourself off this suspension. I don't know what we'll do down here, without your bodies.'

'Looks like you're prepping for a PM. Anyone interesting?'

Drummond laughed into the cup. 'Nobody you can know about.'

Sawyer nodded at the book. 'Good?'

'Bit of pathology porn. Non-fiction. The writer was assigned to Hungerford. Looks like it gave him PTSD. He says something that my old mentor once told me. The worst thing you can be in this job is partial, invested. You just have to get good at turning that off. You have to see the bodies as bodies, not as people. They were people once, of course, fuelled by food and water, driven by electrical impulses. But then, for whatever reason, the power got turned off. The lights went out. They were transformed into meat.' He sat up, leaned forward, rubbed the back of one hand with the knotty fingers of the other. 'People think that makes me a cold bastard. But it's what keeps me sane. Lets me do my job.'

'Don't you feel a responsibility for the bodies? For their history? Loved ones?'

Drummond pondered for a moment. 'I feel responsible, yes. To solve their puzzles, wrap up their stories. Unlike the living, the dead don't lie or exaggerate. I see my work as giving them a voice, a final say. But to do that effectively, you have to learn to stifle the sentiment. The bodies in my drawers used to have possibilities. Options. Hopes and fears for the future. Now, all of that exists in the past. So you have to fade it all down. Stay in the moment. If you get stuck in the past, Sawyer, you might as well be in one of the drawers yourself.'

'You should do some voluntary work. For the Samaritans.'

Drummond closed his book and got to his feet. He was colossal; just shy of seven feet. Sawyer felt a twinge of sadness for him: a beast so formidable, caged underground. 'You picked a bad time to go off grid.'

Sawyer stayed in his chair. 'Oh?'

'I was being disingenuous. It's not just your involvement that brings the bodies. Like my new guest. Drawer C34.'

'Suspicious?'

'Came in early this morning. Late forties. Commuters spotted him in edgeland by Grindleford Station. Nasty.'

Now Sawyer stood. 'Cause of death?'

Drummond smiled. 'Preliminaries for now. Pretty obvious, though. But you'll have to get that from the newspapers, like all the other civilians.'

8

A large round target sat on an easel before a wall-mounted backstop net. The target was divided into concentric sections: blue, white, black, with a central zone in yellow and a bullseye in red. A picture lamp had been mounted high on the wall, casting the target area in vivid light, raising the colours.

A man sprawled on a two-seater sofa at the unlit end of a long hall. He propped up his feet on a chair in front and reached for the crossbow: a Nexgen Pony 335. White axle, black bow. He had selected the Pony, and the colour, for its neutrality; the others had clearly been designed to appeal to the hunter fantasy, with their customised camo skins and thrusting names (Bronco, Stallion). The bow was light in his slender hands—no more effort than lifting a small watermelon—and the stock sat naturally against his bony shoulder.

He stood up, pointed the bow down, and rested it vertically on the floor. He slipped his foot into the stirrup, and attached the cocking device to the hooks on the cable. He used both hands to draw back the cable, priming the bow, and flicked on the dry fire safety mechanism.

He took a long, thin bolt out of the box on the sofa, and studied the symbol etched into the collar around the centre: a crude sketch of two curved lines, forming the shape of a human eye. An imperfect circle hovered in the centre: an iris, surrounded by seven short rays, like a child's drawing of the sun.

He slid the bolt into the flight groove. The Pony could deliver it at four hundred feet per second, penetrating up to six inches from a hundred feet away. A guaranteed headshot kill. The target would feel a millisecond jolt of impact, and then nothing.

He flicked off the safety, opened the lens cover and looked down the sight. He settled the magnified image of the bullseye in the centre of the scope.

Two slow and steady breaths. Halfway through the exhale on the second, he squeezed the trigger, continuing to exhale as the bow fired.

9

Sawyer drove into Sheffield city centre and bought a PAYG phone from Phone-Geekz. He withdrew some money from the Lloyds across Devonshire Green and ate rubbery scrambled eggs in a Kiwi café near the car park. He headed back into the Peak District to the sound of one of his favourite teenage albums: *Maxinquaye* by Tricky, named after the singer's mother, who had died when he was four years old. As the six-year-old observer of his own mother's murder, Sawyer had tried on all the colours of grief: contempt for those, like Tricky, who had been too young to have known their parents; jealousy at his friends' ordered, two-parent home lives; resentment at those who lost parents through disease, with time to reconcile; anger at the children who reduced their creators to providers, and at the parents who used money as balm for abandonment or indifference.

For Sawyer, the cliché applied with an added sting. Not only had he been forced to fast-track his childhood, he was lucky to be alive himself. His mother's killer had wanted to send him and his brother Michael the same way. And now, thirty years later, it seemed he had gone to the trouble of trying to remove one of them from the picture again.

He drove into Thornhill village, and parked the Mini by a farm gate near a cul de sac of stone-built semis. He settled in, listening to music and working through a bag of iced buns, while washing down the chewy bread with sips from a carton of milk. After a couple of hours, when he had resorted to reading the manual that came with his new phone, a boxy, mustard-yellow Range Rover turned into the cul de sac and pulled up outside the house at the far end. Sawyer opened his passenger door a few inches.

A hefty man in a hooded fleece climbed out of the Range Rover driver's seat and lingered, as a woman let herself into the house, followed by a small boy. When they were both inside, the man locked the car and turned to face the Mini. He seemed to ponder for a few seconds, and then began a slow, top-heavy walk in Sawyer's direction. The car dipped as he lowered himself onto the passenger seat and closed the door.

Sawyer kept his eyes ahead, but he could feel Detective Sergeant Ed Shepherd's gaze burning into his left cheek. He took out a notepad and a titanium tactical pen, wrote on the top sheet and held the pad open across his knee.

WIRED?

Shepherd smiled. 'A bit frazzled from the day, but otherwise fine. You ribbed me for using one of those pens.'

Sawyer glanced at him. 'I've seen the light. Anyway, this one's yours.'

'Not any more. I donated it to you, remember? Got a better one.' He looked back towards the house. It was close to dusk, and the street was empty. 'Sir, if just one person sees this, we could both—'

'There's nothing specific in my bail conditions.'

'That's because they assume you know better.'

Sawyer offered him the paper bag. 'Do you want the last bun?'

Shepherd shook his head. 'Sticking to my regime. How many have you had?'

'That's diet shaming.'

Shepherd rubbed at his cheeks. He still took up plenty of space, but had slimmed down recently, and his clever eyes glinted as a late flare of sunshine crept over the car.

'How's work?' said Sawyer.

'If I told you that, I wouldn't have any work to go back to.'

Sawyer nodded. 'Day off today. You booked it a couple of weeks ago. I was worried you'd gone home to Liverpool or something. Do anything nice?'

'Heights of Abraham. Not really the weather for it.'

'Bleak can be beautiful.'

Shepherd toyed with the zip on his fleece. 'Can be. Nice to avoid the hordes. Theo liked the cable cars. We try to do something together whenever we can. The odd day here and there. It'll be over before I know it, so I'm making the most. While he still sees me as cool.'

Sawyer grinned at him. 'I hate to break it to you, Shepherd. But you're not cool.'

'I am to him. In a dad way.'

'Any plans for Christmas?'

'In-laws. Booked the meal out. Wife and her mother always take over the kitchen.'

'Nice of you to give them a rest.'

Shepherd snorted. 'I just can't face the washing up this year.'

'How's the head?' Sawyer watched Shepherd's eyes; he didn't react.

'Keeping it above water. I had a moment in the Trafford Centre last weekend.'

'Christmas shopping will do that to you.'

Shepherd gave a weak smile. 'Calmed myself down. Deep breathing.'

'I've taught you all you know.'

'And I'm grateful for your support. But there's also Google.'

Sawyer closed up the paper bag and shoved it into the glove compartment. 'You know I didn't do this.'

'Of course I do. And you know that I know. I looked into your case, remember? When Keating first paired us up. Due diligence.'

'And you've buffed up your knowledge with Logan's "hero cop" story?'

Shepherd turned in his seat, facing Sawyer. 'I'll tell you what I know, sir. Stop me if I slip into the Logan version. Your mother, Jessica, was murdered in front of you when you were six years old. Thirty-one years ago.'

'Thirty.'

'The guy wore a mask. A balaclava. He also killed your dog, and almost killed you and your brother. They found the weapon, a hammer, nearby. It belonged to a young man named Marcus Klein, a supply teacher who had been seen out with your mother. You don't think he did it.'

Sawyer nodded, sarcastic. 'Good spot!'

'You approached him, Klein, earlier this year when he was due to be released, and you claimed to be a journalist who wanted to write a book about the case, to clear his name. There's a bit where you did some bare-knuckle boxing or something. I'm fuzzy about that.'

'So is Keating. He got sent a picture. I wasn't fighting for fun. It was to follow a lead. To get sweet with the relatives of a burglar from the time just before my mother's murder. He was tasked with stealing the hammer that framed Klein.'

'Right. And you think that the person who tasked him was an officer involved in the case.'

'Yes. An officer who might have killed my mother himself, or passed on the hammer to whoever did.'

Shepherd closed one eye in confusion. 'And not this burglar?'

'No. I met him. He didn't do it.'

'And now, Klein has been found dead. Killed in the same way.'

'With a hammer. All done. You're up to date.'

Shepherd sighed. 'So what's the point of this? Are you after validation from me? Reassurance? I've just told you, I'm positive you didn't do it. That doesn't count for much outside this car, though.'

'Keating said an item of mine was found at Klein's flat. I've never even been there.'

Shepherd frowned at him. 'I think you're mistaking me for your lawyer.'

Sawyer dropped his head back, exasperated. 'This is the point. I'm asking for your help, for your support.'

'And how can I do that without putting my own job at risk?'

'You're not part of the investigation team. Keating wouldn't assign you.'

'No, but—'

'What was the item?' Sawyer leaned forward, held eye contact. 'What did they find that belonged to me? At Klein's flat?'

'DNA. Yours.'

'Could have been transferred.'

Shepherd cast his eyes out to the fields. 'It was on a piece of cellophane. A sweet wrapper.'

Sawyer dropped his chin to his chest and laughed. 'He could have taken that from my car.'

'It's a connection to you. Potentially puts you at the scene.' He raised his head and squinted towards the house. Movement at the window. 'I've got to go. You know how it works. They're building a case, tracking all the moments you were seen with Klein. The DNA isn't much, but along with everything else...' He fixed Sawyer with a flinty stare. 'You need a lawyer. They might interview you again.'

'I can handle that.'

'You told me that it's not a good idea to try and do everything yourself.' Shepherd's phone blipped with a message alert and he sighed. 'Not the best time for you to be out of commission.'

'That's what Drummond said.' Shepherd put his hand on the door handle. 'You must be on the missing children case. Or has Keating got you on the guy they found at Grindleford Station?' He studied Shepherd, didn't get much. 'You're not on my case. That's for Moran, and maybe Myers. Probably coordinating with an MIT unit from Manchester or Sheffield. Special jurisdiction, high-level media management due to internal sensitivities.'

'You've spoken to Drummond?'

'Just visiting a friend at his workplace.'

Shepherd shrugged, opened the door. 'You don't do friends.'

Sawyer raised a hand in farewell. 'That's one thing about getting arrested for murder. You find out who your enemies are.'

10

The immigration clerk held up a hand and beckoned the next traveller forward. He kept his eyes on his screen, as he imported a file of statistics into an overdue report. A shadow loomed at the window to his booth, and he reached up to take the open passport from the shelf.

He cast an expert eye over the photo ID page and entry visa. Netherlands passport. Dates in range. Valid visa. The photo showed a stern, blond-haired man in his mid-forties. His hair had been scraped back into a stubby ponytail: just visible around the back of his muscular neck, which was almost the same width as his skull. He had tilted his head forward slightly, scolding the lens with implacable pinhole eyes set deep beneath an overhanging brow.

'Travelling from Amsterdam, Mr Fletcher?' The clerk looked up. The man at his screen was identical to his passport photo: the poise, the ponytail, the cadaverous eyes. He was well over six feet tall, in a zipped-up black bomber jacket, fitted blue jeans, designer boots. He held a soft, mud-grey briefcase at his side.

'Rhetorical?' said the man. His voice was gruff,

weathered, empty; as if he had left his emotions at home, as unnecessary baggage.

The clerk—young, curious—sat up. 'Sorry?'

'Your question.' The man let the silence hang, showing no discomfort.

The clerk considered a few options: was the man drowsy? Depressed? Doped up? Had he been too focused on his admin and failed to tune in to a mordant sense of humour? 'Yes,' he said, smiling. 'I know that from your flight number. Just making conversation.'

The man offered a barely detectable nod; it would have challenged an auctioneer.

'What brings you to Manchester, Mr Fletcher?'

The eyes shifted. 'Taxi. Aeroplane.'

The clerk tried on a quizzical smile. 'What is the purpose of your trip? Business or pleasure?'

'Both.'

———

Outside, Fletcher climbed into a waiting taxi and set down his briefcase on the seat beside him.

The driver looked up from a puzzle book and checked his shoulder. 'Evening, mate. Where you goin'?'

Fletcher sat back and glowered out at the terminal lights. 'Manchester.'

The driver chuckled. 'We're already in Manchester. Anywhere in particular?'

Fletcher glanced at the driver's eyes in the mirror. He unzipped a side pocket in the briefcase and took out a flask of water and a bottle of pills, marked with a green logo: three overlaid C-symbols, inverted and concentric.

He unscrewed the lid and tipped a pill into the centre of his hand.

He lifted the pill into his mouth and washed it down with a slug of water.

He did the same with a second pill.

He slotted the flask and bottle back into the side pocket and fastened the zip.

At last, he turned his head and looked out of the window again. His eyes flicked to the mirror. 'Deansgate.'

11

Sawyer waited in the Mini, outside the Barley Mow pub in Matlock, listening to a random playlist of drifting ambient music: Eno, Biosphere, Northcape. His previous meeting with the Caseys had ended badly, and he needed time to regroup. He had to take this one steady: don't force it, don't get pushy. He had the private number of Ryan, the family patriarch, and he was still fully stocked on goodwill following his takedown of a Casey rival in the fight at the travellers' farm. But there was no telling which way the murder charge would fall, and he had to walk away today with more than a headful of banter and a skinful of Jameson.

He crossed the road, hitching his collar up against the frigid wind, and headed through into the main bar. The pub was busy for a Wednesday, and the Caseys were already installed in their usual spot: around a far table near the bar, next to a side door leading out to a private car park. It was a poky room, with a low ceiling and walls smothered with knick-knacks and posters: Christmas dinner specials; recruitment for a snow and ice clearance 'hit squad'; a photo montage from the annual Hen Racing event.

Sawyer approached the group. More subterfuge. At the hospital, he had been officially invisible; here, he was known to the Caseys as investigative journalist Lloyd Robbins, named after his favourite pickpocket, Apollo Robbins.

Ryan occupied most of the back bench, with his two beefy sons, Wesley and Ronan, either side. He was showing his seventy-odd years—wispy white scalp hair, flattened nose—but he was sharp and steely, with bright, vigilant eyes. His nephew, Owen, sat beside Ronan, shielded by one of the larger associates who had escorted a seething Sawyer from the same room barely a week ago. Owen was a scrawny man in his late forties, with a grey moustache at the centre of a ratty face disfigured by acne scars.

The group quietened down and watched as Sawyer settled into a chair, a few feet back from the table.

Ryan drained his glass and clunked it back down. 'Mr Robbins. Now, let's keep things friendly this time, eh?'

Owen peered at Sawyer. 'Brought anything more interesting, friend?' He smiled, cracking a ripple of wrinkles around his sunken eyes. 'Have yiz come *equipped*?'

Sawyer kept his eyes on Ryan Casey as he spoke to Owen. 'As we established last time, you were arrested for a burglary in the Buxton area, thirty years ago. June 1988. You said that an older man offered you a deal in return for your freedom. Steal an item, a hammer, from a house near Tideswell. The house of the man who was with me last time: Marcus Klein.'

Wesley Casey sat forward. 'Mr Klein busy today, then?'

'Washing his hair,' said Sawyer. He turned to look at Owen for the first time. 'This man who offered you the deal. Older than the officer who made the arrest.' Sawyer caught himself; he had to be careful not to slip into police speak. 'You said he wore a suit. No uniform. Scruffy brown hair, bushy moustache, a big watch.'

Owen nodded, impatient. 'I got in, found the hammer, met him in a pub car park later. And like I said, he turned pretty nasty. Warned me that if I ever told anyone, then he'd make my life a living hell. The usual shite.'

Ronan Casey wheezed out a laugh. 'Look at him. He's Mr Big Bollocks now. I bet you were shitting it at the time.'

Owen jerked his head at Ronan. 'I fuckin' was not! He gave us a nice chunk of money.' He shrugged. 'I was just honouring a deal. It was a long time ago, though. I'd be more than happy to take another chunk.'

Ronan shook his head, amused. 'To dishonour the deal.'

'To negotiate a new one. He told me his name, yeah. And a rank. Can't remember that, but I do remember the name. The surname.' Owen took a slow, relaxed sip from his bottle of beer. 'And like I said, Mr Robbins, you're operating in a seller's market here.'

'Five hundred,' said Sawyer. 'Here and now.'

Owen grimaced. 'You're pissing way shy of the bowl there, Mr Robbins. You're barely in the fuckin' bathroom.'

Sawyer took out the sketch he'd made on the day before his arrest, after a dream in which he'd momentarily recalled —or imagined—the face of his mother's killer when she had managed to tear off his mask. Heavy eyebrows, black moustache with flecks of grey. 'Did he look anything like this?'

Owen squinted at the sketch and shrugged. 'Hard to say.' He passed the paper back to Sawyer and fixed him with what was clearly his idea of a tough stare.

'A thousand,' said Sawyer. 'That's a nice day's work for one word.'

Owen smiled. 'Mr Robbins. Call it two, and you've got yourself a name.'

Sawyer took an envelope out of his inside pocket. 'There's fifteen hundred in here.'

'Better get yourself down to the Sainsbury's in Matlock,' said Owen. 'There's a fuckin' cashpoint there.'

Sawyer pushed the envelope across the table. 'Mr Casey. I have another couple of new angles that can get me this man's name. But I also have a book deadline, and it'll take time. You can help me speed things up. Once I walk out of here today, we won't be seeing each other again. I won't be popping down to the "fuckin' cashpoint". Now, I can walk out with or without this envelope. Your decision. You're the boss.'

Owen picked up the envelope and examined the contents. He looked at Ryan, then Wesley. No help from either. He folded the envelope in two and slid it into the pocket of his PVC jacket.

Sawyer smiled. 'Don't say it.'

'What?'

'Don't say, "pleasure doing business with you".'

Wesley barked a laugh. 'Give the man his name, Owen. He's suffered enough.'

Owen Casey folded his arms and rested them on the table. '*Caldwell.*'

12

Back at the cottage, Sawyer fed Bruce and sat at the kitchen table with his laptop and a mug of tea. He retrieved the other two envelopes from the inside pocket of his jacket and set them down on the table. One contained two thousand pounds, the other three thousand. He hadn't expected Casey to go for the initial offer of five hundred, but he was surprised that he hadn't played harder for the name. Did that mean it wasn't authentic? Wesley's instruction to Owen implied that the family had discussed the matter and advised honesty. He would soon find out.

He navigated to a website, Spytech, and ordered a GSM4000u micro listening device, making the payment through a private PayPal account. It was a tiny, featureless block of brushed grey metal—around two inches by one inch—with a small aerial cable. It could be planted anywhere, with unlimited range, and dialled into, for instant transmission of surrounding audio: up to a ten-metre radius. It would give him up to eight hours of listening time before he would have to retrieve and recharge it. The website also promised, 'can be used as a tracking device (UK only)'.

Sawyer took out his PAYG phone and tapped in the number of Max Reeves, an old Met colleague. Reeves was a close friend, and their trust was brotherly, but it was safer to keep all official contact off the grid from now on. He switched the phone to speaker. While he waited for the call to connect, he took a bar of Galaxy chocolate from a cupboard and snapped off a couple of segments.

'Reeves.'

'Max. It's Jake.'

A pause. 'Mr Sawyer. I've been expecting you. A burner? This can't be good.'

'I'm on bail. Don't like to sneak around, but it can't be helped.'

'I heard. Are they really pursuing this? Did you do it?'

Sawyer laughed. 'Of course I did it. I thought I'd openly spend time with the man convicted of murdering my mother, and then kill him. The perfect crime.'

'You shouldn't be talking to me. I shouldn't be talking to you.'

Sawyer bit into the chocolate. 'I'm getting that a lot lately. Two things, Max, and I'm gone.'

Reeves paused. Pub noise in the background. The chatter dropped out, as he moved somewhere quieter. A Zippo clunked. 'Right, then. Here I am, round the back of the Horse & Anchor, by the bins. Living the dream. Go.'

'I need detail on a name. Someone who worked at Buxton station around the time of my mum's murder. Possibly a senior officer or official, so keep it off the books. Caldwell.'

'This is the guy who let Owen Casey walk, right? Where did you get the name?'

Sawyer took a breath. 'Owen Casey.'

Reeves drew on his cigarette, exhaled. 'Tidy. I bet he's a delightful soul, these days. I hope you didn't pay too much for that name. It's probably an old parole officer, or someone who once robbed him.'

'That's what I need to know, Max. Is the name authentic? Is he connected to the station at the time? And a photo would be nice.'

'What's the other thing?'

Sawyer sipped his tea, zoning out to a vision of the man in his sketch. 'I saw a car, at a place called Magpie Mine. I went there last Wednesday, with Marcus. The man convicted of the murder.'

'The dead man.'

'Yes. It was around three to four PM. BMW. Burgundy. Check ANPR in the area, in case it's already of interest. If not, CCTV. It's a pretty chunky thing. Hard to miss.'

Reeves took another drag, spluttered. 'This Caldwell's motor?'

'Could be.'

'So, this geezer. You think he was involved in murdering your mum, thirty years ago. He follows you and Marcus Klein. He murders Klein, and, I assume, did a bit of work towards fitting you up for it. And he's driving round in a big, conspicuous car? This fucker must be getting on a bit by now. Brass balls on him, though.'

13

Sawyer parked in his usual spot at Buxton station and stepped out of the Mini, casting around for familiar faces. He bowed his head beneath his collar. It was a bitter morning, and he broke into a trot across the car park, carried to the main doors by flurries of frosty wind.

He strode down the long entrance corridor: a bland gauntlet of evenly placed lime green doors with yellow frosted windows. The glass colour and texture always reminded Sawyer of the cellophane around the bottles of Lucozade fed to him by his mother during childhood illness.

The reception was lively for early morning: suits and uniforms mingling, scattered cliques, murmured apprehension. Sawyer paused at the custody and charge desk, and propped both elbows up on the curved Perspex, resting his chin on his hands.

A rugged man in a short-sleeved uniform shirt emerged from the side office. He spotted Sawyer and handed the main desk over to a younger colleague. 'Sir.'

'I don't think you're obliged to call me that, Gerry. Not while I'm suspended.'

Sergeant Gerry Sherman smiled. 'Hedging my bets, sir.' He gestured to a separate shelf and privacy barrier at the side of the desk. 'Signing in?'

Sawyer nodded. 'What's going on?'

'Press conference. About the...' He caught himself.

'Missing children?'

Sherman handed Sawyer the bail document. 'Yes. You didn't hear it from me, though.'

Sawyer signed himself in and handed back the document, which Gerry countersigned. Two men exited the lift at the far end of reception and crossed past the main desk, heading for the locked door that led to the media room. The man at the front was shorter but large in stature: close to sixty, neat white hair and angular, actorly features. He was stern and swift, in full uniform, with a police cap under one arm. His companion was gangly, with a Nordic air; immaculately dressed in powder blue suit and yellow tie. He hurried to keep up, but slowed when he noticed Sawyer, ensuring the uniformed man would encounter him first.

Sawyer raised himself from the desk. 'Sir.'

DCI Ivan Keating fitted and straightened his cap, as if prompted by Sawyer's presence. He swiped his ID card against the panel by the door. 'Lots going on, DI Sawyer, as I'm sure you can see. Stay close, though. We might need you again soon.'

'Feels like you need me again now, sir.'

A flicker of a smile. 'We'll manage.'

Keating pushed through the door into the corridor beyond, closely trailed by the gangly man: Stephen Bloom, the media relations officer for the MIT unit.

As Sawyer headed back outside, he was interrupted by a shout from behind.

'Mr Sawyer! Not going in, then?'

He turned. A heavyset fiftysomething man in an unflattering suit waddled down the entrance corridor, holding up a hand. Dean Logan was the crime correspondent of the *Derbyshire Times*; an old-school Wapping hack who had scuttled off the sinking Murdoch ship in the build-up to the Leveson Report a few years earlier.

'No, Mr Logan. Not going in. Can you text me the main points?'

Logan reached Sawyer. He was red-faced, his broad forehead shiny. 'One of the station's most illustrious detectives not invited to a key press conference about two missing children? Did you shit in Keating's scrambled eggs?'

Sawyer turned to face Logan, and balked at a waft of body odour: yesterday's sweat, last week's shirt. 'Shall I email you my timesheet?'

Logan smiled. 'That would be wonderful. Look. I've got to go through now. Ten minutes. You don't have to like me or approve of my methods, but I think you'll care about what I have to say. The Source coffee shop. Just round the corner. I'll be straight there once the conference is done.' He leaned in; Sawyer angled his head to the side. 'Nice flapjacks.'

14

Sawyer settled at an isolated table near the toilets, directly below a boxy old wall-mounted TV. The Source was an unremarkable breakfast and lunch joint, with the standard glass display of cakes and sandwich fillings. He was the only customer, and the middle-aged waiter delivered his tea and toast almost immediately.

He spooned a heap of sugar into his mug and pointed up at the TV.

The man smiled. 'Picture's a bit curvy, sorry.' He took a remote from behind the counter and pointed it up at the set. A red BBC News tickertape faded up beneath an image of the police media room: backdrop banner with the Derbyshire Constabulary logo, numbers, web address; a beechwood table of micro recorders and omni mics; Keating at the centre, flanked by DS Ed Shepherd and Stephen Bloom.

Sawyer shifted his chair forward and turned towards the screen. 'Perfect. Thanks.' The man handed over the remote and Sawyer edged up the volume.

'—lines of enquiry.' Keating cleared his throat. A few cameras whirred. 'Holly was last seen nine days ago. We urge anyone who might have seen Holly, in or around the Blackwell area, to please contact us in absolute confidentiality. She told her parents that she was going out to meet someone. Was this you? Do you know someone who told you they were meeting someone on that day, or who was inexplicably absent or late around this time? Holly's parents are understandably desperate to have their daughter back, and we are keen to account for Holly's whereabouts.'

Groaning at the fussy language, Sawyer got to his feet and studied Keating. The DCI always tarted up his diction in public, and dialled back his Welsh twang.

'I would also like to speak to Holly herself,' Keating continued, looking into the camera, which obliged with a slow zoom in. 'Holly. Please get in touch with your mum and dad if you can. You're not in any trouble. They just need to know you're safe. And to the person who might be responsible for Holly's disappearance, I say this. We are aggressively pursuing several lines of enquiry, and I am confident that we will determine what has happened to Holly very soon.'

Sawyer glanced at the waiter, who was also watching. 'They've got nothing.'

On screen, Bloom spoke up. 'We'll take a few questions.'

The camera pulled back. A female voice rose from the audience. 'Is this disappearance related to the case of the other child, Joshua Maitland?'

Keating looked towards the voice. 'In what sense?'

Sawyer shook his head; Keating was being obtuse. He really didn't have anything.

The voice answered, barely audible. Keating responded. 'Joshua Maitland has been missing for over four months now. We're obviously concerned for both children. But at this time, I can't comment on connections between the two cases.'

'DCI Keating.' Dean Logan's voice. 'What progress has been made on Joshua Maitland's disappearance? I'm sure Holly Chilton's parents are desperate to find out what has happened to her, but so are Joshua's.'

Shepherd stepped in. 'We're co-ordinating with local police in Youlgreave, near Joshua's home. As DCI Keating says, there's no evidence that the two disappearances are linked at this time. But we are examining all angles.'

'DCI Keating.' Logan again. 'Could you enlighten us as to why Detective Inspector Jake Sawyer isn't involved in this enquiry? Given that he has a strong track record of success in difficult and complex—'

'Dean.' Keating bristled. 'Given your... writings, I'm well aware that you're a fan of DI Sawyer's. But I'm not prepared to comment on resource or individual staffing issues. We have highly skilled officers working extremely hard on this case, and I have every confidence in their work.' He stood, nodded and walked out of the door at the back of the media room, followed by Bloom and Shepherd.

———

Logan swaggered into The Source and crashed down into the seat opposite Sawyer. He caught the waiter's eye. 'Black coffee, chief.'

Sawyer eyed him. 'Thanks for the support. I don't know whether to be flattered or embarrassed.'

Logan shrugged. 'Column A, column B.'

'I suppose Keating's reaction gives you an angle.'

'Certainly does. Touched a fucking nerve there. Does he really think you might have done it?'

Sawyer scratched at his beard. 'I thought you'd be up to date. How do you know, anyway? Isn't there a blackout?'

Logan laughed, too loud. 'There is. Technically. I know about your arrest, but I can't write anything.' The waiter set down his coffee and retreated to a back room. 'My editor won't touch it. I can't even sell it as a pseudonym job. Keating must have a pretty strong old boys' network. Probably freemasons. Bored middle-aged white men. Rural.' He blew on the cup and took a slurp. 'I suppose it keeps 'em going. Silly rituals, special handshakes.'

'So, what have you got to say? And why will I care?'

Logan dropped his head and gazed into the coffee cup. 'A proposal.'

'We've done this. You ask me for an official interview. I say no. You write a story, anyway. What's new?'

'I'm not sniffing round for an official interview. I want an *exclusive* official interview. Your agony at the death of the man you believe was wrongly convicted of murdering your mother. That's a good way in.'

'No.'

'They didn't charge you, but I take it you're suspended. Hence, *persona non grata* at the conference. That means they have something to pursue.' Logan rested a hand on Sawyer's arm. 'I can take this national.'

Sawyer pushed the hand away. 'My pain, your gain.'

Logan leaned in and ran his fingers through his thinning hair. '*Come on.* When people see how the "hero cop" has been so badly mistreated by colleagues, there'll be all sorts of campaigns. Even if they do charge you, it'll be a sideshow. Like *Making A Murderer* with a happy ending.' He sat back, sloshed the coffee around in his cup. 'I know you didn't fucking kill anyone. But you're being set up, probably by the same person who set up Klein for what happened to your mum. Jake, whoever got to Klein might be the same person who murdered Jessica.'

Sawyer flinched at the use of his mother's first name. 'It's a good job we've got your insight, Logan. That never occurred to me.'

Logan lowered his voice. 'You know what confuses me?'

'The birds and the bees? The metric system?'

He leaned forward again. 'Why not kill you, too? Make a clean break. Nobody else is going to pursue it after all this time. Your dad is busy being the born-again Van Gogh of the North. And your brother is hardly likely to—'

'Shut your mouth, Logan.' A flare of rage. Sawyer cursed himself; it was precisely the reaction Logan was probing for. Raise the discomfort, then apply the balm.

'Okay. I get it. Family ties. How about I sweeten the pitch for you? You know what they say about knowledge.' Sawyer raised an eyebrow but kept silent. 'I know something the police don't know that I know.'

'An unknown known.'

Logan smiled. Nicotine-stained teeth. 'Sort of.'

'I already know it. Male, late forties.' He paused, gauging Logan's reaction. 'Found by commuters at Grindleford Station yesterday morning.'

'Not bad. But I bet you don't know what killed him.'

Sawyer nibbled at an unfinished crust of toast. 'Boredom?'

'Crossbow. Single bolt. Back of the head.'

'How the fuck do you know this? Have *you* been questioned?'

Logan finished his coffee and gave a smug smile. 'It's tough these days, Sawyer, being a journalist. News is spread so fucking thin. It's all so open and easy to access. You have to protect your sources more fiercely than ever. Anyway, that's not all.' He glanced back at the counter; the man was busy in the back room. 'They found another. This morning. Off the Monsal Trail, near the old Hassop Station.'

'Two in two days?'

'I hear this one wasn't quite so fresh. Cyclists reported a bad smell. Rangers traced it. Bloke in his forties. No idea how he died, but I hear your colleagues are looking for connections. I'll do some digging. I've got your number.' He stood up. 'Bad time to be out in the cold, Sawyer. Two maniacs running round. A multiple killer and a child abductor.'

Sawyer forced a smile. 'I like a challenge.'

15

Dale Strickland chalked his cue and crouched low at the side of the table, assessing his angles. 'The cliché applies. You don't shit in your own back yard.'

Marco snorted. 'The whole place is a shithole, anyway. Tea shops and sheep shaggers.'

Dale took his shot: easy red into the corner, leaving a tight angle on a possible blue. 'Exactly. That's why it's prime territory. Full of teenagers with nothing better to do than pass round STDs.'

He took a sip from a glass of whisky and nodded to the far side of the vast, low-ceilinged basement room, where a clique of younger men—almost boys—skulked around an American Pool table. Shaun stood off to the side, talking to a tubby white teenager with dreadlocks and a top-to-toe uniform of branded sportswear.

Marco caught Dale's eye. 'He says they're solid. They've got product, eyes on a few possible bases.'

A match flared in the lamplit booth by the snooker table. Austin Fletcher applied the flame to the unfiltered cigarette in his mouth, flooding the booth with a dense plume of gunmetal smoke. Marco flicked his eyes to the sign tacked above the table: *NO SMOKING.* Dale smiled, shook his head.

Shaun swaggered over. 'Fucking *stinks* over here. Is he doing rock?'

Marco smiled. '*Gitanes*, I think.'

'Turkish', said Fletcher, from behind the smoke.

Shaun shook his head. 'Whatever. We can't have this shit when we're sitting on product.' He jerked a thumb at Fletcher. 'He can fuckin' shoot heroin next week, for all I care. Once we're cleared out.'

Dale took his shot: missed the blue, left an easy red.

Marco stepped up to the table. 'Shaun, I admire your diligence with the smoking regulations, but we're closed down here tonight. Private party.' He polished off the red and lined up the black. 'Why don't you take your brains trust up to the gaming floor? They can show you how to work the Super Mario machine.'

Shaun laughed. 'You sound like my dad. He's got an excuse, mind. Dementia.'

Dale handed his cue to Shaun. 'Take over. And play nice. I want this place clean and those boys set up down there tomorrow. Tell me that won't be a problem.'

Shaun took the cue, glanced at Marco. 'It won't be a problem.'

Dale picked up his drink and headed for a small corner office. Fletcher shuffled to the edge of the booth seat and stood up. He took a final drag of his cigarette and offered it to Shaun, who immediately tossed it to the tiled floor and ground it under the heel of his trainer. Fletcher raised a hand to his head. He fixed his empty eyes on Shaun and smoothed back his blond hair with no hint of hurry. He drew a slow breath, picked up the grey briefcase and followed Dale into the office.

The room was windowless and overlit: two chairs,

cheap desk, bookcase on the back wall with files and ledgers. Dale opened a low cupboard by the desk and took out a bottle of Glenfiddich. He splashed a little into his glass and sat down. Fletcher stayed upright, facing the closed door.

Dale sipped and waited.

Fletcher turned and sat down. He opened the briefcase, took out a slim transparent folder with a black spine and passed it across the desk. Dale opened it and flicked through the pages: photographs of Sawyer at various press conferences and police events; a scaled-down photocopy of Dean Logan's recent *Derbyshire Times* 'Hero Cop' story; assorted documents and clippings from previous cases. The final sheet held a grainy photocopy of the *Daily Mirror* front page from September 1988.

BEAUTY SLAIN BY A BEAST

The main supporting photo showed a headshot of a smiling young woman with long, dark hair.

MURDERED: JESSICA SAWYER (34)

An inset image showed school photographs of two young boys.

TRAGIC KIDS: MICHAEL (9) AND JAKE (6)

Dale looked up at Fletcher; he was unscrewing the lid of his pill bottle. 'Marco paid him a visit a couple of weeks ago. A warning.'

Fletcher kept his eyes down. 'Armed?'

'Yes. Took two others. One's abroad at the moment. And Shaun.' Fletcher snorted. 'He took their car and they found it by Edale station. Marco has a police contact.

They'd had reports of someone on the track near there, playing chicken with the trains. They had a complaint that evening.'

Fletcher raised his eyes. 'He sees a counsellor.'

'I know. If he's self-destructive, suicidal...' Dale took a taste of whisky. 'You could use that.'

Fletcher smiled. 'Could I?' He tossed back two of the pills and drank from his bottle of water.

Dale gripped the edge of the desk with both hands and leaned forward. 'He fought off three capable men. One with a gun.'

Fletcher shrugged. 'Not me.'

16

Sawyer perched on the edge of the black *chaise longue* and took in the room: the mauve armchair opposite; mock baroque side table with teapot, cups and biscuits; glass-topped coffee table; tissues, water jug, fussy frosted glasses. He stared up at the largest picture on the wall: a slow-shutter photograph of the waterfall at Lumsworth, the liquid creamy white and solid, like porcelain. A technological gimmick presented as art.

Alex Goldman entered. She was nearing seventy: flimsy and infant sized, with grey blow-dried hair and muted, functional clothing that almost vanished her into the off-white walls. She shivered, and pulled up the hem of her beige roll-neck as she settled into the armchair. 'Cold snap coming, I think. Earlier than usual, this year. Do you like snow, Jake?'

'That's like saying, "Do you like tunnels?"'

Alex angled her head. 'How do you mean?'

'It's a benchmark, to see how jaded you've become. That childlike feeling when you're in a car and you go into a tunnel, or when you open the curtains and it's snowing outside.'

'Or an aeroplane flies over, low.'

He nodded. She gave him the time to say more, but he stayed silent.

'Well. That's a segue, I suppose. Connection with those childlike responses. After all, our work is all about moving you away from that terrible event you witnessed when you were too young to process it. We're trying to remodel it into something that the adult you can detach from, look back on. A memory you can pack away with the others. Something you control, rather than something that controls you.'

'I thought we tried that, and failed.'

Alex reached over and poured two cups of tea. 'Come on, Jake. Don't be obtuse. You know this. Failure isn't an excuse to give up: it's an important part of learning. I did warn you the reliving process would be difficult.' She added the milk and stirred two sugar lumps into Sawyer's cup. 'How are you coping?'

'Trying to eat better. Watching *Life on Earth*.'

'The original series? How wonderful. I can see how that would be soothing. It ties in with my point about failure.'

Sawyer nodded. 'Of all the species that have existed on Earth, ninety-nine point nine per cent are now extinct.'

'Yes. And some believe we are currently in the grip of a sixth mass extinction. The others were quite sudden natural events, but this one is in slow motion. Triggered by humanity's actions on Earth.'

'Depends what you mean by "natural events", I suppose.' Sawyer reached over for the tea and set it down on the coffee table. He grabbed a couple of biscuits and dunked one. 'Some would say that natural disasters and freak weather are Earth's way of trying to get rid of us.'

'The Gaia theory.' Alex sipped her tea, winced at the heat. 'It's *all* a survival story, Jake. On a grand scale, we're part of that tiny section of life that managed to survive. On an individual level, we all have to find our own ways to live. Adversity, mistakes, failure. It helps us to refine our methods, leads to deeper understanding.'

He munched at the biscuit, spilling crumbs into a cupped hand. 'I dreamt of the killer.'

'Your mother's killer?'

'Another dream where I was there again, as it was happening, as he was hitting her with the hammer. Usually, I can't do anything. But this one was almost lucid. She pulled off his balaclava, and I saw his face. Dark, heavy eyebrows. Black moustache, with a touch of grey.'

Alex pondered. 'It might feel like progress, but it could be just your imagination, filling in a gap. The treatment so far has given you confidence to get up closer to the events, in your dreams. But how are you doing when you're not asleep? Are you still trying to recreate the feeling you experienced in the cave?'

He sat back. 'I haven't felt anything like it since.'

'We've talked about fear. Your apparent inability to feel it, to understand it, how it's part of our survival system. Did you finish the book Maggie gave you? *The Gift of Fear*?'

He nodded. 'Had a couple of days' downtime recently.'

'You're not the only one, you know. We all have a strange relationship with fear. It's a kind of hardwired high. And we seek out the buzz without the bodily peril. Horror films, rollercoasters.' Alex set down her cup and leaned forward, resting her hands on one knee. 'Jake, in the field, when we tried the reliving, you were distressed. You asked why love hurts so much. Love is a deep, complex feeling. And the panic or type of fear you felt in the cave, that's also deep and complex. Despite all of the pain that love has brought you, it's a pain you understand. And so I think you're excited by this new feeling that's equally rich and unfathomable, but that isn't compromised by the baggage from your mother's death.'

Sawyer gave a weak smile. 'So I'm seeking extreme experiences of danger and risk because I'm hoping that the deep and complex feeling of fear will come to replace the deep and complex feeling over what happened to my mother?'

His burner phone sounded with a message alert.

Alex raised an eyebrow at the unfamiliar tone. 'We should have a second try at reliving soon. Take you through the experience again, see if we can get any further.' She stared him down. 'You do realise that we're not working towards improving your vision of your mother's murderer so you can pursue some kind of cold case. We're trying to help you to live a less troubled life in the here and now.'

'Of course.'

She sighed. 'Have you looked into it from a hardware angle? Neurology? You were attacked yourself, with the hammer.'

'My father told me I was examined at nine, and again when I was sixteen. CT, MRI. He insists I was "damaged". I suppose I could get my hands on the imagery. Revisit it.'

He took out the burner phone. Text message from Max Reeves, asking him to call.

'You should get a fresh consult,' said Alex. 'A full picture. New opinion, with current technology. It might help you. As we mentioned last time, my concern over your lack of fear response is that your judgement is impaired, meaning you put yourself, and others, in jeopardy. You can't keep getting away with that.'

Sawyer stood up. 'I'll get the original test results. Got a lot on at the moment.' He waved the phone. 'I need to call someone.'

Alex smiled. 'If you're quick, I can stop the clock.'

Sawyer walked out to the end of Alex's drive and stood by the Mini, staring down to where the lane blended into rolling farmland at the fringes of the Manifold Valley. He called Reeves.

'Mr Sawyer. You're keen. Couple of things you'll be interested in. The name you gave me, Caldwell. First, the good news. William Caldwell was the DCI at Buxton station in the 1980s. So he would have certainly had the authority to let Casey walk.' Reeves took a wheezy breath. 'Got a mugshot from his file. I'll send it. This number safe for media?'

'Yeah.' Sawyer braced. 'Bad news?'

'Might be a problem if you want to talk to Caldwell about what he did with the hammer Casey got for him. He's dead. Well, technically. His wife reported him missing in September 1997. Nothing since. You know how it works: after seven years with no contact, we assume you're not coming back.'

A blast of wind whistled in from the fields; Sawyer turned back to face the house. 'So he's been legally dead for fourteen years now.'

Reeves cleared his throat. 'Good luck with that one.'

'His wife still alive?'

'No idea.'

'What about the burgundy BMW?'

'Fuck me, Sawyer. Give us a chance. This is unpaid freelance, you know. There's a lot of those models registered. It'll take time, off the books.'

Sawyer closed his eyes. 'I need a steer.'

'On what?'

Sawyer opened his eyes: sky white as clay, no sun. 'On a current case.'

Reeves sighed. 'Depends what you want to know. Please tell me this is your special secret phone. I can't help you on your own case. I know nothing. I don't want to know nothing.'

'Anything,' said Sawyer. 'You don't want to know anything. Double negative.'

Reeves laughed. 'Is this how you're dealing with suspension? Turning into the grammar police?'

'The guy they found this morning at the Monsal Trail. Cause of death?'

Silence from Reeves.

'Max. Two bodies discovered in two days. Both adult males, similar age. It'll be on the database. Shared intelligence. Cross reference with crossbow crime in the Southeast.'

'There's no need to fish, Jake. It's a different MO, this time. No crossbow. Someone bashed his head in.'

17

The woman twisted off her yellow gloves and tapped on the door. She paused, and entered. The old sitting room had been cleared of all furniture, apart from a line of bulging bookcases and a new-looking bottle-green sofa against the far wall, below an enormous window.

The tall, slender man lay across the sofa, cast in dappled shadow from the window's Venetian blind. Black hoodie, jeans, luminous red trainers. He was reading by the light of a lamp clipped to his book. Music played from an unseen source: dense and oppressive drone metal, but with the volume almost too low to be discernible. The man tipped his head as the woman entered.

She closed the door behind her and lingered there in the gloom. 'Are you okay, dear? Cold out.'

'I was reading.' His voice was soft, almost whispered. 'Asimov. A story set in the future, where real teachers have been replaced by computers. Not science fiction. Horror, I'd say.' The woman took a few steps forward. 'The children wonder about their counterparts in the past, about how much fun it would have been to have real teachers and real books.'

The woman smiled. 'Not really the future, is it? More like now.'

He chuckled, bitter. 'We used to think of the future as this glorious place of progress. Domed houses. Pills for food. All the corners planed off. All the mess tidied up. An ultimate refinement, driven by science and technology. Living longer, living better. Now, though, that dream is dead. The future's not what it used to be.'

The woman took a deep, steady breath. Her lined face crumpled. 'I have to go out, love.'

The man's head wilted. 'And I was reading Brautigan again. His "pure water touching clear sky". One of the original dreamers.' He sighed, shook his head. 'You have freedom here.'

She moved closer. 'I feel wrong. I need real air. Clear sky.' She smiled.

The man whipped his head round to face her. The light from the window kept his face in shadow. 'Don't try to mirror me. You'll stay here in the grounds. This needs a woman's touch.' He lifted himself upright and stood over her. 'A mother's touch.' He closed his spindly fingers around her shoulders and wrung out a smile. Chipped teeth, yellow around the gums. She flinched as his faecal breath wafted down. He was somewhere in his early thirties, with wide, curious eyes floating behind the dense lenses of his outmoded silver-rimmed glasses. His mousey-brown hair was unstyled and receding, with feathery tufts hanging over his ears. He reached up a hand and cupped his chin, massaging the stubble. 'This is how we change the world, remember? This is how we remodel this future that's been built by phonies. Greatness is achieved when we plant trees, even though we know we'll never sit in their shade.'

The woman trembled, as he turned towards the door.

'Love, I brought them together, like you asked. She thinks she's going to be punished. Or something.'

He walked out into the long hall. 'Let's make sure they know the rules.'

———

The girl and boy sat, side by side, on a long, wall-mounted bench at the far end of the room. She wore a pear-green winter parka; her long brown hair scattered over the fur-lined hood. The boy was a year or two older: pale, unblemished skin; thick black hair, with several curved strands flopped down over his pained, droopy eyes, as if to obscure the view. They were both well fed and dressed in clean clothes, layered for the cold weather. The boy kept his head down, but the girl stared ahead: angry, confused.

The walls were bare, but the room was decorated in cheerful primary colours, and brightly lit from a skylight and a side window that looked out onto the fields at the back of the house. A grid of gym lockers sat behind the bench where the children were seated, with rows of uniform tables and chairs in the centre.

The older woman entered, followed by the tall man. She waited by the door while he walked over to the children and crouched before them. The boy kept his gaze on the floor, but the girl stared him out with bloodshot eyes.

The man spoke in his whisper. 'Joshua.' He laid his long fingers on the boy's hair, giving it an awkward ruffle. 'Have you explained to Holly how the tags work?' Joshua flicked up his eyes, shook his head. The man stood up. He pulled out one of the chairs, flipped it to face the children and sat down. The chairs were child sized, and his knees jutted up high. He smiled and lifted the sleeve of his hoodie to reveal a black bracelet with a steady green LED light. 'It's really easy. The tags on your ankle collars are connected to this sensor on my wrist. I've written some computer code that monitors the distance of the tags to the centre of the house. It's called geofencing. If one of the tags is detected to have moved outside of the distance, then I get a vibration on my bracelet. I wear it at all times, even in bed. And it's waterproof. I can then use my remote to send a mild electric shock to the appropriate tag. It's not too strong. Just enough to cause a muscular spasm and stop your movement.' Holly looked up at the woman, who greeted her with a smile: unreturned. 'I hope you're being kind to Holly, Joshua. It's good to have a companion, isn't it?' Joshua raised his eyes, nodded, dropped them again. 'We might have someone else coming soon. Would you like that?'

Another nod from Joshua. Holly dropped her chin to her chest and started to snuffle and weep.

'Don't cry, love.' The woman stepped forward, but the man held up a hand.

He edged forward off the chair and ran his fingers through Holly's hair, smoothing and tidying the loose ends. 'I'm not going to hurt you, Holly. I'm going to help you.' He waved at the window. 'The hurt is out there. It's all around. In the air. But not in here.'

Holly lifted her face and glared at the man, her cheeks shining with tears. 'I want... to go... *home*.'

He stood up, glanced back at the woman. 'Your parents will see you again. But not yet.' He took out a key and headed for a door at the front of the room. 'Now. It's time for the day's lesson.'

18

Sawyer left the Mini in a lane near an outdoor centre at Thornbridge Hall and joined an off-road walking route towards Hassop Station and the Monsal Trail. Keating would have closed the station and blocked all the roads in and out of the area. Depending on where the new victim's body had been found, he would have also closed the public access points to the trail and Sally's team would soon be conducting line and spiral searches.

Like many cycling routes in the area, the Monsal Trail ran along an old railway line. It told a familiar story: obsolete or unsustainable industry remodelled to serve the tourist trade.

Sawyer hurried along the dirt track, across a ridge which looked down on the section of the trail near Monsal Dale and the Instagram hotspot of the Headstone Viaduct. He knew the route from summer picnics with his father and brother, in the desolate years following his mother's death: cheese and beetroot sandwiches on white bread; hard-boiled eggs in Tupperware; crisps and Fanta and ignored tomatoes. They had slouched on an old Tartan rug—four become three—and tracked the walkers and cyclists with envious eyes: the sibling horseplay; the grinning couples; the unfractured families. His father—normally so sturdy and erudite—had been a black-eyed shell for the first year: wincing through every heartbeat, carried from place to place by a chariot of grief. And then, Sawyer had watched with a mixture of horror and relief, as the arch pragmatist was drawn into the dusty old country churches around Tideswell, in search of something more than just life followed by emptiness. Whatever he found there, it helped him weather the days. As Sawyer approached his teens, there was a sudden shift, as his father seemed to find a new focus. It was more than just religious reawakening. It was as if, after a long time frozen, he had found a way to thaw himself.

After half an hour of walking, Sawyer reached the outer cordon, around the back of the station car park. It was mid-afternoon, but the sky was already greying, yielding to dusk. He stumbled down a slope of frozen mud and caught sight of the yellow-and-white forensic tent, pitched just off to the side of the trail. It was normally a busy spot with lots of two-way walking and cycling traffic; too risky for the killer to engage his victim in the daytime. Although the station wasn't active, it was a busy cycle hire centre and café, so he wouldn't have risked being seen there during business hours. But it was a waypoint; a clear meeting spot. This wasn't an opportunistic killing. He had planned it, probably arranged to meet. So, why would you kill your victim near the station and dump their body further along the trail?

Sawyer headed across the lower part of the ridge and moved beyond the crime scene marker tape, out to the station's natural point of foot entry: a side lane that connected to the main building from the larger Monyash Road. A low wall marked the station boundary, with a short footpath leading to the concourse. He stood against the wall, hidden by a canopy of unruly branches. Through the gaps, he could see the Scientific Services Unit van, and his colleagues—transport police, suited detectives, uniforms in high-viz tunics, FSIs in white Tyvek suits—as they co-ordinated the response, working to ensure the high profile area could be re-opened to the public soon. He shouldn't have been able to get this close; he should at least have been clocked by observers on the outer cordon. Sawyer felt a twinge of professional outrage at the lack of diligence.

He looked around. Plenty of secluded patches—undergrowth, bushes, copses—with a reasonable eyeline on the footpath area. A bright blue station sign was mounted on a pole at the end of the path; an obvious marker. A meeting point. A spot which could easily be scoped and observed by someone off the side of the lane. He took out his phone and turned on the light, keeping it low, aimed towards the ground. He advanced towards the sign, sweeping the light across the width of the path, lingering at the scrubby edges. He was close enough to hear the officers' voices.

He would move in as close as he dared; up to the sign. If he was spotted, he would be challenged and his presence logged. He was on public ground, outside the police cordon, but it would hardly help his case: a suspended officer snooping around an active deposition scene.

A few feet from the sign, his phone light picked up a glint in a thicket of grass at the path edge. At first, it looked like a long piece of coloured paper, maybe a chocolate bar wrapper. Or a pen? Pencil? Sawyer stooped and moved his light closer.

It was a black crossbow bolt: thin and long—fifteen to twenty inches—with a pointed tip and feathered flight.

Sawyer switched his phone to camera mode and took several pictures from the side and above.

Louder voices. If any officers walked out of the station and onto the path, they would be at the opening by the sign in seconds, and would spot him. He backed away and moved off, back along the ridge to rejoin the walking route. At the section that overlooked the dale and viaduct, he took out his phone and studied the photo. The bolt looked new, unblemished. No sign of anything on the tip. There was a raised collar in the centre, with an etched symbol: a reproduction of a sketch. A human eye shape, with an iris-like circle in the centre surrounded by seven rays.

He took out his burner phone and called Walker's number.

'Hello?' Walker sounded suspicious, nervous.

'Are you on scene?'

Walker paused, lowered his voice. 'Sir? You mean—'

'The body. Hassop Station. Monsal Trail.' Walker was silent. Chatter in the background. Female voice: loud and confident. 'It's a PAYG phone. No trail to me. Or you.'

'Yes. I'm—'

'I can hear Sally. You're at the tent.' Sawyer drew in a breath through his nose. The air was crisp and thin. 'He missed.'

'Sorry?'

'The crossbow killer. He arranged to meet the victim out front. He took his shot, missed. Victim spooks, runs down the ridge onto the trail. Killer follows him, finishes him off.'

A pause, as Walker moved out of the tent. 'How do you know it was the same killer?'

Sawyer smiled. 'I'll show you mine if you show me yours. What are the victims' names?' Silence from Walker. 'Come on, Matt. They'll come out soon, anyway.'

'Grindleford vic is Lee Cunningham, forty-seven. Monsal guy is Adrian Little, forty-five.'

Sawyer took out the tactical pen and noted the names in his pad. 'Go to the front entrance, just off the road at the station concourse. There's a footpath. Low wall. Search the edges of the path. For extra brownie points, wander out there yourself before Sally's team get to it. You need to check on any other crossbow killings recently. Be generous. Give it a year. Probably up north, but don't restrict yourself. Cross ref for connections between victims. Focus on motive. I don't think you'll find DNA. But get the why and it'll give you the who.'

19

Sawyer studied the menu; Eva studied Sawyer. 'Not hungry?'

'Not a lot I can eat here, really.'

She slumped over the table. 'Seriously? A mainstream Italian joint and there's not a lot you can eat?'

He glanced up. 'Intolerance.'

Eva took off her Tom Fords and polished the lenses with a napkin. 'Lactose? Peanut?'

'Weird food.'

She shook her head. 'Can you cope with pasta?'

He gave her a little boy grimace. 'Not too spicy, though.'

'This is like having dinner with my ten-year-old son.'

Sawyer sipped at his Coke. 'That's the sexiest thing you've ever said to me.'

The restaurant—Antonio's, in Buxton town centre—was rustic and cramped, the walls cluttered with Italian memorabilia of dubious origin. Eva ordered the 'green burger'; Sawyer asked for lasagne. Despite his protests, she took the executive decision of a shared dish of steamed greens.

They looked at each other, caught in the limbo between the waiter's arrival and departure. Sawyer had overreached with his dress: blue suit jacket, white shirt, orange tie. Eva, as ever, was elegant in a black cocktail dress and grey shrug, perfectly pitched to shine against the scenery.

Sawyer raised his eyebrows at the silence. 'How are things at home?'

Eva rested her hands on the table. Sawyer glanced down and darted his eyes back up. She smiled. 'Yes. Still wearing the wedding ring.'

'Why?'

'I like it. As jewellery.'

'And you don't think of it as a mark of ownership?'

Eva poured herself a glass of wine. 'Are you virtue signalling or making a passive aggressive comment against Dale?'

'My feminist credentials are without question, surely? Has Dale been around?'

She took a drink. 'He came to the house with a few others. Marco wasn't there.'

'Shaun?'

She nodded. 'Couple of new faces, too. Kids, really. I have some information for you. Don't know how useful it is, though.'

Sawyer took out his pen and pad. 'That's what witnesses say when they know they've got something good.'

She balked. 'Witnesses? You're off duty, remember?'

'No such thing. It's a myth.'

'Even under suspension?'

'It's a grey area. Tell me the thing. You know you want to.'

Eva took another long sip of wine, holding the moment. 'Dale has a room at the house where he meets friends and associates. I think he thinks it's private, but you can hear bits and pieces from the bathroom on that floor, depending on who's speaking. I overheard a few things. There's another club, as well as the one in Manchester. Closer.'

'In the Peak District?'

'Somewhere near here. Fairfield. Just outside Buxton. They're calling it "Players".'

Sawyer frowned and drummed his fingers on the table. 'Did he stay over?'

'No. It had the feeling of him dropping in for a quick visit, to approve something. Normally, people come to visit him. But he'd been out and they all arrived together. They were only at the house for an hour or so.' She lowered her eyes. 'He didn't even see Luka.'

'How is he?'

She looked at him. 'He asked after you again.'

'I'll come to see him tomorrow.'

'Let me know first. In case Dale is there.'

'Does that matter?'

'Yes. It matters.'

The food arrived. Sawyer leaned in to Eva's plate. 'That looks healthy.'

'It's made from quinoa, kale and beans. I assume you haven't eaten any of those things.'

He took a small block of grey metal out of his pocket and nudged it across the table. 'This is a micro listening device. There's a magnetic strip at the side. Is there anywhere in Dale's special room you could hide it?'

Eva unwrapped her knife and fork, unfazed. 'Loads of places. But why would I do that?'

'Dale wouldn't move out of town if he was opening some social club franchise. And he tried to spook me into backing off. There's something deeper going on here. It's why he wants the distance. I need to know more, though.'

She shook her head. 'He sweeps the place with a little handheld detector thing. Paranoid. I don't want him finding it and accusing me—'

'Take him a drink or something. Slip in the device when he's halfway through a meeting. Remove it straight after.'

Eva laughed. 'Jake, we're not living in a spy movie. You might not like Dale, but don't dismiss him as stupid. I wouldn't normally do that. Bring him a drink, slip out again. He'll notice, and he'll assume I'm up to something. You'll have to find another use for your special bug. Was it expensive?'

Sawyer toyed with his lasagne, sulking. 'Very.'

'So, you're Batman now? An outlaw with gadgets?'

He laughed and pocketed the device. 'Chapel-en-le-Frith is hardly Gotham City.'

'Luka is big on Batman at the moment. The Nolan films.' She took a small bite of her burger. 'Bit too young for it, I think. But it's so hard to gauge, these days.'

Sawyer dug into his lasagne. 'They grow up so fast, right?'

She eyed him. 'It's true. Faster than ever. They have to. There's so much flying at them, from the internet, peers. So much to keep up with. Luka is even getting fashion conscious now. He's ten! Do you remember worrying about your clothes at that age?'

'I wasn't a particularly happy ten-year-old.'

'In contrast to your bright and sunny adult self, you mean?'

He snorted, forked in some pasta.

Eva smiled at him, caught his eye. 'I realise it's a bit early to talk about stepfather duties, but Luka could certainly use a good male influence.'

'Let me know when you find someone who isn't suspended from their job, accused of murder.'

'You're a master deflector, you know. Seriously. He's always talking about how you picked the lock, got him out of that cave.'

Sawyer sighed. 'It feels big to him, but it was just me at work.'

'Right. Outwitting a killer and kidnapper. Just another day at the office.'

He darkened. 'I'm not a superhero. Luka shouldn't build me up in his mind. I'll let him down.'

'You don't have to be an ideal father figure or role model. Luka might want to show everyone how sharp and sophisticated he is, but he's ten years old. He thinks in black and white. To him, you're... somebody who does good. Somebody who does the right thing.'

Sawyer nodded. 'Like I said, I'll let him down.'

———

Back at the cottage, Sawyer looked online and found a basic one-page website for the Players club in Manchester, with a *Coming Soon* splash for the branch in Fairfield. It was as Eva had described: two floors, one with snooker and pool for adults only, and another for all ages, with retro and contemporary arcade cabinets and LAN computer gaming. It was plausible, but not Dale's style, and the numbers didn't add up for such aggressive franchising.

He searched for the crossbow victims: Lee Cunningham, Adrian Little. Cunningham's murder was showing up in local news, but Little's hadn't filtered through yet. No related stories. He took out his phone, navigated to the photo of the crossbow bolt, and cropped the image to the sketch on the collar. He sent it to his laptop and tried a reverse image search. The algorithm delivered plenty of close-ups of eyes and eyeballs, but nothing that resembled the hand-drawn look, with the seven rays surrounding the central iris.

Movement in the corner of his vision. He turned.

Bruce had hopped off his usual spot by the sofa and was creeping towards the front door, staying low, in stalking mode. A mouse, bold enough to venture inside for shelter from the cold?

The cat stopped at the front door and sat there, staring up at nothing. Sawyer walked to the door and opened it, flinching at the frosty air. Bruce gave him a curious look, and stayed where he was.

Sawyer gazed out into the blackness, listening.

Swishing trees, an occasional distant car.

20

Sheila Caldwell led Sawyer through a narrow entrance hall into the bungalow's musty sitting room. She was stooped and slow, barely mobile. Late seventies, maybe early eighties. She opened the door and shuffled through, keeping her head down, as if in shame.

The room was overrun with outmoded chintz—doilies, a barometer, Toby jugs—and baked in the heat from two wall-length radiators. Sawyer touched a finger to one and had to withdraw it immediately. 'Nice and cosy in here.'

Sheila raised her head and searched the room, eventually fixing her rheumy eyes on him. 'No sense in being cold. Plenty of time for that when you're dead.'

Sawyer laughed; Sheila faked a smile and gestured towards an olive-green velour armchair opposite the matching sofa. The fireplace had been tiled over, and the shelf above was jammed with knick-knacks and sterile Royal Doulton figures. He leaned in and studied the one photograph: a framed black-and-white shot of a younger Sheila on a beach in a chaste bikini, squinting into the camera. A man—shorter, older—stood beside her in T-shirt and shorts, folding his arms, grinning. No moustache or watch. Sawyer took out his phone and compared the image of the man with the bland file photo sent by Reeves; the expressions were different, but it was the same individual in both shots.

Sawyer dropped down into the armchair, sending up a puff of dust. Sheila took the sofa, staying oddly in the centre, between the two cushions. The years had lined her face in all the expected places, but her short, dyed black hair bought her a decade.

She licked her thin lips and gazed ahead for a few seconds, then caught herself and looked up. 'Oh, I'm sorry. Would you like a cup of tea?'

'I'm fine, Mrs Caldwell. Thank you for seeing me. As I said on the phone, I'm a Detective Inspector and I work at Buxton station. My boss used to work under your husband.'

She gave a wheezy laugh. 'I'm sure he did.'

'My dad was there, too. When he was a young copper.' Sheila's head drooped again. Narcolepsy? 'He's an artist now.'

Sheila startled. 'Very good.' She shook her head, suddenly angry. 'What is all this about?' She kept her eyes fixed on the worn tartan rug in front of the fireplace.

Sawyer leaned forward and rested his elbows on his knees. 'Just a few questions about your husband.'

She raised her eyes to him. 'Ex-husband.'

'Did you marry again? After his disappearance?'

She started to laugh but lapsed into a coughing fit. 'No, no. I mean he was declared legally deceased.'

'After seven years. You would have been in your fifties, though? I thought you might have—'

Sheila waved a hand. 'Yes, yes. I *saw* people. What do you want? A fucking life history?' She spat out the expletive with enough venom to jolt Sawyer back in the chair.

'Do you remember much about the night of William's disappearance?'

Sheila sucked in a breath. 'Of *course*. It still feels like it was last week. He went out, on business. Didn't tell me what it was about. He never did. Why would he? That was his job. And he didn't come back.' She sank forward, deflating. 'William never saw the job as something he picked up and put down. He was so deeply involved in his cases. And he brought them home. Never spared me any detail. I was always worried that he would go out and not come back. And then one day, that's just what happened. Nobody has seen him since.'

'Did he mention someone called Owen Casey?'

Sheila thought for a second. 'Not that I remember. He was distracted that evening, though. More than usual. It was as if something was eating at him. Boring into him. He seemed... angry.' At last, she raised her head fully and blinked her eyes, focusing on him. 'I *know* you.'

He nodded, patient. 'From the newspaper?'

'From what happened. To your mother. To *you*.'

Sawyer staggered to his feet. The room swayed.

She looked down again. 'I was a teacher, too. A lecturer.'

Too hot in here. He glanced at the door; it seemed smaller, miniaturised.

'My goodness, Mr Sawyer. We both lost so much. So long ago.'

Sawyer steadied himself on the fireplace and stared into the photograph of Sheila and William, caught in the centre of a sun-bleached half-world: a frozen eternity, drained of colour, cast in monochrome.

'I used to read poetry to William. I don't think he ever clicked with it, but he was tolerant. There's a poem I love, by an American writer. Delmore Schwartz. He has a great line: "Time is the fire in which we burn." Isn't that wonderful?'

———

Sawyer drove, too fast, away from the Caldwell house in the wild countryside of Padley, down to soothing, touristy Hartington. It was a lousy day—gloomy, flecked with sleet —and he pitched the Mini around blind corners, half expecting a tractor or lumber truck to pick him off at any moment.

He called a number on his burner phone, set it on speaker, and mounted it in the dashboard dock. It rang twice before pick-up.

'Frazer Drummond.'

'Civilian Sawyer speaking.'

Drummond paused. 'You're using a secret phone. That's so cute.'

'For the greater good. I've got an idea. A theory.'

A pause as Drummond sat down. He was in his office, probably alone. 'Go for it. I'm too busy for more bodies at the moment.'

'Adrian Little. The guy they found off the Monsal Trail.'

'You *are* keeping your hand in.'

'Battered to death. What with?'

Another pause from Drummond. 'Looks like something flat, metal. Spade, probably.'

Sawyer braked as he turned into a narrow lane, and crawled past an oncoming SUV. 'The crossbow. It's not about efficiency.'

'You think it's the same killer?'

'Yes. He missed with the second vic. The spade was back-up.'

'Why not use a knife? Easier to conceal.'

'It's about proximity. The spade still keeps him at arm's length. He can't stand to be close to them.'

Drummond clicked his tongue. 'A revulsion.'

'Yes. He isn't using a distance weapon for security. It's because he can't touch them, can't look them in the eye.'

'Hold on. How do you know he tried the crossbow again and missed?'

'Like you say, keeping my hand in. They might even bother to tell you officially soon.'

Drummond chuckled. 'So, how does this help?'

'There's something longstanding here. Something enormous that embedded itself a long time ago. Revulsion, yes. Maybe even anger. And yet he's denying himself the pleasure of being close to their pain, the sadism of seeing their awareness of their final moments. Why so squeamish? If we can answer that, we might be able to ease your workload.'

21

Maggie had taken a central table at the Nut Tree, a compact café on the main road through Hartington. She was pouring from a teapot, filling two large mugs as Sawyer entered.

He crashed down into the seat opposite and shovelled a heaped spoonful of sugar into his mug. 'Nice timing.'

She added the milk, glanced up at him. 'I've worked you out, after all these years. You used to be late for everything, but now you're early.'

'Is that a marker for anything? Sociopathy?'

Maggie smiled. 'My charitable assessment would be borderline personality disorder.'

'Alex isn't so coy. She's stuck on PTSD.'

She balked. '*Jake*. Confidentiality.' She nodded to the tray on the table. 'I got you a rock cake. It's technically confectionery, but the raisins mean you're getting one of your five a day.'

'Thanks, but I heard it's seven now. You not eating?'

'Had breakfast with Mia and Freddy before I dropped them off.'

Sawyer caught Maggie's gaze. Her red hair was

94

uncombed; dark circles underscored her eyes. 'Not sleeping? You on FLO work for Keating?'

She sighed. 'We've done this. Conflict of interest. I need the work.'

'So, yes. Is Justin being difficult?'

Maggie bought some time with a sip of coffee. 'It's all difficult. Freddy is oblivious, but Mia has worked it out. She's moody, in her room all the time. More like a teenager than a ten-year-old. I just wish they were more in sync. She bosses him around, he bites back, I break it up. It'd be nice if they'd just be kids and enjoy... kid things.'

Sawyer picked a raisin-free edge off the rock cake. 'Kid things?'

'Yeah. Justin's taking them swimming on Sunday. He always seems to do the fun stuff, while I'm the one who gets them to school, nags them about phones and whatever.'

'Try and focus on the good bits. At least you know they're safe.'

Maggie eyed him. 'I saw Holly Chilton's parents yesterday. The poor mother, Jake. Jesus Christ. She just paces and paces. She reminds me of one of my clients. He can never sit still, never settle. It's like he's worried that if he stays in one place for too long, he'll get taken out by a sniper or something.'

Sawyer gave a dark laugh. 'What about Joshua Maitland's parents?'

She stared into the mug. 'They're in a different place. More resigned, expecting the worst. The Chiltons are full of that awful hope. Alert to every noise, expecting every call or contact to bring some news. They're still clinging to the possibility that their daughter might come back one day. But the Maitland parents have lost that sense of bracing.'

'The acceptance stage of grief. Sounds like the Chiltons are still in denial.'

95

'It's a crude model, but it often works that way.' She took a drink. 'Now. Please tell me you've hired a lawyer. I could talk to Justin—'

'I think they're alive.'

'Who?'

'The children. Holly and Joshua.'

She slumped. 'Based on what?'

'Experience. The time between the disappearances. Couple of other details. I spoke to Shepherd. I know he's on it. Wouldn't give me much else. Don't tell him I told you I'd spoken to him, though.'

She raised her eyebrows, sarcastic. 'Of course not. That would be unethical.'

Sawyer munched on the cake, spoke with his mouth full. 'Holly told her parents she was meeting a friend.' He swallowed, took a swig of tea. 'Joshua left school alone and didn't return. Couple of months ago. But Shepherd said Joshua's parents think he might have been meeting someone, too. Right?'

Maggie took a slow sip of tea, watching him. 'Shepherd wouldn't give you that much, Jake. He's Mr By-The-Book. Not long a DS.'

Sawyer fussed with the cake, avoiding eye contact. 'He didn't tell me directly, no.'

'Tell me you haven't spoken to Walker.' Now she was playing him, gauging his position. She could have heard about his hospital visit from Drummond, or maybe Walker himself.

'Not about this case, no.'

'But about a different case?' She smiled. 'The two station murders, right?'

'Mags. I'm trying—'

'To help?' Maggie bristled and leaned forward. 'Help *yourself*. You're under investigation. Leave this to Keating and Shepherd. This is your condition, steering you. Jake, you're not the centre of the universe. Things can get fixed without you. Let other people do this work and focus on getting professional advice to make your accusation go away. Then you can help to find these children. Officially.'

Sawyer sifted through the pile of raisins on his plate. 'I'm on it.'

———

The sleet had solidified into a squall of hail that rattled down onto the windscreen. Sawyer sped over Sterndale Moor, hemmed in by the leafless hedges, and joined a rickety A-road down to the outskirts of Buxton. As the weather calmed and a low winter sun cracked through the clouds, he played *Mezzanine* by Massive Attack; another favourite from his nineties teenage wilderness years. The car trembled with the pummelling drums and pulsing bass. It was a blissful fusion of private audio and natural visual. One of those soundtrack moments; the feeling that he was the dark star in a film of his own life.

Logan met him at The Source; same table. He looked soggy and ragged and didn't bother to shake Sawyer's hand as he sat down. 'Fucking weather!'

'It's winter. You not used to it by now?'

Logan swiped at his head, spraying water. 'No, I'll never get used to it. I miss London.'

'Rains there, too.'

'Yeah, but... It's proper rain here. No buildings to soak it up. Anyway, I got your message. I was worried it was a hoax. New number?'

'That's the one I'm using for this. Think of it as our own little hotline.'

Logan waved to the man at the counter. 'Two teas.'

Sawyer hitched up his jacket collar against the cold of the café. 'Let's not get too cosy. Business over pleasure.'

Logan grinned. 'Go on then, boss. What have you got for me?'

'I need you to get your snout in the trough, if you'll pardon the imagery.'

'And implication.'

'I've got a name. William Caldwell. He was the DCI of Buxton station in the 1980s. Hands-on type, according to his wife. I think he was involved in my mother's murder, and he might have had something to do with Klein's death, too.'

Logan spluttered. 'He'll be cracking on.'

'Yeah. Seventies, at least.' Sawyer went quiet as the man brought their tea over. 'Thing is, he walked out of his house one fine day in 1997. Never came back. No sign since. Declared legally dead in 2004.'

'So why would you do a runner, nearly ten years after you've got away with murder?'

Sawyer ran a teaspoon across the film on top of his tea. 'That's what I need to find out. I want you to dig into prison visitor records, for HMP Sudbury. That's where Marcus Klein did most of his time before being moved to a Cat D when he got his parole. Did he get a visit from Caldwell? Also, check for "Owen Casey".'

Logan winced. 'That's a lot of work, Sawyer. Few favours to call in, too.'

'Don't get too excited. This is not the beginning of a beautiful friendship. But it could work out for both of us. If you can help me find the person who really killed Klein, I'll give you the exclusive. I can see the headlines in your eyes already. You could make it all about your favourite subject: yourself. "*How I helped clear hero cop's name.*" Cast me as the incidental beneficiary. Pulitzer might be a stretch, but you'd be up for the Paul Foot Award, at least.'

Logan slurped at his tea, nodded. 'It's a good angle. You might have evolved into a decent hack yourself, you know.'

Sawyer leaned in. 'There's one thing I'd like to clear up first. Someone took a picture of me at the travellers' camp fight. The picture somehow found its way to Keating. Anything to do with you?'

Logan smiled, sheepish. 'As I said, Sawyer, it's all spread so thinly, these days. You have to duck and dive. A contact sent me the shot, yeah. I thought it would help me get something out of Keating, since you weren't helping. The fucker is sewn up tight, though. And then you were arrested for murder and the leverage became irrelevant. Events overtook us.'

'Have you heard anything about the investigation into Klein's death?'

Logan looked out of the window. 'Not a sniff. Sorry to be the bearer of bad news, but in my considerable experience, a watertight operation suggests they really do think they're onto something with you.' He sat back. 'The media blackout on your arrest can't last forever, you know. Whatever you want to call me, Sawyer, I'm a journalist. I'm paid to break big stories. And at the moment, you're the biggest unbroken story in town.'

22

Luka Strickland hopped up onto a chair, opposite Sawyer at the kitchen table. Eva's family home was the largest semi in a quiet estate on the edge of Bakewell. She kept it clean and uncluttered, with little evidence of the domestic turmoil beneath the surface. Sawyer's eyes drifted up to the wall portrait: an enlarged studio shot of Eva with toddler Luka. She had since dyed her white hair black, but Luka had barely changed; he was still small and skinny, with scruffy blond hair. The ten-year-old version before Sawyer at the table wore a pair of glasses with cherry-red frames.

'How are you, Luka?'

'Okay. Just playing PS4. *FIFA*.' He shrugged, took a slurp from a can of Fanta Zero. 'It's awesome.'

'I heard *Pro Evo* was the better football game.'

Luka gave a theatrical scoff and scowled at Sawyer. 'No way! All the teams are wrong. Chelsea are, like, "London Utd".'

'You support Chelsea?'

He scowled again. 'No. Just saying why it's rubbish. I support Man Utd, like my dad.'

'I'm Liverpool. So you're supposed to hate me.'

Luka shrugged. 'Not bothered.'

Eva brought Sawyer a glass of Coke. 'I'm glazing over at the football talk. Brought some work home, so I'll leave you to it.' She trotted out.

Sawyer watched her leave, his gaze lingering. He snapped his eyes away and ran straight into Luka's. 'I've got *FIFA*. Don't play it much, though. I think it's a bit old. Most of the players in my version have retired.'

'You have to get the new one every year. It's a rip-off.'

Sawyer took a drink. 'They should just update it with the new players. Downloadable content.'

Luka frowned, shocked at the idea. 'But they wouldn't be able to charge as much money for it then.'

'Exactly. As you said, it's a rip-off.'

Luka nodded. He drank some of his Fanta, avoiding eye contact.

Sawyer took a pair of handcuffs out of his jacket pocket and laid them on the table. Luka brightened and sat forward. 'Have you heard of Harry Houdini, Luka?' He shook his head. 'He was a magician. A very clever man. He became famous for escaping from special traps, jackets, cases.' Sawyer took out an oblong black case. 'He said that his brain was the key that set his mind free. It's a good line, but he was just a showman who knew how to make things seem more complicated and dangerous than they really were.'

Luka took out his phone. 'Hey, Siri. *Harry Houdini.*'

Sawyer smiled. 'Did it work?'

'Yeah. Wow. He was Hungarian. My friend Tamas is from Hungary.' He looked up. 'Did he get out of handcuffs like these?'

'Much harder than this. But he probably used other

tricks. It's pretty easy to get out of these, though. Or to get into basic locks. You just need the right tools for the job.'

Sawyer opened the case and took out a pair of kirby grips. 'Your mum will have plenty of these hairpins lying round.' He opened up one of the pins until the ends sat at a ninety-degree angle. 'You just have to practise the technique. Takes a while, but you get used to it.' He slotted the bent pin into the keyhole and turned it to the side, creating a kink. He coiled the other part around the kinked section, until it functioned like a makeshift handle. Luka leaned in close. 'See? Now you push in the other pin just above it, and you use one to feel out the tension, and the other as a pick.' He slid the second hairpin into the keyhole above the first. 'You're trying to feel your way through to the tiny pins, like jaws, that keep the lock closed. Then, when you feel the plug that holds the pins move, you push harder with the wrench. Have a try.'

He pushed the handcuffs over to Luka, who held on to the wrench pin and twisted at the pick.

Luka frowned. 'What does it feel like when the plug moves?'

'It takes practice. You get to know it. Keep trying. You're looking for the plugs that aren't loose. The ones that have seized. You can keep the handcuffs and pins. I've got spares of both. I'll give your mum a key, just in case.' Luka worked with the hairpins, twisting and pushing.

Sawyer held the handcuffs firm. 'How are things with your counsellor? Last time I saw you, you said he was alright. Didn't shout.'

Luka glanced up. 'He's fine. We talk about the same stuff all the time, though. Gets a bit boring.'

'Do you talk about other stuff with mates?'

'You mean online? Gaming?'

'Sometimes. You know. Social media. Stuff like Facebook.'

Luka laughed. 'Facebook is for old people.'

'Snapchat?'

He shrugged. 'Yeah. Instagram, too. Some people use the chat in games. And there's a few other networks. MEETUPZ, uChat.' He raised his head, eyes wide. 'Oh! I've got one that's not moving.'

Sawyer smiled. 'That's one of the seized plugs. Now maintain the tension with the wrench pin and push up with the pick pin. *Slowly*.'

'I felt a click!'

'Now find the next one that's seized. You're trying to line them all up. That's when the lock will open. Tell me more about the networks.'

Luka continued to work on the lock. 'We had a presentation at school, about online safety. There was a policeman there. He told us about the dangers of the chat apps and a few other things. Most of the kids just made notes about the apps. They hadn't heard of some of them.'

Sawyer sighed. 'Do you always know who you're talking to?'

Luka shook his head. 'Course not. But everyone can tell if there's someone trying to pretend they're older or a boy pretending to be a girl. They try the same things. I know what it is. At the school they called it "grooming". They make you trust them, ask if you want to meet.'

'Does anyone you know ever go to meet people they talk to on the apps?'

'I don't know anyone who does that. But nobody bothers about the age rules or whatever. My friend, Jaden. His brother is older. He just uses his password.' Luka shoved the handcuffs back across the table and tossed the pins aside. 'This is so *hard*.'

'Nothing good is easy. Keep practising. Watch the YouTube videos.'

'When you got me out of the cave, you did it so quick.' Luka finished his Fanta, looked back at his phone. 'I don't think my dad would be happy about you showing me this.'

'I wouldn't worry about your dad. I think he's busy with his work at the moment.'

23

Sawyer stood before his bedroom mirror and worked through the first of the Wing Chun Kung Fu forms: *Sil Lum Tao* ('Little Idea'). The controlled, meticulous movement was designed to strengthen the core principles of economy and efficiency, but it was also meditative: to fade out the chatter and improve focus.

He hooked a towel around his neck, just above his tattoo: a series of Greek characters that ran across his back, dipping into the valley between his shoulder blades. *Κατά τον δαίμονα εαυτού* ('True to his own spirit').

He showered and changed into jeans, T-shirt, hoodie. It was early evening, but he made himself a milky coffee and settled in to resume an episode of *Life on Earth*. Bruce curled in his usual spot at the foot of the TV stand, regarding Sawyer with a dubious stare.

On-screen, David Attenborough explained how a species of stinging ant defends an acacia tree and in return gets nectar and thorns for nesting. Symbiosis.

He lowered the volume and activated the subtitles, then phoned Walker on the burner. The call connected instantly. 'Did you find the bolt?'

Walker paused. 'Of course. Hold on.' Movement, as he took the phone into another room.

'Can you talk?'

'Just about. Sir. Yes. Found the bolt.'

'And did you look into other crossbow murders?'

A sigh. 'There were two earlier in the year. Stations up in the Dales.'

'Yorkshire? Similar age? Men?'

'Yeah.' A slight hesitation. 'One in his late thirties. Brendan Manning. Another, fifty-one. Cecil Boyd. Couple of weeks apart.'

Bruce had settled his head down between his paws. Sawyer stared at the TV screen: translucent ants swarming over a flailing beetle. 'What about the symbol?'

'Symbol?'

'There's a little sketch engraved into a collar around the bolt. Looks like an eye. Circle in the centre with sun rays around it. Did you get to it before Sally's team?'

'Yes, but it's with her now. Didn't see the symbol.'

Sawyer closed his eyes. 'Check the first bolt. Is the symbol on it, too? Could just be a brand or something, but you might get a hit on where the bolt was bought. If not, reproduce it. Blow it up. But don't release it to the public as a line of enquiry yet.'

Bruce's ear flicked. Sawyer looked around, alert. No car noise. Animals?

'Sir?'

'Now, what's the thing you're not sure you should tell me?'

'What thing?'

Sawyer smiled. 'You hesitated before you told me about the Yorkshire vics.'

Walker cleared his throat. 'Sir, I can't... You should be on your own case. Clearing your—'

'People keep telling me this, as if I'm not doing that. I am. I can multitask.' He stood up and walked to the front door. 'You've got two missing children. No trace. Given the press conference, I'm sure Keating has put most of his resources on it, with Shepherd leading. He's got Moran keeping tabs on me. That means you're on the crossbow murders, probably under DS Myers. I've just gifted you a major find. You're teacher's pet right now. Give me a bit more.' Silence at the other end. 'I won't tell.'

Walker sniffed, lowered his voice. 'One of the Yorkshire victims was on the registry.'

'Sex offender?'

'Yeah. Boyd. Not at the time of his murder, but he had been on it for five years due to an offence against a child committed just over ten years ago.'

Sawyer peered out of the gap between the blind and the front window. Nothing but the moonlit front porch. 'What about the other one? Manning?'

'Nothing. But they found some underage stuff on his computer.'

Sawyer held a few seconds of silence and listened. A slight shuffle from the porch. A footfall? He turned away from the window and kept his voice low. 'And what about the two here? Cunningham and Little.'

'Yeah.' Walker's voice was flat, resigned now to giving away more. 'Cunningham wasn't on the register, but Little was. Coach driver. He was under a Sexual Harm Prevention Order. Something on a school trip.'

'Has Rhodes looked at their computers? Anything on Cunningham's?'

'Some imagery. Nothing hardcore.'

'He was exploring. Early stages.' Sawyer's nose wrinkled. An unfamiliar smell? On-screen, Attenborough crouched in the jungle. The subtitles spoke of how humans

107

have tried many techniques to conquer insects but haven't managed to kill a single species. 'Anything on Cunningham and Little's computers that links to the Yorkshire murders?'

Walker hesitated again, but continued. 'Nothing we can see so far. The usual social networks. Good hygiene with browser history. No obvious chat logs, although Rhodes is still rooting around. Definitely a link, right?'

'I think it's fairly clear that we're looking for a guy who's killing child sex offenders. But what does the connection with the Yorkshire murders tell you?'

'He travels a lot?'

Sawyer slipped on his jacket. He opened the front door and stepped out onto the porch. The smell was more acrid out here; it tickled the back of his throat. Tobacco.

'It tells us that the murders aren't impulsive. He's meticulous. A planner. I'm thinking that the Yorkshire killings might be practice, away from home. We also know that he missed his shot at Hassop Station. So he's not a professional. He's still learning. And now he's up and running, he's not going to stop. He missed, but he still finished the job.' Sawyer closed the door and went back inside. 'But what's *really* interesting is his method.'

'Hunting?'

He flopped back down on the sofa. 'More than that. There's no sport, no pleasure. It's more like a cull.'

24

A dense swirl of snow settled over Buxton High Street. Robbie Carling stepped out of the clinic side door and turned down the alley, away from the street. He walked with a simian slump, head listing from side to side as if scanning the ground for danger. He was in his mid-twenties, but with the stature of a child: coltish and curious.

He cut through a suburb of uniform semis and headed for the Ecclesborough Road Community Centre: a brutalist two-storey block of grey and beige concrete, with the upper floor propped on columns. A group of men had gathered outside the building, by the low railings near the entrance: three small, one large. Robbie tossed his head, shifting his long, greasy hair out of his eyes. He squinted at the men, but didn't slow. He would just breeze past and rest for a while in his flat, giving them time to leave before venturing back out.

To Robbie's horror, the largest of the men—thickset, in a black leather jacket—called to him as he passed. 'Give us a sec, mate.'

Robbie kept walking.

'Oi, oi!'

He glanced back. The men had moved away from the building entrance and were following close behind. The large one loitered, as the other three caught up, led by a chubby white teenager with ratty dreadlocks and a pristine but cheap-looking red-and-white puffer jacket.

'Slow it down, bruv. We come in peace.' The boy clapped a hand on Robbie's shoulder and squeezed, forcing him to stop and turn. 'Just lookin' for a bit of advice, y'get me?' He released Robbie's shoulder and held out his hand to shake. 'My name's Ash, yeah?'

Ash was flabby and leering, with dirty teeth. His dreadlocks looked matted, and he had scrunched them together at the roots, rather than restyle. When he didn't get his handshake, he leaned down, trying to make eye contact, without success.

'Got your dollies, Robbie?' The large man sauntered over and nodded to the paper pharmacy bag in Robbie's hand.

Robbie flashed his eyes up. 'Methadone.'

The big man laughed. 'That's what I said.' The other two gathered round; both teenagers, both uniformed in sportswear. One sucked on a pipe and puffed out a sweet-smelling cloud of vapour. 'Listen. My name's Shaun. You live round here, right? I'm trying to find a place for meself and friends. Nice and cheap. Out of the way.'

Robbie hesitated. He looked at Ash, then Shaun. 'You have to get on the list. It's hard. How do you know my—'

Shaun laughed and shook his head. 'I'm not a fan of waiting, Robbie.'

Ash nodded. 'Life's short, innit?' He clapped his hand back on Robbie's shoulder. 'Let's take a look at your place, yeah? Show us round and we'll sort you with a fix.'

Robbie led the way to a shabby estate of social housing: repurposed flat blocks, bordered by untamed edgeland. They walked down a long, uneven path towards the largest block: five storeys. Robbie paused at the front door, in front of a card lock.

Shaun stepped up beside him. 'Don't worry, Robbie. We just want a look round. This is perfect for me. Do us a favour and I'll get you a proper taste. Never mind that substitute crap.' He took out a white plastic bag, filled with a grainy tan powder. 'No fuckin' fentanyl, either. This is *decent*.'

Robbie looked around. It was approaching dusk, and the street lamps were sparking up. The snow was heavier now, tumbling through the pools of light. 'I'm on a programme.'

Shaun stepped closer. 'That's no problem, Robbie. Really. This is just a little treat. It won't blow your progress. It's like if you're on a diet: having a doughnut from time to time won't kill you. Trust me, we just want a quick look round the place.'

Robbie pocketed the bag and swiped his card to release the door. He led them up a staircase to the second floor. Stale bleach, fresh urine.

The corridor was lined with the entrances to six flats; three on each side. Robbie unlocked the door at the end and entered, followed by Shaun, Ash and friends.

It was surprisingly large, with a spacious central living room, bathroom and kitchen, and, at the end of a short corridor, an open door revealing the bedroom. Shaun stepped into the kitchen, looking the place up and down. 'I'm fuckin' gaspin' for a cup of tea, Robbie. Please tell me you've got fresh milk.'

Robbie brightened. He sidestepped Shaun and checked the fridge. 'Yeah. No problem. See? Got biscuits and that.'

'Nice! Tell you what. Ash here can make us all a nice cup of tea. You can cook up if you like. Where's yer works?'

Robbie frowned; he was breathing fast. 'Bedroom.' He stood there, staring up at Shaun, caught between hunger and suspicion.

Shaun smiled and nodded. 'You're a bit simple, aren't you, mate?'

Robbie turned and slouched into the bedroom, closing the door behind him.

Shaun fell back into the sofa and spread his arms across the back. 'Kettle on. And coats off.' He nodded to the snow at the window. 'Not going out again in that.'

25

The woman reclined in a broad, padded chair at the back of the playroom. Her black woollen hat and yellow gloves sat on a side table next to the chair. She had taken off her black sensor bracelet and rested it on top of the hat.

She held her head on her shoulder, eyes trained on her book: Michelle Obama's autobiography, *Becoming*. She had slotted a remote handheld into the groove between the seat cushion and side of the chair.

The room was vast and bright, with foam patchwork flooring and educational wallcharts: geography, human anatomy, kings and queens. The far wall was lined with shelves full of books, DVDs and Blu-rays. A widescreen TV was mounted on the corner of a recessed wall, beaming down on a central sofa with a high backrest.

Joshua Maitland and Holly Chilton sat side by side, gazing up at an animated movie: *Chicken Little*. Joshua was dressed in light paisley pyjamas, while Holly remained in her day clothes: jeans, jumper. Despite the snow outside, the room was cosy; perhaps too warm. Earlier, despite her clothing, Holly had asked the woman to turn up the heating and dim the lights so she could see the screen better.

Holly glanced at Joshua; he was already looking at her. His eyes widened and he shook his head. Holly slowly turned to peer around the sofa backrest at the woman behind. She kept her voice low, but loud enough to be heard over the movie. 'Can we have a glass of milk, please?'

Normally, the woman would shift in her chair and turn down the request, saying it was too late or they'd had enough for the day. But she didn't respond. The book had dropped onto her lap, and her head had lolled to the side. Holly edged off the sofa and walked to a table near the wall with a stack of books. She made a show of sorting through them, turning her head to check on the woman.

Eyes closed now. No movement.

She looked back to Joshua; again, he shook his head. She smiled, nodded, and walked to the door. It was an unthinkable risk, but if the woman woke, or the man came home, she could always claim she had been heading for the kitchen to get her drink.

The woman didn't wake, and Joshua watched as Holly Chilton walked to the door and slipped through it.

A few minutes later, something caught his eye and he turned to look at the woman. The LED light on the sensor bracelet flashed red. Joshua turned back to the film, queasy with anxiety. Would he be blamed for Holly's departure?

He turned again, and saw the moment the light switched from flashing red back to green.

———

Soon after, the main door at the front of the house slammed shut and the tall man walked in, head bowed.

The woman stirred. 'Cold out there, love?'

He took off his hat and scarf and looked up at the

screen. 'More Disney. They should watch things with more substance.'

'They like those. It keeps them happy. How did you get on?'

He winced. 'Nothing. Didn't show.'

He looked at the woman's side table, at the bracelet. 'I told you not to take that off.'

She smiled, sat up in the chair. 'It's okay. It's right there.'

The man lifted the bracelet off the woollen hat. 'Keep it on a hard surface, so you can hear the vibration.' Jerking his head to face the high-backed sofa, he strode over and peered around the backrest, at Joshua who lay there with his eyes closed, either asleep or pretending to be asleep. He turned and stared at the woman. 'Where's Holly?'

'What's that?'

'*WHERE'S HOLLY?*'

Joshua startled at the shout.

The woman scrambled out of the chair. 'Toilet? Kitchen?'

He glared at her for a second, then dived for the door. In the kitchen, he opened a drawer and took out a heavy torch. He crashed out of the side door and ran down the garden, crunching into the thick snow. He stopped, and shone the torch at the ground ahead.

Footprints. Leading out through a gap in the hedge.

He ducked and barged out into the open field, white and shining in the darkness. The footprints were fresh, but were already being sealed over by the snowfall. He dug in his heels and followed them, up towards the distant treeline. How long had she been gone? Could she have made it to the road?

He stumbled forward, up a shallow slope, staggered by the snow. After a few minutes, he reached the trees and had to hunt around for the footprints among a snarl of bracken and fallen branches. He picked them up again—clearer under the shelter of the trees—and followed them down towards a thicker patch of woodland that faded to scrub at the edge of the road. It wasn't a busy area, but there was a chance she would get lucky and catch a passing car. It was tough underfoot, though, even for a tall adult. Had she overreached?

He dragged himself through the snow, and almost toppled forward at a sudden dip in the slope. As he righted himself, he saw her: just on the edge of the thicker trees.

Face down, motionless. Her foot twisted at a sickening angle under a snow-covered tree root.

He reached the body and squatted, panting. He wore his heavy brown leather jacket with a couple of layers underneath, but he could still feel the depth of the cold. Holly was wearing jumper, jeans and socks. No shoes. It must have been a superhuman effort for her to even make it this far.

He pulled on his gloves and reached down to her. He brushed aside her long brown hair and squeezed her neck, feeling for a pulse.

Nothing.

A convulsion rippled through him: rage, grief.

Ten years.

He reached down to the right leg of her jeans and rolled it up at the hem. He took a small key from his jacket pocket and unlocked the ankle collar.

His eyes pricked with tears, but he held them back. No DNA.

He pocketed the collar and rolled the fabric back down over Holly's frozen ankle. He checked her pockets. She had died with nothing, wearing clothes bought by her captors.

He stood up, battered by the biting wind.

The snow swooped around Holly's body, eager to claim her.

He steadied himself, breathing deep and slow.

He bowed his head, raising the base of his neck above the jacket lapel and exposing the tattoo: a sketch of an eye shape with a sun-like circle in the centre, surrounded by seven rays.

26

The Snake Pass was a broad, undulating A-road that rippled through the Pennines like a cracking whip. Today, it was scudded with melting snow, and even Sawyer took care on the bends, despite the urgent guitar music: Queens of the Stone Age. The scenery commanded something more expansive, but he was hazy and sleepless; he needed the wake-up.

He turned off and pushed north, up through the bucolic sweep of the Longdendale Valley: smothered in white, twinkling in the morning sun. The dirt track that led to his father's house was a swamp of icy slush, and he had to twist and bully the Mini up through the steep section alongside the Langsett Reservoir.

He parked next to his father's laurel green Volvo. As usual, the house door opened before he could get out of the car. The building sat in splendid isolation, overlooking the reservoir valley, on a high point outside the village of Upper Midhope. It was built as the residence of a mining company manager in the 1700s, and since retiring from the service, Harold Sawyer had reinvented himself as an abstract artist and remodelled the cottage as his classic Englishman's castle.

Harold's German Shepherds, Rufus and Cain, lolloped across the porch to greet Sawyer as he climbed out of the car. He fussed them, and looked up to see his father, bent forward on the porch, brushing away a mush of melted snow. Harold was a couple of inches taller than his son; hefty, but light-footed for a man in his late sixties. He had a long, distinguished face with a permanently furrowed brow hanging over narrow but bright eyes, and a flop of unkempt black hair, grey at the temples.

He swished away the snow, gripping the brush with his vast goalkeeper hands. 'This won't stick around. Not cold enough in November, really. January is the month where I usually have to go survivalist up here.' He smiled at Sawyer and drew him into a hug. 'Do your bail restrictions stretch this far?'

'Spoken to your old mate, Keating?'

Harold led him inside. 'He's briefed me, yes.'

'*Briefed* you?'

'About Klein's death. The man who murdered my wife. Courtesy, I suppose. He says he's getting grief from the brass about transferring you from the Met without first considering the potential issues with Klein's release.'

Sawyer scoffed. 'So, he thinks I did it?'

'Of course he doesn't.' Harold turned and led Sawyer through to his reading room at the side of the house. He stopped and stared out of the enormous French windows that overlooked the valley and the near end of the dirt track.

Sawyer cast his eyes around the room: walls lined with bookcases, sky-blue armchair, upright digital piano. 'Are you going to say you told me so?'

Harold fiddled with a coffee machine by the window. 'Told you what?'

'To leave Klein alone. Accept his guilt.'

Harold shrugged. 'Well, he was obviously into *something* we didn't know about. Tea? Coffee?'

'No, thanks. Why do you say that?'

'Somebody wanted him dead.'

'I can see your old police skills haven't deserted you in old age, Dad.'

Harold eyed him, smiled. 'Could have been a botched burglary or something. Maybe not so much to it.'

Sawyer unwrapped an orange boiled sweet and slipped it into his mouth. He held up the cellophane and pocketed it. 'They have my DNA at Klein's flat. On a wrapper. Klein could have taken a sweet from my car without realising.' He sat in the armchair. 'And anyway, Keating looked into my interest in Klein's release. He told me he had concerns. I told him I didn't think Klein killed Mum. I've never been secretive about that.'

Harold turned and took a mug from a cupboard below the coffee machine. 'The Crown lawyers will interpret your openness as a double bluff, if you're charged.'

'Someone didn't like me getting close to the truth, and so they clipped Klein and put me in the picture as the most plausible scapegoat.'

'Jake. If a sweet wrapper is the best they've got—'

'I don't know that for sure. The custody interviews were sloppy.'

Harold slotted the cup into the machine and switched it on. 'Well. It's circumstantial. Where did they find the body?'

'At his brother's place in Castleton. He was staying there.'

'And I assume they're questioning the brother?'

Sawyer stood up. 'Klein's brother didn't do it, Dad. Whoever did used a hammer on him.' Harold flinched.

'That's someone speaking to *me*, Dad. To you. Even to Mike. About Mum. That's someone taunting us. Taunting our family.'

Harold pushed his fingers through his hair. 'Trolling. As the kids call it.'

Sawyer waited for a few seconds, letting the silence settle. The aroma of coffee smothered the room's standard fug of detergent and dog breath. 'I want to get myself checked out again. You said I was examined, after the attack. Once when I was nine, and again when I was sixteen. Do you still have the brain scans and reports? CT? MRI?'

Harold sipped his coffee. 'Of course. All my admin is in my studio. I still have all your old school reports, police certificates, Michael's stuff.'

'I'd like to take the scans and reports.' Sawyer moved off, towards the door that led to the back of the house.

Harold hurried after him, getting ahead. 'Hold on. I don't want the dogs getting in there.'

The studio was a large, open space in a converted outhouse. It had a modest window that looked out on the open fields at the back of the house, and Harold had laid the floor with brushed white parquet tiles, arranged in a chevron zig-zag pattern. It was clean and ordered, with his blank canvases neatly stacked in the far corner, and his paints and accessories stored on colour-coded shelving: yellow for paint, blue for tools, red for filing.

Harold browsed through the paperwork in a multi-drawered cabinet on the red shelf, while Sawyer studied his current work in progress, propped on an easel in the centre of the room. He was keen on abstracts, and his father's art was normally bold and primal. But this was a different direction: a layered central smear of dark and bright reds, blended over each other, increasingly chaotic as they fanned out towards the greys and white at the edges of the canvas.

Sawyer leaned in, surprised by the jagged peaks which had formed in the paint; his father's brush strokes were normally so measured and uniform. 'This your Rothko phase, then?'

Harold sighed. 'I keep hearing that, yes. There's no patent on that palette, you know. Deep colours, big emotions. By the way, I went to see Michael. I've arranged for some more speech therapy.'

Sawyer looked up, surprised. 'You told me that would be pointless, because there's not enough to work with.'

'Change of heart. We have to keep trying.'

'Did he speak to you?'

Harold turned. 'Of course not.' He handed over a black folder which contained smudgy photocopies of two consultant reports from 1992 and 1999. He had also kept copies of the letters to Sawyer's GP. The CT imaging hadn't reproduced well, but the MRI scan showed a series of top-down slices of Sawyer's brain.

Sawyer browsed the notes and letters. *Focal bilateral amygdala lesion... suggested isoproterenol infusion...* He looked up at his father. 'Surprised you kept these, after your conversion from science to God.'

Harold closed the cabinet drawer. 'One day you might grasp that faith can be private, personal. It doesn't have to be preachy. Life is a struggle. We all have individual ways of coping.'

'Yes, but I just can't see why you would switch from a world based on gathering evidence and hard facts, to some comforting fairy story.'

Harold downed the rest of his coffee. 'Seems to me you might be going the other way. From denial of the evidence to a kind of acceptance. Why do you want these scans? Are you at last considering the possibility that you might have been physically damaged?'

Sawyer slumped down on his father's vermillion corner sofa and scanned the spines of a stack of novels. Hemingway, Roth. A couple of recent Booker winners. 'Dad. Somebody murdered the man who was convicted of killing Mum, and they have either tried to point the finger at me, or Klein had taken a sweet wrapper from my car and the whole thing is an almighty reach from Keating.'

Harold nodded. 'Because he's embarrassed at accepting your transfer. Being seen as naïve.'

'Whoever it was, he committed the murder with a hammer. Not a knife or a gun. It speaks to Mum's death. It speaks to us. You know the score. Look for what stands out.'

'Does the killer think the connection with Mum's murder will make it stick to you more?'

Sawyer frowned. 'It's MO, not signature. He doesn't need to do it that way. It's not for the feels. It's referring back to the method of a previous murder, which was signature based on anger, hatred, resentment. Maybe humiliation. Given that we haven't had an ongoing thirty-year hunt for a hammer-wielding serial killer in this area, I don't think the person who killed Klein is the same person who killed Mum.'

Harold angled his head. 'I wouldn't use this theory as the basis for your defence.'

'I think it fits with my innocence. Someone killing the man who killed Mum using the same method. Symmetry. Biblical justice. An eye for an eye.'

'It's not meant to be literal.'

'Atheists can read the Bible, too, Dad. Leviticus. "Fracture for fracture, eye for eye, tooth for tooth."'

Harold smiled. 'Most of the naysayers get bored before

the New Testament. That's where Christ clarifies. He taught love, not pain. Not vindictiveness. That just leads to a cycle of resentment and violence. It's all in the interpretation. Commensurate justice. You take a life, you have your life taken away. Some people read that as capital punishment, some see it as life imprisonment.'

Sawyer got up. 'So, how is Keating? I was hoping to ask him a couple of questions myself about the day they arrested Owen Casey.'

Harold bristled. 'This again.'

'Yes. This again.'

'With everything else hanging over you?'

'Owen Casey was let off a serious burglary charge, with no paper chain. He's told me directly that he was tasked with stealing a hammer from Klein's house. The murder weapon.'

'We've been through this, son. A senior officer with a moustache and a big watch. Casey is a chancer, telling you what he thinks you want to know. I assume you paid him?'

Sawyer leaned back on the storage shelves, scrutinising his father's reaction. 'I saw him again, the other day.'

'I told you. I don't remember him, or anyone who was involved in his arrest.'

'He gave me a name. William Caldwell.'

Harold dropped his gaze and seemed to run his eyes along the patterns in the floor tiles. He looked back up. 'How much did that cost you?'

'You don't recognise it?'

'No. I was pretty junior at the time. I didn't really connect with the senior staff, even if that name is authentic.' He opened a drawer in a wooden desk beneath the shelves.

Sawyer took a few steps forward, ending up close to his father's shoulder. 'Mum's last word to her killer, according to Michael: "*Why*?" She knew him. And I've got another one-word question, Dad. *How*? How did she know him? Was it this Caldwell? And did he kill Klein, too? Or have him killed?'

Harold took a circular coin of around an inch in diameter from the drawer. 'Have you heard of the French painter, Philippe de Champaigne?'

Sawyer sighed. 'No.'

'Seventeenth century. French Baroque. He produced a painting called *Still Life with a Tulip, Skull and Hourglass*. It showed the three essentials of existence. A tulip, representing life, a skull for death, and an hourglass for time.' Harold held the coin up to the light. 'It was part of the Vanitas genre: works that featured symbols of mortality, and encouraged reflection on the ephemeral nature of life. How it all seems so limitless, yet only happens to us for a short period of time. This is a *Memento Mori* medallion. It's meant to be carried with you, to remind you that life is fleeting.'

Sawyer took the coin. On one side, a profile illustration of a skull sat between the words *MEMENTO* and *MORI* at top and bottom, with an hourglass on one side and a tulip on the other. On the other side, six words were stacked in the centre.

YOU COULD LEAVE LIFE RIGHT NOW

He nodded, glanced up at his father. 'Marcus Aurelius.'

'Yes. Your original Stoic. The full quote is, "You could leave life right now. Let that determine what you do and say and think." He was urging people to live a life of virtue in the moment, rather than wait. The coin was created at a mint in Minnesota in 1882 by a man who wanted to help recovering addicts not to succumb to temptation. But it also serves as a reminder not to obsess over trivial things or make plans too far into the future.'

'Like going to Heaven?'

Harold smiled. 'My faith is about my actions on Earth, not to get a reward in the afterlife.' He bowed his head, avoiding his son's gaze. 'You and Michael are survivors, Jake. You've both come so far. Please focus on being there for each other, in the here and now.'

After Sawyer had left, Harold headed back into the studio and took a paint pot from the yellow shelf. He shook out a small key and unlocked the side door, which led to a rugged outbuilding with a stone floor and metal wall shelving, crammed with labelled boxes containing various supplies: groceries, medical items, accessories.

In the corner, a heavy steel door had been installed at the top of the staircase that led down to the old wine cellar. Harold pulled out a short stepladder and climbed up to reach the ledge of a high, frosted glass window set into the building's slanted roof. He slid a protective wallet from a groove in the brickwork and climbed down.

As Harold snapped the stepladder shut with a clang, Rufus and Cain bundled into the studio door, scrabbling and whining.

'Exercise time, boys.' Harold took the swipe card from the wallet and held it against the reader on the steel door. A red light on the panel to the door's left turned to green, and the locking mechanism clunked open.

27

Shaun swaggered up the path, away from Robbie's flat block. Ash shouldered out of the main doors and caught him up, panting.

'Those two gonna be okay in there?'

Shaun fiddled with his phone, nodding. 'They'll be fine. Think of it as their apprenticeship. Looking after a junkie mong. If they can manage that, I'll promote 'em to watching the door at the club or something. I want to get the fuck out of here as soon as I can. Stick to the plan.'

Ash frowned. 'I am not fucking with Dale, bruv.'

Shaun glowered at him. 'We're not "fucking" with anyone. I'm managing the business here. That Marco cunt is covering Manchester. Dale knows him from prison or whatever. We'll get this done. But we'll do it my way.'

They walked into town, across a large park bisected by the River Wye, close to its source. Most of the snow had melted, and the grass was squashed and sodden.

'Are they *ducks*?' Ash waved a hand at a group of white-feathered, red-faced birds loitering by the edge of the river.

Shaun squinted at them. 'Geese? I dunno. What am I? Bill fuckin' Oddie?'

'Who?'

Shaun slapped Ash on the chest, bracing him. 'Here we go.' He nodded to a group of teenagers playing football on a patch of open grass between two sets of jacket goalposts. 'You okay there, lads?'

The biggest of the group stood by the nearest goal. He turned and glowered at Shaun and Ash. 'We're fine to play here, mate.'

Another one spoke up. 'We asked yer man at the gatehouse. All good.'

Shaun smiled. 'Nah, nah. I'm not police or anything.' He strode out into the middle of the pitch, forcing the boys to stop playing. 'I'm just wondering if you'd be up for a bit of work, lads. Nothing dodgy, yeah? New club just out of town. Pool, LAN gaming, some arcade games. Bit of money in it.' The teenagers gathered, and Shaun handed round a few business cards: thick cardboard, professional design; icons of a number eight pool ball and a console joypad beneath the word *PLAYERS*; address and mobile number on the back.

The goalkeeper studied his card, looked from Ash to Shaun. 'Is it cash?'

'Course. Totally legit, mind.' He winked. 'Just trying to cover set-up costs. The taxman will get his nibble further down the line, yeah?'

Ash smiled. 'Victimless crime, you get me?'

Shaun flashed him a withering look, and squeezed the boy's shoulder. 'Listen. Come down later; we'll sort something out. Tell your mates. Fuck all to do round here, yeah? Somewhere to go when the weather is shite. Might be a few perks in it, too.'

Shaun's phone buzzed in his pocket. He checked the screen. It was Clem, one of the tech guys at the Buxton branch of Players. He turned away from the group and took the call. 'What's the story?'

Music in the background. Clunking pool balls. 'You need to get down here.'

Shaun sighed. 'This is your gig. Buy a bigger signal booster. I told you the Wi-Fi would be shit.'

'It's not that. There's a weird guy. Been sitting here for a while, saying nothing. Freaking me out, man.'

————

Shaun parked his white Mercedes on the main road alongside the Fairfield golf course. He dived out of the car and hurried through the side streets, pursued by Ash.

The Buxton branch of Players was housed in a refitted pub building on the corner of a residential street. There was no obvious shop front, but a portable sign stand had been propped by the door, displaying the business card logo and name. The ground floor walls were lined with contemporary and retro arcade cabinets and a couple of pinball machines. At the back of the room in a low-lit, roped-off area, gamers in headphones huddled around a connected hub of laptops. In the far corner, a few casual tables had been arranged near a serving hatch in the wall. The place was busy with a young, mostly male crowd. All of the machines were occupied and a few stragglers with plastic coffee cups hung around the tables by the hatch.

Clem stood behind a raised desk near the entrance. He was thirty-odd, tall and solid and well groomed, with a heavily gelled quiff. He nodded as Shaun approached and leaned in to his ear, shouting over the cacophony of twittering games and stomping techno. 'He's at the back. Been on the same cup of coffee for a good half-hour now.'

Shaun craned his head around a group of gamers at the front. Sawyer sat at one of the tables by the hatch: head back, eyes closed, jacket collar folded up. 'And he's asked for me?'

Clem nodded.

Shaun turned to Ash. 'Keep watch.'

'Mate of yours?'

'Shut your fucking mouth and keep your eyes open.'

Shaun sauntered over. As he approached the table, Sawyer opened an eye. 'How's the nose, tough guy?'

Shaun plonked himself down in the seat opposite. He smiled. 'We know where you live.'

Sawyer closed the eye again. 'I know you know where I live.' He opened his eyes and sucked in a breath. 'But now I know where you work. And who pays your wages.' He squeezed the coffee cup, denting it. 'You haven't hung around, I'll give you that. The website says this place is "coming soon". Gold star for hitting your schedule. But is this really all Dale trusts you with? A glorified community centre. You must feel a tiny bit patronised by that? How's Marco? And Hector?'

Shaun leaned in. 'Try something like you pulled back at your house here, Sawyer. Go for it. I've seen your moves now. So you took a few karate lessons. You're not fuckin' Bruce Lee.'

Sawyer grinned. 'You're mixing your martial arts there, Shaun. But I take your point.' He looked past Shaun, to the front door. 'Who's the dude with the dreadlocks? He needs to lose weight if he wants to be the Laurel to your Hardy.'

'Hey. This is a business, alright? Snooker and pool upstairs. No license yet. Bit of mark-up on the coffee and tea. Tenner to get in, with all the play you want.'

'Hence the name. I'm not saying I don't think this is a good idea. Personally, I'm a purist. I could live without the rhythm games and the pay to continues. But I suppose I'm not the target customer, right?' Sawyer waved an arm. 'I'm just not sure this is Dale's style. Nurturing the disaffected youth.' He leaned further forward and lowered his voice, close to a whisper. 'And I don't think you'd take a job like this without significant benefits. Maybe a few benefits you've awarded yourself.'

Shaun shrugged. 'Is there a point to this? Are you here to make an arrest? If not, might I politely suggest that you fuck off?'

Sawyer stood up, smiled. 'Shaun. That's robust, but fair. No arrests. I've got bigger issues on the go at the moment. Just suggest to your boss that he introduces a loyalty card scheme. I think I'll be spending quite a lot of time here.'

28

Austin Fletcher stayed low and silent as he crept through the galley kitchen towards the sitting room. He wore latex gloves, and plastic shoe protectors covered his boots. He paused at the fridge, dipped his head, and scanned the kitchen and sitting room.

Sawyer's car wasn't out front, and Fletcher was certain he wasn't home. But he would stick to his key principle: assume the worst. He had watched Sawyer drive away, but there could be someone else, asleep in the bedroom. Or Sawyer might have spotted, or heard, Fletcher's approach and driven away as a decoy, then doubled back and seen him enter the house.

When he was on unfamiliar territory, Fletcher always remained on high alert until he had scoped out every millimetre, assessed every threat, identified all the entry and exit points. Side door: lock easily picked, now ajar. Front door: unknown, probably locked from the outside. At the end of the kitchen, he could see the open door to Sawyer's bedroom, and another door ajar to the bathroom beyond. The place was a mess, with half-empty glasses and unwashed dishes, but there was no way to tell how long they had been there.

As ever, his supplements had dried his mouth, and he opened the fridge door in search of water. Cellophane-wrapped pizza, a few mouldering tubs and condiments. He reached his huge gloved hand to the back of the middle shelf and pulled out a bright yellow plastic pot. Cadbury's Flake Chocolate Dessert. He wrinkled his nose, and replaced it. He lifted a half-full litre bottle of Diet Coke from the door compartment and unscrewed the top. He tilted back his ponytailed head, opened his mouth wide, and tipped in some of the liquid, taking care not to touch the lip of the bottle with his mouth. He replaced the bottle, and froze.

A noise, off in the bedroom.

Fletcher dropped into a squat, using the kitchen table as cover.

A black-and-white cat padded in and dug its nose into a food bowl by the side door. Fletcher moved towards it, but it darted away and slipped outside.

He crept through into the bedroom and studied Sawyer's wooden man dummy, recognising it from a teenage fling with classical martial arts. He sifted through a few items on the bedside table and poked around the bathroom. No revealing medications, no clues on secrets or weaknesses.

As he stepped back into the sitting room, his phone vibrated in the inside pocket of his bomber jacket. He took it out, checked the ID, and connected the call. 'Yes?'

'We need to move things forward. This weekend, if you can.'

'No.'

A pause from Dale. 'This isn't a negotiation, Fletcher. He's sniffing around, getting too curious.'

Fletcher's gaze drifted to the cat's food bowl. 'Not smart to phone.'

'How about you let *me* decide what's smart?'

Fletcher gave a strange little grunt, somewhere between contempt and despair. 'Haven't finished the preliminaries.'

'Improvise.' Dale hung up.

Fletcher stood there in silence for a few seconds, gazing at the floorboards. As expected, his fury surged up through his core: scorching, volcanic. He closed his eyes and kicked into his breathing exercise: deep and slow, deep and slow, spacing out the inhales and exhales.

He opened his eyes and walked back to the fridge.

29

Sawyer strode through the main doors of the High Peak Bookstore, a bookshop and café at the edge of a gusty tract of moorland outside Buxton. The converted warehouse was dank and cold from the melting snow, but it was a busy weekend spot, with two large, well-stocked rooms of new and used books.

Dean Logan lurked at a corner table by a glass door fridge, rendering its contents temporarily unpopular. He grinned at Sawyer as he approached. The small table was overloaded with Logan's tea, a tall mug of milky coffee and two plates with hefty slices of cake.

Sawyer took his seat. 'Nice spread. Bit disturbing, though. A selfless gesture from a journalist.' He sipped at the tepid coffee. 'Is this part of a religious conversion or something?'

'I'm not a spiritual man, Sawyer. Unless—'

'Unless we're talking about the other kind of spirits? Yeah, yeah. So what have you snuffled out?'

Logan cut into his cake with a miniature fork; it looked comically dainty in his bloated fingers. 'You don't have to keep this up, Sawyer. The pass-agg comments about my profession. This is mutual now, remember? We're working together.' He mashed the cake into his mouth and carried on talking. 'The outlaw and the truth seeker. Each no better than the other.'

Sawyer shrugged. 'I see our relationship as more symbiotic. Transactional. "Mutual" makes it sound too warm and fuzzy.' He sliced into his cake. 'Come on. What have you got?'

Logan slurped at his tea. 'Couple of interesting things. I checked Marcus Klein's visitor records for HMP Sudbury. Just to clarify, Sawyer, that wasn't easy. The eighties and nineties records were archived, on paper. I had to get creative.'

'You mean, lie?'

'Lose the moral revulsion. I got what you asked for.'

Sawyer ate more cake, watched Logan. 'So, did Caldwell visit him, or try to visit him? How about Owen Casey?'

Logan smiled. 'Neither. But there was one name that popped out. Your dear old dad, Harold. He showed up in October 1997. Tried to visit. Klein refused. His name doesn't come up again.'

Sawyer scowled. 'Why would he want to see Klein? Presumably, the governor would have screened him as family of the inmate's victim.'

'He was a copper at the time, though.' Logan leaned back. 'I'm no detective, Sawyer, but it looks like your old man might have been a few steps ahead of you, if he had reason to question Klein almost ten years after his conviction.'

Sawyer stared at the froth patterns on the inside of his coffee cup. 'And a few weeks after Caldwell's disappearance. What's the other thing?'

Logan scooped in another forkful of cake. 'Not so good. They've found another body. Crime scene up at

Hollinsclough. Open field, not too far from the primary school. Can't get near the place.'

'Another forties male?'

Logan shook his head, wiped his mouth. 'Young girl. They think it's Holly Chilton.'

———

Sawyer took the short, straight drive across the moor to the village of Earl Sterndale. He parked outside The Quiet Woman Pub: a stained grey building with a sign featuring a macabre illustration of a headless woman and the legend, *Soft words turneth away wrath.*

He took a pair of binoculars from the glovebox, changed into walking boots and slipped down the side of the pub onto a farm track. He bore down through a dry valley to the foot of Chrome Hill: a steep, limestone spike that Sawyer remembered Keating once claiming as 'the only proper peak in the Peak District'. He joined the concessionary path and heaved himself forward. It was crusty underfoot, and he stumbled in places where the snow lingered. After half an hour of vertiginous hiking, he merged with the main ridge path and reached the summit.

Sawyer crouched down and gathered his breath, stung by the churning winds. He rose up, tipped back his head, and held out his arms to full span: palms out. Far below, the chequered fields, speckled in white, swung across the Dove Valley, to Hollins Hill and Staffordshire, and he found himself submerged in a late afternoon lightshow: a yolk-orange winter sun, flaring through the clouds.

He raised the binoculars and aimed them down, towards a patch of activity by the school just outside Hollinsclough village. Police vehicles, Scientific Services Unit van, officers, detectives, TyVek suits. The yellow-and-white forensic tent had been erected at the edge of a field, close to a treeline.

He called Shepherd. It rang for a while before connecting.

'Detective Sergeant Shepherd.' He sounded flat, defeated.

'I want to help.'

Shepherd sighed. 'Where are you?'

Sawyer turned away from the wind. 'Don't worry. I'm not hiding under the forensic van.'

'Sir. You can't help.'

'I can.'

Shepherd hung up.

Sawyer marched along the entrance corridor, head down, past the lime-green doors and yellow-frosted windows. It was quiet: a few uniforms, no detectives. Sergeant Gerry Sherman sat at the custody and charge desk; he clocked Sawyer's approach and shuffled over to the privacy barrier.

'Afternoon, Gerry.'

'Sir.' Sherman had the bail document ready by the time Sawyer reached the desk.

Sawyer glanced up at him as he signed. His eyes were dull and distant. 'How's the grind?'

Sherman forced himself alert. 'Usual. Grim. But we didn't get into this work for the jollies, did we?'

Sawyer handed the document back, and Gerry countersigned. 'Not much happening.'

'Lot of 'em are on a call.'

'Anything I shouldn't know about?'

Gerry gave a weak smile. 'See you again soon, sir.'

Sawyer walked back down the corridor, towards the lift. He slowed and lingered before he reached the doors. The ground floor alert pinged and three uniforms got out and pushed their way past him. Sawyer slipped inside. Essence of BO and mid-price cologne.

'Sir!' Gerry called from the desk.

Sawyer waved and pressed the button for the MIT floor. 'I'm just picking up something from my office. Keating is aware.'

The doors closed and the lift carried him up to the Murder Investigation Team unit, which occupied the whole of the first floor. It was an open plan set-up, with private side offices for senior staff. The place was normally brash and bustling, with detectives scurrying along the corridors between the desks, hopping between jobs. Today, the atmosphere was muted, with only a few DCs present, slouched at their desks.

Sawyer strode around the edge of the room, heading for his office. A few heads turned. He held up a hand. 'Won't be a second. Need to get something.'

A skinny detective pivoted his chair at the sound of Sawyer's voice. He took off his wire-frame glasses and cleaned the lenses with the hem of his shirt. 'Are you authorised to be here?'

Sawyer unlocked his office door. 'I am, DC Moran.' He nodded towards Keating's empty office. 'Dad said it was okay.'

Inside, he made a show of fussing with his desk drawers, and took the micro listening device out of his pocket. He checked it was live and held it steady in the groove of his palm.

As he left his office, Moran was outside, waiting. 'So, if I call DCI Keating, he'll confirm that you've been authorised to be present on police premises, despite being suspended?'

Sawyer locked his office and turned to face Moran. 'At the moment, I'm not sure DCI Keating would have a lot of time for a suspended officer retrieving a personal item from his office.'

He moved off, towards the window at the back of the room. Moran overtook him and turned the case whiteboard to face the wall. As he struggled to balance the legs of the board, Sawyer fixed the listening device to the magnetic frame underneath Moran's desk.

'Don't worry, Moran. I'm not here to snoop.' He leaned around the corner: another pretence. 'Just seeing if Bloom was in.' Sawyer turned and retraced his steps to the lift; Moran escorted him all the way, and stood nearby as he waited for the car to arrive.

Sawyer stared at the lift doors. 'This could be a career-limiting moment, Moran. I might get off this accusation.'

Moran smiled. 'And you're going to have me directing traffic, right? Just doing my job. Upholding the law. Sticking to the rules. Someone has to.'

'If you haven't already, I would get a rural observation point on me, if I were you. Not easy in this weather. Not much tree cover. You're the man for the job, though. There's a lot of sneaking around, lurking in the shadows. It plays to your strengths.'

'Seems to me that's been your main skill since you got back here, Sawyer.' He scoffed. 'Sorry. *Sir.*'

Sawyer turned. 'Questions. Good stuff for the CPS, this, so maybe make some notes. If I'd planned to kill the man who was convicted of murdering my mother, why would I go to such little effort to conceal the fact that I'd been spending time with him? And what gives Keating the idea that I believe he did it? I've told him the opposite.'

Moran shrugged. 'Hiding in plain sight. Classic tactic.'

'There's a clear paper trail of the investigation work I've been doing with Klein. Witnesses, who can testify that we were following a specific line of enquiry that would lead us to the person who murdered my mother.'

Moran inched forward. 'Gypos, yeah. A bunch of Irish freeloaders whose lifestyle is outside the law. They always play well in court.'

The lift doors opened. Sawyer wedged his foot inside. 'Moran. You're a decent detective. Park your animosity for a second. You must see there would be no sense in me doing this. Somebody didn't like me getting close to the truth, and so they hit on a good method to get me out of the picture and off the scent. They weren't prepared to kill a police officer. But an ex-con...'

Moran dropped his voice; more of a hiss than a whisper. 'You came back here for some good old-fashioned revenge, Sawyer. You've muddied the water with this phantom investigation rubbish. You told anyone who'd listen that you didn't think Klein was guilty. And you did what you had to do.'

———

Sawyer crossed town to The Source coffee shop. He ordered a cheese toastie and gazed out at the early evening procession of cars, rumbling through the slush down Terrace Road.

It was 4:30pm. He nursed the food and grazed on a few phone games. The briefing would be on the next hour.

At 5pm, he slotted in his noise-cancelling headphones and navigated to the phone app that controlled the device. He activated the listening option and adjusted the volume.

His heart jolted; the sound was pure and unmuddied, as if he had been sitting at the desk next to Moran. Scraping chairs, murmuring.

'*Any evidence of sexual assault?*' DC Myers.

He'd missed the start. They must have convened as soon as Keating had returned.

'*Nothing obvious.*' The plummy voice of Sally O'Callaghan, the MIT unit's principal SOCO. '*She seems well fed and otherwise pretty healthy. No obvious injuries. We won't know for sure about sexual assault until we can... Drummond won't be able to make a full examination until the body has defrosted. It'll take a few days. Until then, no cause or time of death, no DNA, no toxicology.*'

'*Can't he do it any faster?*' DC Walker.

'*He could. But then the outside of the body would decompose, while the inner organs stayed frozen. We might lose evidence.*'

'*So, she was just left out in the cold?*' Myers. '*Her captor got bored with her, but couldn't face killing her?*'

'*Well...*' Sally again. '*My best guess is that she froze to death. But it's impossible to paint a clearer picture until the body has been fully thawed. There was a little light bruising around one ankle, but no other external anomalies.*'

'*And it's definitely Holly?*' Keating.

'*A hundred per cent.*' Sally sighed.

'*No tracks? Trace evidence?*'

'*Weather has killed all that.*'

Sawyer took out his burner phone and texted Walker.

Maybe she escaped? Not dumped?

'*Why would her body be left out there?*' Myers.

'*We can safely assume the body wasn't left close to where she was being held.*' Moran. '*That eliminates some location.*'

'*The bruising around the ankle.*' Walker. '*Could it be from some kind of restraint? And she broke free of it?*'

'*No telling when, though.*' Keating. '*We need to wait for Drummond. See if there's DNA.*'

Walker cut in. '*We should do house to house, in a catchment area around the deposition scene.*'

A snort from Moran. '*He wouldn't just leave her on his doorstep.*'

Walker continued. '*Maybe he didn't leave her. Assuming we're dealing with a he. Maybe Holly escaped.*'

A moment's silence, broken by Keating. '*Drummond has got to be our next step. We have the body, but we can't move until we know more about how she died.*'

31

'Dad came to see you?'

Michael Sawyer flicked his eyes up to his brother, and aimed them back down at the screen of his handheld console. Michael's en suite room at the Rosemary House care centre had the look of a well-worn Travelodge: single bed with pastel sheets; boxy, wall-mounted TV; cheap kettle with a single cup. In contrast to his brother, Michael was burly, with greying buzz-cut hair and an uneven beard. His eyes were a similar shade of green, but without the sparkle of Sawyer's. He wore a violet winter hoodie, and chewed on one of the white drawstrings as he played his game.

Sawyer sat in the high-backed chair, facing Michael on the bed. 'Is the therapist decent? Any help?'

Michael ignored him, kept his focus on the game.

Sawyer pulled the chair closer. 'I know this is hard. But I need to know if you saw what I saw. I need to know that my brain isn't just making this shit up. Telling me stories.' He leaned forward. 'I've got a name. William Caldwell. Anything? Did you hear Mum use that name? Do you recognise it?'

Michael gave a short shake of his head.

Sawyer reached into the inside pocket of his jacket and took out the tactical pen, and the piece of paper with the sketch he'd made on the day before his arrest. He opened the paper out and laid it on the bed next to Michael, alongside the pen. 'Mike. I saw this man in a dream. Please could you pause your game and take a look?'

Michael sighed. The chirping from the handheld fell silent and he hauled his vast head to the side and looked down at Sawyer's sketch: heavy eyebrows; deep set eyes with dark irises; black moustache with lighter pencil strokes representing the dabs of grey hair.

Sawyer shifted closer. 'Do you recognise him? Is there anything you can add?' Michael picked up the sketch and studied it. 'Mike. Was this man there on the day? Was this the face under the balaclava when Mum pulled it away?'

Michael lowered the paper and looked across to the closed door, sifting through his splintered memories.

Sawyer reached out to him and rested a hand on his knee. 'He also had a big watch. Maybe designer.'

Michael's shoulders rose and fell with his breathing. The motion became deeper, quicker. He batted Sawyer's hand away and locked eye contact. He squeezed his eyes shut, opened them again. 'Couldn't see.' His voice was soft and low, close to a whisper.

'Couldn't see what, Mike?'

Michael squinted, his eyelids flickering. 'The sun. On the watch.'

'Reflecting off the man's watch?'

Michael nodded. 'It hurt my eyes.' He looked back to the handheld screen and restarted his game.

Sawyer tried for more. 'Do you remember the face? The moustache?'

But Michael angled his body away, towards the wall. Lost again.

32

Sawyer drove back to Edale in a daze. Too many moving parts: the Klein investigation; Caldwell's disappearance; Dale and Eva. Worst of all: his impotence in the face of the missing children enquiries and murders. The listening device was useful, but how long could he afford to leave it at the station?

At the cottage, he fed Bruce and poured himself a large glass of Coke. He paced at the sofa and took out the burner phone. Call Walker? Shepherd? The meeting with his brother had sapped his will; he needed time to recharge. He tossed the phone onto the sofa and opened the side door to let Bruce slip outside.

His nose twitched. That smell again. Tobacco. Scorched, exotic. Was it fresher than before? He stepped outside, walked round to the front porch, and looked along the lane towards Hayfield village. It was a cold but calm evening: midnight blue beneath a gauzy moon.

He slipped back inside, switched on the PlayStation and opened his favourite 2D shoot 'em up: *Bullet Symphony*. A relentless onslaught of enemy spaceships, swarming geometries of glowing missiles. Almost, but not quite, impossible to navigate. Blast the enemies, weave through the channels, dart into the pixel-wide gaps. To onlookers, the game was unfathomable, demented. For Sawyer, it was soothing: a mind-clearance technique; a safe space where he could power down and let his primal instinct run the show.

Tonight, though, he was off form. Overreaches, obvious mistakes. He could usually see the paths and patterns, but his timing was behind, his moves clumsy.

Between levels, he pulled back his head, stretching his neck muscles. It was only early evening, but his eyelids prickled and felt leaden. His remaining lives dropped from five to three with no memory of the moments where he had lost them. He had managed to get through the previous winter without catching a cold; was this payback time?

Tea.

He paused the game and rose to his feet. The room lurched, and he gripped the sofa, nudging his leg into the coffee table. The half-full glass of Coke wobbled and he reached down to steady it. But again, his timing was out, and the glass tilted and spilled its contents onto the floor.

A wash of black. Unconsciousness tugging at him. He shook his head, gulped back a deep breath and aimed for the kitchen.

He was suddenly holding an overflowing kettle underneath the tap, with no memory of the journey to the sink.

Then, more water. Splashing from the tap to his hands to his face. He was in the bathroom now, again with no memory of getting there.

He stared at himself in the mirror, holding his eyes wide between thumbs and index fingers. His head throbbed, and his stomach tingled with nausea.

Not tea. Bed.

But then he was in the sitting room again, stumbling towards the side door.

A knocking sound. He switched direction and hobbled towards the front door.

Then, he was on the sofa, lying back, his limbs spent and hollow.

A man with a stubby blond ponytail and black bomber jacket moved around the room. Latex gloves, shoe protectors. He turned off the PlayStation, shifted a few items around, righted the glass. He took the bottle of Coke out of the fridge and slipped it into a mud grey briefcase, humming as he worked. He replaced the Coke with a fresh bottle.

Sawyer was up, with the man pushing his feet into his shoes, and his arms into his jacket. He lashed out, but flailed at air. The man watched his efforts, waiting.

Another wash of black, stronger this time.

And he was gone.

33

Sawyer jerked awake as his head clunked forward into the Mini's steering wheel, sounding the horn. He was travelling fast, no lights, down an incline.

He pushed himself back into the driver's seat, clawing back to consciousness. Outside, the world scrolled by.

His stomach lurched at a second of freefall, as the car shunted forward, lost contact with the ground, and reconnected to a steeper incline, pitching him into the wheel again. He dug his thumbs into his eyes, trying to shock himself alert.

The engine whined as the car rolled forward at a terrible angle: so acute that the front wheels would surely catch at any moment, flipping the vehicle into a forward somersault.

He stomped on the brake pedal; the wheels skidded uselessly over the rough ground. He felt for the handbrake in the darkness, and summoned the will to lift it. The wheels skidded again as they locked, and the car spun.

Sawyer was now pushed back in his seat, facing up the incline, rolling backwards.

He grabbed the wheel, but the steering was locked. The car drifted and spun, aiming forward again. The wheels shunted, more fiercely this time, pitching him into another moment of freefall. His legs and body strained against the fastened seatbelt as he dropped.

He flopped forward as the car lurched into a heavy landing, killing the momentum. He held his head up to the window and squinted, cupping his hands around his eyes. He was floating: in a vast lake or reservoir that filled the lower half of a steep-walled basin. Langsett? Ladybower? Too dark to tell.

The engine whined again, and cut out, smothered by the water.

Sawyer sat there for a moment, in stupefied silence. Fragments of memory: the blond man; the videogame; his eyes in the mirror, stark and bloodshot. The sudden peace and silence soothed him, and as the adrenaline spike eased off, he had to fight to stay awake. The exhaustion was profound, deep in his bones. It squeezed at his brain, shutting him down.

Icy water seeped into his shoes, shocking him awake. The footwell was flooding. In the time it took for him to reach down and unclip his seat belt, the car had tilted forward and taken on more water, gushing in through the doors and the gaps in the bodywork. He was sinking.

Sawyer had read somewhere that you should always leave the doors closed in this situation, to keep the car afloat longer. Try to escape through the windows.

He pressed the window switch, but there was no connection, no movement. He felt around the door. No manual rollers.

The water seeped up, covering his knees. The cold ripped through him, and he sucked in a juddering breath. Despite the shock, his head lolled again, desperate for sleep.

The front of the car was almost full: a fibrous soup of murky water. Sawyer scrambled between the seats, into the back end, which was tipped higher and only half submerged. His breaths became laboured; the water was thinning out the oxygen.

He gripped the back and front headrests, clamped his feet together, and kicked at the driver's side window. But the impact was feeble, dampened by the water's density.

And then. It came again. The tingling sensation: prickling at the base of his neck, spreading over his shoulders and down into his core. His breathing grew rapid, staccato. He shivered: all-over tremors, unstoppable. His hands trembled. It wasn't just from the cold; there was something deeper. The same panic he had felt in the cave network during the Crawley case. Dread. Desolation. Something close to how he imagined the sensation of fear.

The front of the car was fully submerged now. In the back seat, only the top half of his body remained above water.

He cried out, fought against the tremors, forced himself to slow his breathing. And still it tugged at him: whatever was in his system, whatever had laid him out. The adrenaline was keeping him in the fight for now, but his strength was waning, and he would soon be lost in the eternal night, claimed by the deep.

He kicked at the window, sloshing his legs through the water. But the impact was too broad to resist the pressure on the glass from outside the car. Lit by only the faintest shimmer of moonlight, he had no way of telling if the car was sinking horizontally or vertically.

Sawyer felt in the inside pocket of his jacket. His wallet was still there, along with the notepad and tactical pen. He dug out the pen and gripped it in his fist, with the titanium tip pointing out. He held his elbow above the water for purchase and stabbed the tip into the edge of the glass, using quick, powerful jabs.

A crack appeared, and he worked at the centre, speeding up the jabs. Fragments of glass spat back at him as water seeped through the crack. He pulled back his elbow and jammed it into the weakened pane.

The window collapsed, caving inward under the weight of the flooding water. Sawyer snatched his head away, drew in a deep breath and held it. He grabbed the edges of the frame and heaved himself through the gap, into the water.

He turned and watched, as the car sank away, out of sight.

He was deeper than he'd imagined, and it was difficult to tell up from down. He swam away from the direction of the car's descent, thrashing his way through the freezing water, tracking a cluster of rising air bubbles. He had a minute, maybe two, before the exhaustion would shut off his muscles. And after that, a new threat: hypothermia. He had to get out of the water, find shelter, reheat himself.

Sawyer surged up and surfaced. He opened his mouth and held his head back, gorging on the air. He trod water and looked around. The lake was at the base of a steep valley, surrounded by a narrow lip of shoreline.

A car engine, and lights: on a road up above, beyond the ridge. The lights flared, then faded.

He dug in, aiming for the shore. He mistimed his breathing and took in a gulp of water. Stringy, brackish. He was numb now, all over. But there was no option; he had to keep going, keep moving forward.

Sawyer dragged himself onto the shore and stumbled on, heaving his battered body up the incline. He scrambled forward, clawing at the earth.

More car lights from up above, now with the crunch of tyres on the road.

At the top of the ridge, he stayed low and scanned the

153

roadside bushes. He had expected the blond man to be watching and waiting. Ready to finish the job.

Another car approached: a hefty 4x4. Sawyer hobbled into the road and held out his arms. The car pulled up onto the verge.

There was nothing left now. If this was the blond man, he could offer no resistance.

The driver got out. He was a broad, middle-aged man wearing a woollen hat and a fleece-collared jacket. Another man—younger—got out and hung back by the open door.

Sawyer noticed he was shivering.

'You okay, mate? What's happened?'

He spoke. Something about coming off the road. It was hard to speak. Jaw frozen, in spasm.

Down on his knee; hand on the cold earth.

The second man, wrapping something round him. Coat, blanket.

Inside the car, across the back seat. Shivering, shivering.

The first man. 'Don't think you'll be seeing your car again, son.'

Driving away. The second man watching him from the passenger seat.

And laughter: retched up, sweeping over.

Dark, uncontrollable laughter.

34

Sawyer sat up in his temporary bed. The corridor flared into focus: too bright; everything moving, everything amplified.

A man stood at his bedside: smiling, waiting. Early twenties, goatee, man bun. He wore olive green scrubs, with a stethoscope draped around his neck. 'Mr Sawyer, my name's Lyle. I'm one of the doctors here. Do you know where you are?'

Sawyer winced at his fierce headache. The doctor handed him a plastic cup of water, and he downed it in one. 'Hospital? Cavendish?'

'Yes, you're in A&E. You've been here a couple of hours. You were quite confused when you came in. You were shivering and your clothes were wet. Do you remember that?'

He did. Just. The car, the lake. Already, it seemed so distant and dreamlike. 'What time is it?'

'Just gone eleven PM. You had a mild touch of hypothermia. We've dried you off, warmed you up.' Sawyer looked down; he was wearing a hospital gown, his arm attached to a drip. 'The line is just warmed saline. You've been monitored, and I'm happy that you're out of the woods. But you need to take it easy. Your body's been through quite a shock.' He disconnected the drip. 'You had a few cuts to your arms. Some bruising. Did you fall? Into water?'

He reached for a clearer memory of the time before the lake. Nothing. 'Yes. Might have drunk too much.'

The doctor eyed him. 'Have you taken anything else this evening?'

'No.'

'Is there a possibility that you might have ingested something without your knowledge?'

'Yeah, there's a possibility.'

'Your saliva test came up negative for GhB. But, judging by your behaviour when you came in, I would suspect flunitrazepam. Rohypnol. Roofies. Do you have any dependency issues, Mr Sawyer?'

He managed a smile. 'No.'

The doctor nodded. 'Well, you're awake. You have some recall. However this got into your system, it seems you had a mild dose. If your drink was spiked, then that's a criminal offence. You should inform the police.'

A flash of the glass of Coke. Half drunk, spilled. The blond man taking the bottle out of the fridge, replacing it.

'Who brought me in?'

'I didn't see you at that stage. You must have been triaged quickly, though, given your state.'

The doctor gestured to a chair at the side of the bed. Sawyer's clothes sat in a folded pile with his boots underneath. 'We've dried out your things. Your phone is in the coat pocket. Not in the best shape, though.' He frowned. 'Do you *remember* coming in? Giving us your name?'

Again, he flexed for recall. But there was little beyond

the house, his brother. He sat up, hopped out of bed. 'Got to go.'

———

Sawyer took a taxi back to the cottage, paying the unimpressed driver in 20p pieces from his change jar. He checked each room, looking for missing items, anything out of the ordinary. The Coke glass had been placed back on the coffee table, and the spillage cleaned away. He took the bottle out of the fridge and sniffed the contents. Nothing unusual.

Bruce reappeared, and as he scraped some food into his dish, Sawyer noticed his wallet was still there on the coffee table. He checked it: no cash removed. He reached into the inner pocket and pulled out the polaroid of his mother, standing at the garden gate on Christmas morning, 1987. Orange bathrobe; long, raven-black hair gathered into the hood; uncertain smile. He took out his phone; it was clammy, with a clouded screen, and wouldn't turn on.

He shuffled into the bathroom and turned on the shower, hot taps only. He stripped and stood there in the billowing steam, with his chin on his chest. Reviving, reheating.

He dressed and checked around the sitting room again. He dug a hand down the side of the sofa and pulled out the burner phone. Text message from Max Reeves.

Call me when you can.

That could keep. There was someone else he needed to speak to first.

His thumb trembled as he made the call. It rang for a long time before connecting.

'Hello?' Eva sounded wary but sleepy.

'It's me.'

'Jesus, Jake. What now? It's late.'

He flopped back on the sofa. 'Whatever Dale is up to, he must have a lot riding on it.'

Eva yawned. 'What do you mean?'

'Because I think he just had someone try and kill me and make it look like suicide.'

35

Sawyer slept in his clothes: clenched and foetal, buffeted by a collage of leering nightmares. The doctor, tending him, transformed into the blond man, manipulating his drip. And the blond man became the man with the moustache from his dream: holding down his mother, raising the hammer. Sawyer lunged forward to stop him, but the man smiled and dazzled him with the shine from his watch.

His brother, flat out on the bloodied grass. His dog, motionless.

His mother called out to the man. '*Why?*' He replaced the balaclava and brought the hammer down into the centre of his mother's face.

For the first time, he saw something close to distress in the man's eyes. A loathing. As if the hammer blows were inflicting pain on himself.

'*Jake! Run, my darling. Don't look back.*'

He woke with a shout, on the edge of the bed, clinging to the headboard. His breaths came in juddering rasps, and he realised he was convulsing: half laughing, half crying.

He showered, changed, and took a taxi to Enterprise Rentals, a car hire garage in an industrial estate on the edge of Buxton. The office was manned by Howard, the grim-faced but friendly South African clerk who had sold him the Mini.

Howard stood up and shook Sawyer's hand. 'Nice to see you again. Looking for something new already?'

'Just a rental. Had a slight mishap with the other car.' Howard squinted at him, waiting for more. 'Whatever you've got for a couple of weeks. I'm not fussy.'

He signed off a white Corsa and drove into town, where he bought a new official phone from the same contract provider and set himself up in The Source with tea and white toast. As the phone restored everything from his back-up, he called Reeves on the burner.

He picked up straight away. 'I'd hoped you would spare me on a Sunday.'

Sawyer dug a knife into the butter. 'The law doesn't rest, Max.'

Reeves ignored him. 'Got something for you.'

'Me first. You need to look into a character called Dale Strickland. Work connections in Manchester. He's got a club. Players. There's one in Deansgate, and he's set up a second in Buxton. The timing is indecently efficient. Snooker. Videogames.'

Reeves lit a cigarette. 'Sounds like an upstanding business to me.'

'Strickland is a crook, Max. I think we're talking county lines here. Drugs.'

'Teenager-friendly businesses. Plenty of buyers.'

'And sellers. I think he's got a lot riding on this. I would love to do some deeper digging myself, but obviously...'

Reeves puffed out smoke. 'You are a tad compromised right now. Alright. I'm on it. My turn. Your burgundy

BMW. Plenty of them registered in your area. I've got a data services intern working through ANPR catches in the period following Klein's release.' A rustle of paper. Sawyer looked up, made eye contact with the owner, who averted his gaze. 'There are four burgundy BMWs active in Derbyshire between Klein's release and his death, but only one was clocked in the area near Magpie Mine on the day you gave me. It's a 2008 X5. Current owner bought it second hand in 2014. DVLA registration certificate transferred online to a Charles Kelly.'

Sawyer stirred his tea; the owner was still sneaking the odd look in his direction. 'Kelly. Is he a GP? That's the name of my old family doctor. Lived near Wardlow. He was good friends with my dad. I remember him being around the house a lot when he was struggling after my mum died. Bit of a Bible basher.'

'Address near Wardlow. Must be the same guy.'

'So, what the hell is my old family doctor doing, snooping on Klein?'

Reeves took a long drag on his cigarette. 'I've got a better question. What the hell is your old family doctor doing driving his car around when he died three years ago?'

'Someone stole the car?'

'Or acquired it and never transferred the registration. That explains why it's not pinging ANPR as stolen or illicit. It's fallen through the admin cracks. Whoever has it now is probably keeping it legit with cash in hand MOTs. You might get lucky if you check local garages, but not as a civilian.' He lowered his voice. 'Jake. There's one more thing.'

Sawyer crunched into his toast. 'Go on.'

'You made the papers again.'

161

36

Austin Fletcher pushed open the door to the basement snooker room. As soon as he stepped inside, two weighty men in branded black polo shirts abandoned their game of American Pool and barred his way.

Fletcher took out a packet of cigarettes, tapped one out.

One of the men shook his head. 'No smoking down here, boss.'

Fletcher took out a match and slowly turned it around in his fingers. He struck it and raised the flame to his cigarette, puffing it into life. The men eyed each other.

He tossed the spent match to the floor; he still hadn't made eye contact with either of the men. 'Strickland?'

The men took a step closer.

'He's good!' An even larger man in a caramel blazer and white shirt called from the door of the corner office. The men stepped aside and Fletcher strolled past the lit but unoccupied snooker tables, into the office. The blazered man followed him inside and closed the door.

Dale sat at the desk, with Marco stood off to the side. He nodded to the blazered man. 'Austin. This is Hector.'

Fletcher ignored him.

Hector moved further into the room and perched on the desk, between Fletcher and Dale. 'What happened?' He was square jawed and angry-looking, with a slight Slavic accent.

Fletcher pulled on his cigarette, exhaled an opaque fog of smoke. 'He got out.'

'We know that,' said Hector. 'How?'

Fletcher raised his head, laid his hollow eyes on Hector. 'Too rushed. Not prepared enough.'

Hector shook his head. 'Not good enough.'

Dale held up a hand. 'Gents. We're celebrating. It looks like our dear friend might be on his own way out of the picture.' He passed a copy of the morning's *Sunday Mirror* across the desk. Fletcher leaned forward to read it. The main splash story—*RED ARROWS HERO DIES*—dominated most of the front cover, but a second story occupied the left-hand column, with a picture of Sawyer, under a stacked headline.

TOP COP IN MURDER PROBE

Dale tapped the story. 'He's been bailed, under investigation. We might not need to do anything. Let's hang back, focus on the new business, and revisit if we need to.'

Hector spluttered and waved a hand through the air. 'Put the fucking cigarette out.'

Fletcher raised his head, stared at Dale.

Dale pulled a crystal ashtray from a desk drawer and set it down on the desk. 'Stick around. Enjoy the bright lights of Manchester. We're finished, for now.'

Fletcher took another drag on his cigarette, expelled the smoke through his nose. 'We didn't start.'

37

Sawyer stood before his bedroom mirror, in T-shirt and hoodie. He would normally train topless, but the memory of the cold water still clung to his bones. He plugged his iPhone into an ancient speaker dock and set his Spotify nineties playlist to shuffle.

McAlmont and Butler – 'Yes'. He smiled at the irony: the euphoric tone, lyrics about feeling better, escaping a toxic past.

He slipped into Wing Chun horse stance and drilled out a series of double punches. As he switched into the *Sil Lum Tao* form again, he saw Sheila Caldwell: alone with her chintz, abandoned, recalling the last time she saw her husband, his father's boss at the time.

'*It was as if something was eating at him. Boring into him. He seemed angry.*'

And her poem. Delmore Schwarz. A lament for the fleeting nature of life.

'*Time is the fire in which we burn.*'

He pondered Logan. His father's refused visit to Klein.

'*It looks like your old man might have been a few steps ahead of you.*'

His old doctor, Charles Kelly. The burgundy BMW.

And, always. His mother's final words.

'*Jake. Run, my darling. Don't look back!*'

He broke out of the form and sat on the bed, letting his thoughts drift and settle. He made a call on the burner phone.

'Richard Jensen.'

'Jake Sawyer.'

A laugh at the other end. 'Calling from a secret number on a Sunday evening. Who are we planning to piss off this time, Jake? The Mossad?'

Jensen was an old friend from Sawyer's time at Keele University. He'd began post-academic life as a self-styled 'supernatural investigator', but had evolved into a professional sceptic, and author of a series of pop psychology books. He was a little rough round the edges, but they had developed a solid mutual trust, and Jensen had helped Sawyer with the Crawley case.

'Just one man, Rich. No international incidents. And if we're careful, we might not even need to piss him off.'

'I love it. Talk cryptic to me.'

Sawyer sipped at the Coke. 'I'm embracing technology. After our triumphs against Mr Viktor Beck, I was hoping you could help.'

'I'm sure I can. You around tomorrow? I'm in Birmingham later that day with our mutual friend.'

'Professor Ainsworth? How's the book going? I heard you might do a podcast? Debunking the bullshitters?'

'It's going really well. But our ambitions are at different ends of the scale. He wants podcast, I want Netflix series.'

Bruce scratched at the side door and Sawyer got up to let him out. 'Tell me more over lunch tomorrow. I'll text with details.'

'Cheerio.'

He made cheese on toast and slumped on the sofa with an episode of *Life on Earth*. A herd of zebra milled around an African plain, watching a lion and lioness prowl past. David Attenborough's half-whispered narration settled over Sawyer like a familiar blanket.

'Provided they've got a start in the race, the lions will never catch them. The lions' only chance is to get really close and rely on their spectacular acceleration.'

His iPhone rang: still in the speaker dock. He sprang up and hurried into the bedroom.

Maggie.

As he connected the call, she was already midway through a sentence, talking to someone else. She sounded shrill, panicked.

'Mags?'

'Jake! Please. Will you... What do I...' She spluttered, struggling to measure out her words.

Sawyer sat on the bed. 'It's okay, it's okay. Take it slow. What's happened?'

Maggie breathed fast, sobbing. 'I don't... Justin. He took them out.'

'The swimming? Mia and Freddy.'

'Yes! He took them. And they went to a Christmas market in Bakewell.'

'Maggie—'

'He was... he was buying something. With Freddy. He says it was busy.' She broke down again, pulled herself back. 'Mia went off.'

'Went off? Where?'

'To look around. But it was dark and busy. He shouldn't have...'

Sawyer stood up. 'Mags. *What happened*?'

She let out a cry: bereft, angry. 'We can't find her, Jake. We can't find Mia.'

PART TWO

SOUR TIMES

38

The woman pocketed her yellow gloves and tapped on the door of the old sitting room. She took a breath, and walked in.

The blind was closed, and the woman had to squint to spot the outline of the man, sprawled across the bottle-green sofa. He flicked on the reading light clipped to his book and looked up. The music was much louder this time: deep, droning guitar and plodding, time-delayed drums. He reached for a control and lowered the volume.

The woman nodded. 'She's safe, dear. I settled her.'

'Already?' The voice: strangled and watery.

'I gave her something.'

'Name?'

'I'm not sure. I think it's Mia. I heard her father shouting.'

The man rose up. He stretched his spindly limbs and put on his silver-rimmed glasses, then stalked over to the woman. She braced, but he walked past her, out into the hall.

She followed him, into the room with the gym lockers.

Joshua sat at the far end of the wall-mounted bench, eyes down, while Mia perched on the floor below: arms around her knees, head down. She wore a bright pink duffel coat, striped bobble hat, white mittens.

The man approached Mia and crouched at her side. She was trembling, but not crying. He reached out and eased away the bobble hat with twig-like fingers. Mia glared up at him, then pulled it back down, burying her face back into her knees.

The man shuffled over, near to Mia's feet. He glanced up at the woman, and she leaned in and took a firm grip of Mia's wrists. He held her left leg and rolled up the end of her jeans. Mia raised her head again and offered a few feeble kicks from the other leg. The man clipped the collar tight around her ankle and stood over her.

The woman released Mia's wrists and she scratched and scrabbled at the metal. 'It's okay, my love. Just for security. It won't hurt you.'

The man looked up to the skylight and the starless night. Flurries of rain rattled the glass. 'Don't be frightened, Mia. You don't need to struggle any more. I'll look after you.'

Mia scowled at him. 'Where's my dad?'

The man nodded at the woman and they walked back out into the hall. As they closed the door, Mia repeated her question, louder, and buried her head between her knees again, sobbing.

The man faced the wall of the corridor. 'She's emotional.'

'It'll settle.'

'I'll need to take more time. She can't accept things if she isn't calm.' He turned his wide eyes on the woman. 'I'm out tonight. Can I trust you this time?'

She gave a strained smile, distorting her lined face. 'Yes. Holly was difficult. I think this one will be easier.'

The man bowed his head and gripped a handful of his mousey brown hair. 'Holly was *perfect*. She just... needed time. And now, thanks to your negligence...'

She inched towards him. 'I need time, too.'

39

Sawyer drove hard, through the rain, down to the Staffordshire Roaches: a rocky ridge that overlooked the borderland town of Leek. He sped past the Ramshaw Rocks lay-by and turned into the lane that led to Maggie's home. He slowed as he approached the converted barn; Shepherd's boxy Range Rover was out front, beside two other civilian cars and a yellow-and-blue police vehicle.

He parked near the end of the road and turned off the Corsa's lights. He hunted around the glovebox and opened a fresh packet of chocolate eclairs: toffee, soft centred, long lasting. He sat there, chewing, watching the house. He couldn't risk going in: it would get back to Keating. Better to keep his head down and wait for an opportunity.

After half an hour, Shepherd emerged with Patricia, Maggie's assistant Family Liaison Officer. Sawyer texted Shepherd: *CORSA*. Shepherd checked his phone and looked up. Sawyer flashed his lights, and Shepherd walked over to the car. He dealt with another brief call, then got in.

Shepherd swished the rainwater off his shoulders. He looked as bad as Sawyer felt: ashen, emptied.

'How is she? What's happened?'

Shepherd glanced at him. 'Her husband had the kids, Mia and Freddy. Bakewell Market. Took his eye off Mia while he paid for something. No sign.'

'CCTV?'

'Nothing we can see yet. The market was busy. Rhodes is on it. Shop cameras. *Everyone's* on it. Blocks on all the perimeter roads. It was too busy. Hard to get in there and start working quickly. Fucking weather is no help.'

Sawyer swiped away the windscreen condensation, opened his window an inch. 'Why kill Holly and not Joshua?'

Shepherd dropped his head. 'She disappointed the captor? Didn't fit the bill, for whatever reason?'

Sawyer offered him the eclairs; he refused. 'We need to know cause of death.'

'*We?*' Shepherd scowled at him. 'With respect—'

'We've done this. Don't say that. Let's take it as read. It's mutual.'

'Sir. I know it's difficult, but you're not part of this investigation.'

Sawyer nodded. 'Mia's disappearance might not be related to Holly and Joshua. You need to keep that option open.'

'Obviously.'

Sawyer unwrapped a second eclair. 'Strange, though, if there is a connection. If he was done with Holly, for whatever reason, it's odd that he didn't take Mia and *then* kill Holly. Feels like the wrong way round. It's also interesting that he's changed his method of abduction. Holly and Joshua were both out, and didn't come home. Probably groomed online. This one is opportunistic. Rushed. As if he needed a quick replacement, whatever the risk.'

'You're clued up, then. Been following the case.'

Sawyer caught Shepherd's eye. 'I'm a man of leisure, remember? Plenty of papers to read.'

'And you can read about yourself, now you've made the front page.'

Sawyer slipped the eclair into his mouth. 'That's why I'm sitting in a dark patch of road in a bland rented car.'

'Where's the Mini?'

'Garage.'

Shepherd studied him. 'Keating has moved your case to an outside team. Moran was working it, with a few others. He's shifted them all onto the missing kids.'

Sawyer frowned. 'Myers and Walker on the crossbow murders, I suppose. Dead middle-aged men don't rank as highly as abducted children.'

'*Very* clued up. Reading some pretty sharp papers.'

Sawyer rolled the sweet round his mouth. 'Concentrate on the time between Holly's body being found and Mia being taken. It's too short. Emotional. Impulsive. What's he reacting to? He's lost control of something. I think that was Holly. You don't kill someone and dump their body in full view, on the edge of a treeline. You go into the trees. You hide it, bury it. She got out. Maybe she was injured, couldn't go further. Died from exposure by the time he got to her. I don't think he intended to kill Holly. I think she escaped, and you need to find out where she escaped from.'

'We might learn more from Drummond. He says the body will be thawed enough to do preliminaries tomorrow.' Another marked car arrived up ahead. 'Need to go.'

'Work back from Holly. Assuming there's a connection, her body holds the key to finding Mia, and Joshua. There's a story there. She'll tell it to Drummond.' He dug his fingers into his eyebrows, worked them around. 'Holly is the mouth of the river. To understand who's taking these children, and why, we need to sample a handful of water, study the elements, trace them back. How did the water get there? What's the source?'

Shepherd climbed out of the Corsa and approached the marked car. Two uniforms got out and Shepherd guided them to the front door, where Patricia let them all inside.

Sawyer took out his iPhone and called Maggie's number. As expected, it went straight to voicemail. 'Mags.' He stared out at the teeming rain, brimming around the dormant wipers. 'I'd be in there if I could. You know that. Please. Call me when you want to, when you think you can. It feels like the world has ended. Everyone is telling you how sorry they are. But please don't think that Mia is lost, Mags. Not for a second. We just misplaced her, okay? And we'll get her back.'

40

Snatched fragments of sleep: half an hour, an hour. Left side, right side. Too dark, not dark enough. The constant hiss of the rain outside: soothing at first; but then enclosing, claustrophobic. The drains splashed and spluttered, sending Sawyer back to the car and the lake. A phrase, circling in his mind like a mantra: *a watery grave.*

He was about to give in, when Bruce nosed his way into the bedroom and hopped onto the bed.

Sawyer sat up and petted the cat. 'No action tonight, big man?'

Bruce broke into a fruity purr and curled up in a groove in the duvet.

And in a moment, he was awake, in a brightened room.

He reached for his phone: 8:30am. *Fuck.* Had he missed an early briefing?

He opened the app and activated the listening device. General office chatter, ringing telephones. Keating's voice, further away.

Sawyer opened his bedroom blind to a rare dazzle of morning sun.

He made coffee, carrying the phone around with him.

At nine, he heard Keating's voice: loud and present. He set the phone down on the bedside table and worked out on the wooden man while he listened.

'*Good morning, everyone. As you all know, we're facing a complex situation and I want you to focus all of your resource and efforts on the new development. Mia Spark, ten years of age. Her mother, Maggie, is a colleague. An FLO. Mia was with her father, Justin, and brother, Freddy, at yesterday's Christmas market in Bakewell. Her father says he became distracted for a few minutes at a stall, and Mia disappeared into the crowd. Because of the busy streets, it was a challenge to conduct the initial enquiry inside the first hour, and we currently have no leads on Mia's whereabouts.*'

'*We're looking over street and shop CCTV.*' Shepherd. '*But as DCI Keating says, the time of day and weather conditions will make it a challenge to pick out Mia in the crowds. FLOs will talk more with the parents today.*'

'*Connections with the other missing children?*' Moran. '*And the dead girl?*'

'*You mean Holly.*' Shepherd again. '*Holly and Joshua left their homes and didn't return, but it seems that Mia was taken. More opportunistic. There's a chance that she was groomed and arranged a meeting during the Christmas market, but it's slim. She didn't have her own phone, but there's a family computer we'll take a look at.*'

Sawyer crashed his forearms against the wooden struts, relishing the pain, pushing his full core strength into each movement. He paused at a moment of silence from the briefing, wondering if he'd lost connection. But then, Sally O'Callaghan spoke.

'*We have preliminary findings from Frazer Drummond on Holly Chilton. No sign of sexual assault. No external trauma. Most likely death from exposure, although we're still awaiting toxicology, fibre analysis.*'

'*Let's get everything on finding Mia for now.*' Keating again. '*Sally, let me know if Drummond finds anything else from the Holly Chilton PM.*'

Shepherd spoke up. '*If there is a connection, then Holly might be the key to finding Mia, and Joshua.*'

Sawyer smiled, and towelled himself down. He took a slurp of coffee.

Keating made a non-committal noise. '*Myers, Walker. Any movement on the crossbow killings? Little and Cunningham?*'

Walker cleared his throat. '*Rhodes has been looking deeper into the computer and phone history of the two murdered men. Looks like they were both active on a network called MEETUPZ. Can't get any specific chat histories or logs, though. The company's based in Korea. Plenty of pictures on their home computers. Cunningham's collection was pretty low on the COPINE scale, but Little's was further up. Mostly sevens and eights, a few nines. We've liaised with North Yorks Police on the two crossbow murders from earlier this year. Boyd and Manning.*'

'*Any joy with this symbol yet?*' A noise, as Keating tapped the whiteboard.

'*No. It's on all four crossbow bolts. Could be from an obscure manufacturer or something custom. Drawing a blank, either way. But it does suggest the killings are connected.*'

Sawyer dug out the burner phone and sent Walker a text.

Two perps? For each abduction, the killer takes a paedophile?

'*Get me more on MEETUPZ.*' Keating sounded flustered; it wasn't like him.

'*Sir.*' Walker. '*Could there be a link between the children*

178

and the crossbow killings? The victims are registered child sex offenders. Maybe he's killing them in response to the abductions?'

Another moment of silence. Sawyer held his coffee cup suspended before his mouth.

'*Nice thinking,*' said Keating, '*if a little baroque. Talk to your North Yorks contacts and check child disappearances around the time of Boyd and Manning's deaths.*'

'*And let's see if he clips another nonce down here,*' said Moran. '*In response to Mia.*'

Keating snorted. '*I don't see how this helps us right now, though. Stick to the crime in action. Mia. And keep it confidential. We've already had an internal enquiry leaked out in the open yesterday.*'

Bustle, as the meeting broke up.

'*Vigilante paedo killers and missing kids,*' said Moran. '*Shame the mighty DI Sawyer can't be with us. This is right up his street.*'

41

Richard Jensen crashed through the main doors of The Bull's Head in Castleton. It was a cramped traditional inn, with a few minor concessions to the North Face crowd: leather settees, easy on the display plates. Sawyer had claimed a spot by the ground-floor window, away from a horde of loud, layered-up hikers, eager to tackle the nearby 'mother hill': Mam Tor.

Jensen spotted Sawyer and grinned. He wore his standard normcore combo: black pullover and brown leather jacket, with a chunky, striped scarf coiled high over his angular chin. His silver-rimmed glasses lent an academic air, but the eyes behind flashed with a puckish charm.

He flattened his thinning hair and clamped Sawyer in a crushing handshake. 'Jake. Freezing out there. Hardly a revelation, I know.' He looked around. 'Need a piss. Can you get me a beer? Dizzy Blonde. Are you eating?'

'The homity pie is good. Cheese and veg.'

'Sold!' Jensen dropped his backpack at Sawyer's table and disappeared into the toilet. Sawyer bought Jensen's beer, and ordered two pies. He took out his phone and pulled up the picture of the crossbow symbol. Rays of light around the iris. An all-seeing eye? An implication of vigilance? Exposure?

'Nice place.' Jensen took a seat opposite Sawyer and poured out his beer. 'They sell fucking *pheromone wipes* here. There's a machine in the toilet. It says you can use them to "boost your pulling power", and that you should "use responsibly".' He laughed and slurped beer through the head of his drink, wiped his mouth. 'It gives me an image of some irresistible lothario being followed by a train of salivating women. Like little ducklings.'

Sawyer smiled. 'Are you implying that's something you don't need personally?'

Jensen recoiled in mock horror. 'I'm forced to rely on my natural magnetism. The Prof sends his regards, by the way.'

'How's the book going?'

'Well! Some terrific stories of the people who tried to win his old Paranormal Challenge. And I've always loved Edinburgh. Ainsworth's profile is giving us plenty of publisher options. He's also working on some side project. Criminology, psychology. British serial killers. He says he might talk to you.'

The food arrived, and they gathered their cutlery. 'You're doing a good job, Rich.'

'Job?'

'Of not mentioning my arrest.'

Jensen looked at Sawyer over the top of his glasses. 'What *is* that all about, anyway? Surely it's not going to stick?'

'I'm working on that.'

Jensen nodded, and muted the moment with a forkful of pie. 'I can't stick around, Jake. Got to get down to Birmingham for this thing with Ainsworth.'

'You still seeing the woman from Sheffield?'

Jensen smiled, nodded. 'As infrequently as possible. That's how you keep it exciting.' He lowered his voice. 'That's the secret, you see. The smug marrieds look on serial monogamists like me with pity. But the moment you domesticate, you're on a downward spiral. You can't maintain an exciting sexual relationship with a woman who peels your socks off the barrel of a tumble drier. Life is to be enjoyed. Shades of intimacy. Yes. But you shouldn't make yourself a slave to compromise.'

'Did you get the thing I asked for?'

Jensen forked in another mouthful, nodded. 'What's it for, anyway? Do I want to know?'

'No. Do you mind if I keep it confidential? In case I have to go to Plan B?'

Jensen eyed him. 'I would actively prefer you kept it confidential. I'd like to maintain plausible deniability, if possible.' He took a small pouch out of his backpack. 'This is a hangover from my ghost-hunting days. It's pretty straightforward. A micro mini spy camera. 1080p. HD. Wireless, of course. It even has a night vision mode. People use them for home security, spying on nannies. No storage. You can follow the footage on your phone, via an app.'

'I've got something else that works that way.'

Jensen smiled. 'I'll assume that's also something I'd rather not know about. The camera has a motion sensor. You can turn it off, but it can be useful if you're leaving it somewhere quiet where there isn't much activity. It'll just sit there and send you a notification when it detects movement. You can also turn that off, though, and just keep it always active. Runs off a battery that lasts about three days at always on, and about a week on motion sensitive.'

Sawyer took the pouch. 'Thanks, Rich. Do you want anything for it?'

Jensen shook his head. 'Just buy me lunch. I'd offer to pay, but I can't seem to find my...' He patted his pockets, smiled at Sawyer.

Sawyer passed Jensen's wallet across the table. 'I was going to—'

'Of course. It was a sloppy lift. Apollo would be appalled.'

They ate in silence for a moment. Sawyer nodded at his phone. 'I've got something to show you.' He navigated to his photos and brought up the image of the eye symbol. 'Have you seen anything like this on your arcane travels? Scary secret societies?'

Jensen studied the image. 'There *is* a touch of illuminati about it. Interesting that the rays radiate out from the centre of the iris. It's vaguely familiar. Send it to me. I'll have another look when I'm stuck in Spaghetti Junction.'

'One more thing.' Sawyer set down his cutlery and nodded over his shoulder. 'Can you leave first? Get a face picture of the big guy sitting at the café across the road.'

Jensen looked past Sawyer, through the window. 'Guy with the baseball cap and ponytail? Bomber jacket? I don't think he's here for the scenery, Jake.' He gathered his things, stood up. Sawyer got to his feet, and they man hugged. 'Your car near here?' Sawyer nodded. 'Leave a couple of minutes after me. I'll keep tabs on your friend for a while and send you the picture. Go easy, Jake. And get yourself cleared. Next time I see you, I don't want it to be in a visiting room.'

42

Sawyer parked in the road by Alex's house. He took out his iPhone and sent a text message to Maggie.

Thinking of you. Always here. x

He opened Jensen's pouch. The spy camera was a black plastic cube around the size of a 50p piece, with a blue lens in the front and brackets around the back for fixing. Jensen had included a fold-out manual and a black cable tie, thin enough to thread through the brackets. He rolled the camera around between his thumb and forefinger, put it back in the pouch, and shoved everything into the glovebox.

His phone blipped. Text from Jensen, with a clear, high-quality picture of the man at the café. Sawyer zoomed in to his face: forties, well preserved, with deep-set, pinhole eyes. Flat expression, distant. Sawyer groped into his memory, searching for detail of the night with the car and the lake. But it was still vague and misted over. The short ponytail seemed familiar, but he couldn't be sure it was the same man who had been in his house. He read the message.

Followed our friend for a bit after you came out. You drove off and he got into his car soon after. Same car park. Not sure if he followed you. Got his reg. See you soon. Don't die. –Rich

Sawyer pulled back from the close-up of the man's face and zoomed in to the café table. Newspaper, coffee cup, and a small bottle with a green logo of three concentric C symbols.

He zoomed out and swiped away the image. A second picture showed a close-up of a car registration. He tapped out a quick message to Max Reeves and sent him the images.

He got out of the car and walked up the path to Alex's front door, looking from side to side. There was nobody waiting in any of the parked cars, and he hadn't noticed anyone following him on the journey down from Castleton. If this were Dale's man, he didn't expect a high level of professionalism, but just because he hadn't seen him didn't mean he wasn't there.

————

Alex poured the tea. 'Did you get the scans from your father?'

Sawyer nodded. 'Haven't had a chance to do much with them, though. Quite a few things going on right now.' He kept his eyes down, on the thin beige carpet.

'Did something happen?'

He looked up. 'What?'

'You're barely here at all today, Jake. Four fifths of you is off elsewhere. Scheming, stressing.'

'Sorry. Something did happen. The tingling sensation.'

She sat forward. 'Fear? Panic? You felt it again?'

'Yes. Like the cave. In a place with limited oxygen.'

'That's consistent with what we talked about. Studies have shown how patients with amygdala damage have an inhibited fear response, but not in situations where they're deprived of oxygen. The low oxygen level seems to stimulate their amygdala and induce an extreme fight or flight response. In other words, a panic attack. The body convincing itself it's in extreme danger.'

He snapped back his head. 'I *was* in extreme danger.'

'Really? And did this involve a lack of oxygen?'

'Yes.'

She lowered her voice. 'Is this something you can talk about?'

His eyes searched the walls. 'Can, but won't.' He drew in a deep breath through his nose. 'It's ongoing.'

Alex nodded. 'I know it might not seem like it right now, but this is good, Jake. It's more evidence that the damage you suffered at the hands of the man who attacked your mother is repairable. The reliving therapy will help you come to terms with the psychological effects of what you witnessed, and you can now use the brain scans to explore the physiology.'

He glared at her. 'And then what? Closure? A normal life? A normal fear response?'

She smiled. 'Sometimes, there's a tendency to embrace dysfunction, to hold on to it. There's a feeling that it's part of the package, the uniqueness. To fix it or lose it would make the person less exceptional.'

'I don't need fixing. I just want to find the bastard who murdered my mother.'

Alex took some time stirring her tea. 'I'm sure you've heard of Hans Eysenck. English psychologist, German born. He did some interesting work on extroverts and introverts. We think of extroverts as loud and outgoing, and introverts as shy and retiring. But he said that extroverts are just people with low levels of natural arousal, who need more stimulation from their environment. The standard rhythm of the world around them just isn't enough. They often need to create this stimulation with aberrant or criminal behaviour.'

Sawyer nodded. 'You've seen the papers.'

'Oh, I'm sure you're not guilty, and it will all be cleared up somehow. But how have you reached this point, with all this going on? The world hasn't conspired against you. It's your choices that have brought you here. Like we said before, you're seeking out stimulation similar to the complexity of the feelings you have for your mother. And you're constantly disappointed. And so you escalate. And this escalation keeps getting you into difficult, often life-threatening situations. And this new fear or panic that you've felt, in the cave and again recently... It's exciting because it feels like a shortcut. All the feeling without the baggage, without the emotion.'

Sawyer held her gaze. 'If it works, it works. Does it matter how or why?'

'You can't hack yourself, Jake. Modify your brain to only feel what you want it to feel. You are what you are, and our work is all about giving you the tools to accept that, before this desire to seek arousal, with no regard for consequence, leads you to a place you can't talk or fight your way out of.'

43

Sawyer headed out for a late afternoon run, down through Edale village, along the edge of the farmland at the base of Kinder Scout. No headphones, no easy distraction. He had hoped the activity would clear his mind, but his worries tagged along, hounding him like gnats. He jogged along the sodden track: a wanted man, probed by his own colleagues, stalked by criminals.

On the path back down to the cottage, he was scoured by a deluge of icy rain. He bowed his head and drove forward; by the time he had reached the front door, a weak shaft of sunlight had squeezed through the blackening cloud. It would be dark by 4pm. He longed for the winter solstice, still weeks away; his side of the earth at its furthest tilt from the sun, but with the eternal promise of return and rebirth.

He towelled off and checked his phone: two messages, from Eva and Max Reeves, both asking him to call. He poured a glass of milk and opened a large packet of Revels. He pulled out a spherical chocolate. Coffee for Reeves; orange for Eva. He gnawed away the outer layer.

Coffee.

Reeves answered on the first ring. 'Still a free man, then?'

Sawyer chewed on the sweet, wincing at the synthetic coffee flavour. 'Always running, Max. Found anything?'

'Strickland. Good call. Manchester vice are on it. Contact says they're watching the Players club there.'

'Are they planning anything?'

Reeves struck a match, cursed, tried another. 'Don't know. My source wouldn't give me any more, which suggests they might well be.' He puffed on a cigarette.

Sawyer laughed, chewed on a flat, saucer-shaped chocolate. 'My "source". You sound like someone else I know. What about the car and the guy from earlier today?'

Reeves paused. 'Car was hired. Silver Ford Fiesta. Picked up at an Avis in Manchester last Thursday. The guy in your pic was on a flight from Amsterdam the previous day.'

'Why not pick the car up from the airport?'

'Dunno. Too conspicuous? Not sure if he'd be staying until he'd been into town?' Reeves blew out smoke. 'Name of Austin Fletcher. Ex-Marine. Served in Afghanistan in the early 2000s. Tried to join the SAS and got as far as jungle training, but was bumped back to his unit after allegations of sexual assault from locals in a Brunei village. Then he really pissed on his chips. Put his commanding officer in hospital. Broken jaw. Anger issues, or the jungle heat?'

Sawyer took a slug of milk. 'I'd go for anger issues. I think he takes creatine. Associations with Strickland?'

'Nothing obvious at the moment. But he did go to the same college. Maybe that was the beginning of their bromance. Dropped out and joined the army. Look, do me a favour. Well, two favours. Get yourself off this charge so you can do some work of your own. And I know you're a big boy, Sawyer, but don't fuck with this geezer.'

Later, Sawyer made spaghetti, and resumed his previous episode of *Life on Earth*. He laid his laptop on the coffee table and opened the Google home page.

He ducked forward and shovelled in a forkful of pasta.

Text to Eva.

Come see me tonight?

He typed 'paedophiles grooming' into the Google search box. The results were as grim as he expected: definitions, documentaries, explainer pieces for parents, articles on grooming methods via live streaming and YouTube.

'A lioness begins to stalk, keeping low and almost invisible in the tawny, sun-withered grass.'

He browsed a *Guardian* article—*Rise Of The Hunters* —about the culture of paedophile hunter groups in London. During Sawyer's time in the Met, his specialist unit colleagues had frequent run-ins with hunter groups and their high-profile stings: posing as children and tricking paedophiles into meetings that would be streamed live on social media; then informing the police and restraining the offenders until they arrived.

Sawyer typed 'paedophile hunter manchester sheffield leeds' and found a group based in Sheffield called JFK: Justice For Kids.

Text from Eva.

Can't. Dale around. I'll call tomorrow.

'Predator exposure'... 'Net justice'...

Sawyer tapped the blue F icon and found the JFK

Facebook page. He logged in as Lloyd Robbins—his journalist alias account—and opened the Send Message box. He wrote a quick private note, with the number of his burner phone and a request for an interview.

'But only one in five of these solitary hunts is successful. Scavenging is an easier way of getting meat.'

44

Sawyer hustled the Corsa up the track to his father's house. As usual, Harold was already at the door with Rufus and Cain. He turned back into the hall as Sawyer approached, letting the dogs do the greeting for him.

In the reading room, Harold settled himself in the sky-blue armchair. 'I saw you made the papers.'

Sawyer shrugged. 'Who reads newspapers, these days?'

'I do.' He reached over to a side table and held up a chunky copy of *The Sunday Times*.

'I don't suppose I made the front page there?'

Harold shook his head. 'You're in the Home News section. Small piece. I expect they'll push you nearer the front if you get charged.'

'Any inside track on that?' Sawyer walked to the French windows and looked down to the reservoir, shimmering through the morning haze. 'From your old mate, Ivan?'

Harold waved a hand. 'Keating is an old colleague. Hardly a "mate". And, no. Nothing coming through on the Freemasons' grapevine. I've been busy, preparing for a festival in Sheffield. Art student intake.'

'You exhibiting?'

'Yes. Seminars. Part of a panel discussion on analogue versus digital media. Did you do anything with the scans?'

'I wanted to ask you about that, among other things. Since I'm not allowed to investigate other people, I've been working on myself.'

Harold nodded. 'That's good, Jake.'

'Do you have any more stuff in your family file? Out in the studio?'

'One or two bits and pieces, yes.' He stood up and moved out into the hall. 'I have a couple of letters from a therapist you saw in your teens.' Harold looked over his shoulder and grinned. 'Might be a few clues there.'

Sawyer followed his father into the studio. His work in progress hadn't really progressed since Sawyer's last visit: a neat grid of blended browns, reds and blacks, collapsing to a distorted blur in the centre of the canvas. Again, Sawyer leaned in close to the picture, studying the unusually jagged brush strokes. 'Do you remember Charles Kelly, Dad?' He watched his father's back: no reaction.

'Dr Kelly? He was a friend. Our family doctor for years. He was a huge support after Mum's death.'

'Another man of God?'

Harold laughed. 'It is possible to embrace both science and religion, you know.'

Sawyer stood upright. 'Doublethink.'

Harold opened another drawer. 'What about him?'

'Nothing. He just... came to mind the other day. There is something else, though.'

Harold turned. 'Here's the letters. I also have a couple of bits from school. Don't know if it'll help with your self-investigation, though.' He handed Sawyer a folder and tidied the contents of the cabinet. 'What else?'

'You tried to visit Marcus Klein, at Sudbury. October, 1997. Klein refused the visit.'

'Did I?'

'You did. Nearly ten years after Klein's conviction. Makes me wonder if some new information had come to light, and you wanted to ask him a few more questions. I'm assuming it wasn't a social visit?'

Harold strolled over to the vermillion corner sofa and sat down. 'Maybe some detail we wanted to clarify. Something that might have helped us with another case, and could have helped his pitch for parole. I don't know. I don't remember. It's over twenty years ago, son.'

Sawyer pulled his phone out of his pocket and looked at the empty screen. 'Need to take this. Private.'

He walked out to the back garden: a manicured patch of weather-beaten grass edged by a modest fence. The ground outside the fence sloped up to a flat private field, where a dry stone wall marked the start of a steep incline down into the valley. Sawyer held the phone to his ear and strode out to a group of trees that lined one side of the patch.

He turned to face the house. Harold's studio was connected to a small outbuilding with a single window set high into the wall. A detached garage had been recently built, further up towards the road.

Sawyer couldn't see into the studio, but his father would have no reason to follow or watch him. He turned to the thickest of the trees and took out the camera: pre-fixed with the black cable tie. He attached the camera to the thick end of the highest branch he could reach, pointing towards the main house and studio. He tidied the end of the cable tie into a groove at the back of the branch and took a few steps back, holding the phone to his head again. The camera was small enough to blend in to the texture of the wood. It would be easy to find if you were actively looking for it, but unlikely to be spotted in passing.

His phone buzzed, making him jump.

He walked back to the edge of the house and checked his messages. Text from Walker.

Another one. Crossbow. Briefing in half an hour.

45

Sawyer made it to Sheffield in twenty-five minutes: haring down through the Bradfield dales and popping out of the National Park, into the raised western suburbs. He parked at a Starbucks near the University and hurried inside, squinting through a shower of hail. By the time he'd settled with coffee and signed in to the Wi-Fi, he was a few minutes late for the briefing, but half an hour early for his other meeting.

He screwed in his earphones and opened the listening device app.

Shepherd was in full flow. '*The body was discovered off the side of the platform at Chinley Station, by a rail worker starting his shift at six this morning.*'

'*Another nonce?*' Moran.

'*Parking attendant.*' Shepherd. '*Barry Abbott. Thirty-nine. Did eight years for the sexual abuse of his nephew. 2005–2013. Quiet for a few years, but served with an SHPO earlier this year for sharing of indecent images and inciting sexual activity online, with a thirteen-year-old girl. Looks like he used lots of social networks, including MEETUPZ.*'

Hopefully, we'll have more detail when we get deeper into his computer history.'

'Tell me more about the body.' Keating.

Shepherd continued. *'Again, single crossbow bolt to the back of the head. But this time, he's gone further. Drummond is expediting the autopsy, but it looks like the attacker inflicted PM injuries. Several stab wounds to the back, and the back of the head.'*

Sawyer took out the burner phone and texted Walker.

He's angry. Something changed.

Walker spoke up. *'The eye symbol is on the crossbow bolt. Still no joy on that. The bolts seem generic, customised.'*

'Keep the symbol private.' Keating. *'I don't want to alert the killer to the fact we're investigating it. DC Walker, any more on your theory that the killings and abductions are connected?'*

'Spoke to North Yorks contacts, sir. No abductions around the time of the Boyd and Manning murders.'

Keating sighed. *'This new killing is too close to the new abduction. There has to be a connection. Where are we with Mia?'*

'Not a lot in the family computer.' Shepherd. *'Nothing to suggest that she was meeting someone. We're talking to her friends. She may have been using computers elsewhere and arranged to meet that way.'*

'Mr Robbins?'

Sawyer looked up, took out the headphones. A man was leaning down to his table, holding out a hand. He was vast —borderline obese—with a grey beanie hat pulled low over his brow.

Sawyer disconnected the app and shook the hand:

puffy, but with a strong grip. 'Yes. You Craig? Can I get you anything?'

'I'm alright, thanks.' Craig Bailey stripped off the beanie and squeezed himself into the booth seat opposite. 'Sorry I'm early. Bad habit.' He scratched at his thinning ginger hair. 'Doing a bit of work, eh? Dunno how you can concentrate in these places. D'ya work for the papers, then?'

Sawyer had to strain to tune in to Bailey's thick Sheffield accent. 'Yeah, sometimes. Mostly online, these days, though.'

'Y'said you were working on a book? Give us a shout and I'm happy to help. We don't really want to give too much away, mind. Keeps us ahead of the predators.'

'No, no. It's just research at the moment. I'm thinking more of a guide for parents. How to spot the danger signs that their children are vulnerable or being groomed. I thought groups like yours would be able to help. How long have you been running Justice For Kids?'

Bailey tilted his head left to right, cracking the muscles in his neck. 'I've been leading it for about five years. The previous lad died. He used to take me on stings. I loved it.'

'In what way?'

'Just... seeing their faces change. When they realise they've been done. Feeling like you're doing something, making a difference. It's easy to post comments on Facebook or Twitter or whatever. Not many people actually get up off their arse and do something about it. I got into it when my partner told me she'd been abused as a child.'

'What do you do? For a living?'

Bailey laughed. '*This*. I'm a postman, but it sometimes feels like that's my part-time job and hunting paedophiles is what I actually do.'

'Are there many hunter groups in this area? Derbyshire? South Yorkshire?'

'There's a few, but most are amateurs or #MeToo types. Some just do the exposing. Not all do stings. And hardly any do the live streaming. We do that because it helps us get support. We get contributions from all over. JFK is definitely the biggest round here.'

Sawyer sipped his coffee. 'By contributions, you mean money?'

Bailey smiled, curious. 'Well, yeah.'

'How do the predators groom the kids online?'

'Loads of ways. Apps, social media, YouTube comments. Plenty of routes in. A lot of 'em share leads to YouTube channels. Kids who stream themselves live, in their bedrooms or whatever. They download the videos and screenshot any bits where the kids show some underwear or something. Share 'em round. That's the low-level stuff. You often see that with the ones who haven't plucked up the courage for live contact. It's a grey area. Low risk. Then they go further, to the live streaming channels and apps. Direct the action, pretend to be kids themselves.' Bailey scrubbed at his stubble. 'It's the adults that make this possible, Mr Robbins. The parents. They use the apps as babysitters. They haven't got a clue how deep it all goes, or how easy it is for their kids to get drawn in. Some parents think they're sharp by keeping an eye on WhatsApp or whatever, but there are apps that masquerade as games, and have live chat features. They flatter the kids, talk them up, slowly make it sexual. Send pictures, ask for pictures. Arrange to meet.'

'Kids are sharp, though, right? They know the score about this kind of thing.'

Bailey shrugged. 'Most are, yeah. But attention is seductive. The kids who are most vulnerable are the ones who aren't getting attention at home. Domestic troubles, distant parents. They feel unloved, ignored. So, some stranger starts to pay them compliments... Feels good.' He shuffled his hands together, over and over, in and out, as if washing them.

'How do the groups work? How do you work?'

'First, we identify the predators. We sometimes use Sarah's Law to get disclosure on someone we suspect. Then we use the apps, with decoys, to try and get them to suggest meetings. Places and times.'

'Decoys? Kids?'

'Yeah. Relatives of group members, volunteers. They don't get involved themselves. We just use their pictures. Whatever makes the profile authentic.'

Sawyer had a general understanding of how the groups worked, but he wanted to play dumb to work down to the deeper details. 'How do the police feel about all this?'

Bailey grimaced. 'I think they have to publicly disapprove, but as long as we're legally careful, they tolerate us. There are so many of these... people out there. The police just don't have the resources to deal with them. It's the internet. It's given the predators so much easy access, and it's made it almost impossible to keep track.' He held up his head, jutted out his chin. 'We can't stop them all. But for every one we take out of circulation, that's one kid who isn't getting abused. Better than doing nothing.' He leaned forward. 'The law does fuck all, really. The sex offender registry system. They find ways to get round it. It's stronger in the US, with Megan's Law. Harder for them to hide.'

'As far as I'm aware, the registry itself doesn't have any impact on sexual offences. It's seen as too broad, and an invitation to vigilantes.'

Bailey narrowed his eyes. Had he sounded too official? Police-like?

'We're not *vigilantes*, Mr Robbins. We are voluntary

assistants to an overstretched and underfunded police force.'

Sawyer forced a smile. 'Have you ever had to knock someone back? Kick them out? Because of their behaviour?'

'There's been one or two who've pushed it at the live stings, but nothing scary. Like I say, not everyone gets involved in the confrontations. Most just help with the online stuff, provide child pics for decoys, do the profile set-ups on the networks. I have to be careful how I dish out the work. Not everyone can cope with the real-time contact. They get sent pictures. It stays in their heads.'

Sawyer took out his phone and navigated to the photo of the eye symbol. 'Do you recognise this?'

Bailey studied the image and raised his eyes. 'I do, yeah. That looks a lot like the avatar for a profile from one of the networks, MEETUPZ. We get a lot of information from it. We've also received a few anonymous donations, and I think they're coming from this profile. I might be able to dig out a few chat logs, but, assuming it's a bloke, he never gives us any more than names and other profiles, sometimes addresses. Where did you get the pic?'

Sawyer smiled. 'A source. Could you trace him from an IP address or whatever?'

Bailey shook his head. 'They use masking software. Rock solid VPNs.'

'Is there any more detail in the profile ID itself? Is it named?'

Bailey took out his phone. He swiped through a few screens and turned it to face Sawyer. 'This is the ID from the MEETUPZ app.'

Sawyer leaned in close. Black background, with an 'MTZ' tab and menu access bar in the top corner. The avatar image was a perfect match: a rough sketch of two curved lines, forming the shape of a human eye; crude circle in the centre, surrounded by seven short rays. The only other info was the profile name, directly under the image: *HOLDEN82.*

46

Back home, Sawyer worked out on the wooden man, watched by Bruce. He flopped down on his bed, opened his laptop, and logged in to the web version of the micro camera viewer. He had set the camera to non-motion sensitive, because of its outside location. The image opened in a small window and Sawyer switched it to full screen; it was clear enough, with the occasional wobble from a blast of wind.

The garage sat just off to the left of the picture, with his father's studio and adjoining outbuilding in the centre. He assumed that the door by the sofa in the studio was the only access into the outbuilding. All was quiet, apart from the odd leaf flitting across the screen.

He called Walker on the burner.

'Sir.'

'You still haven't asked me.'

'Asked you what?'

'How I have access to what's being said at the briefings.'

Walker paused at the other end. 'Do I want to know?'

'No. It's just plain, old-fashioned second sight. You

wouldn't understand. How's the mood there? How are you coping?'

'Fine.' He hesitated. 'Not sleeping well.'

Sawyer watched the camera feed. The ground by the studio side window was illuminated by a faint glow; his father must have entered the room and turned on the light. 'You seeing it all again?'

'Not the attack itself. Just you, wrapping your shirt sleeve around my neck, stopping the bleeding. And I remember you saying something about how I had to take myself away, somewhere happy.'

Sawyer winced. 'I thought you were done. I was trying to send you off with a positive memory.'

On-screen, the high window in the adjoining outbuilding lit up. Harold had moved in there from the studio.

'Got something for you. The MEETUPZ network. I think the crossbow killer is using it to pick his victims. Maybe other sites, too. But there's a profile on there using the illustration of the eye as its avatar pic.'

Walker sighed. 'It's a nightmare, sir. We can't get to any metadata or IP addresses. The companies that own the apps are all based abroad, and we just keep hitting brick walls when we request access.'

'The profile with the picture has connections to a local paedophile hunter group, Justice For Kids. JFK. I spoke to the leader. He says he thinks whoever is behind the profile has been sending anonymous donations. Look into the profile name. *HOLDEN82.*'

'Look into?'

Sawyer leaned in closer to the screen. The light from the small window in the outbuilding flickered as a shadow passed over it. 'Holden. First name and second name. Cross-check. Convictions, arrests, crossbow sales, everything. And maybe the '82' is 1982. Focus on that as his year of birth. We might get a hit that links him to the killings, gets us closer to who he is, or what the symbol is all about.'

'Okay. Great work.'

Sawyer smiled. 'You'll never make DCI giving easy praise like that.'

Walker laughed. 'DS Shepherd gave me an evil stare for checking my phone during the last briefing.'

'Stay out of his eyeline. Shepherd's sharp. He'll have logged that.'

'So how *do* you know what's happening at the briefings?'

The light from the outbuilding window dimmed, as a darker shadow blocked it from the other side. His father must have been passing by, or standing in front of it, moving. It didn't make sense; the window was too high in the wall.

Sawyer leaned in close to the screen, as the shadow disappeared. 'I'm just being creative.' He glanced at Bruce, curled into a ball by the pillows. 'There's more than one way to skin a cat.'

47

Shaun Brooks closed the tin box and locked it in the top drawer of his desk. He unlocked the drawer below, took out a second tin, and patted it with a meaty palm.

Ash sat in the chair facing the desk: elbows on knees, dreadlocks hanging down. Clem hovered in the corner. It was a tiny storeroom, with a whiff of blocked drains. Shaun had strong-armed the fitters into clearing the room for use as an office, but it was barely big enough for the three of them.

Shaun leaned back in his Formica chair, falling into the light from a frosted window that faced out to the Fairfield golf course. 'The start-up has started.' He pointed to the locked drawer. 'Official takings.' He swung his finger to the second tin and grinned. 'Petty cash. How's our new host?'

Ash nodded. 'Spaz Boy? He's good. He's cool. Keeping him well supplied, you get me?'

'Any visitors? Nosy neighbours?'

'No. Don't think he's much of a social animal. Gets his rent paid, so no landlord visits. He's had the speech. He knows what's good for him, what'd be bad for him.'

Shaun frowned. 'Make sure he attends meetings.

Doesn't get missed. No surprises. Not now we've got product there. *You get me?*' Ash nodded. Shaun looked over to the corner. 'This place turning over?'

Clem sniffed, phoney tough. 'Good enough. Better if we could get some fruities.'

'That'll come. Booze in the snooker room will do for now.'

A knock on the door. Shaun glanced at Clem and Ash. He tucked the second tin box into the bottom drawer. 'Yeah?'

The door opened. A huge, shaven-headed bouncer in an undersized suit stepped into the room; he was so tall he had to duck under the door frame. 'Sorry to interrupt. Fella to see you, boss.'

'Tell him I'm in a meeting.'

Austin Fletcher walked in; the bouncer barred his way to the desk.

Shaun sat back in his chair. 'I'm in a meeting.'

Fletcher dropped his head, bored. 'Money. For Dale.'

Shaun laughed. 'Fucked up your one job, so the boss has demoted you to courier, eh?' Fletcher took a step forward. The bouncer held up a hand to warn him off. Shaun grinned and spread his arms out wide. 'We're all friends here. But, like I say, I'm in a meeting. I know you're at a loose end, mate, but I don't need babysitting. So, fuck off and make yourself useful somewhere else. In fact...' He sat forward. 'Here's a suggestion. You could fuck off back to Amsterdam. Go to the Red Light District. Get yourself a girlfriend for the night.'

Fletcher shouldered into the bouncer, knocking him off balance. The man crouched, stumbling to steady himself. There was a crisp *crack* as Fletcher landed a headbutt square into the middle of his face. The bouncer roared and fell back against the bare wall, blood spilling down over his white shirt. Clem pushed himself into the corner; Ash sprang up and backed away, towards the window. The bouncer scrambled to his feet, cursing, holding a handkerchief to his nose. Fletcher stood square to him, tracking him all the way as he hobbled out of the room.

Shaun reached for another drawer, but Fletcher grabbed the corner of the cheap desk and swept it aside. He held Shaun by the neck and drove him into the wall by the window, forcing Ash to scurry past and watch from the door.

Fletcher took out a short-bladed hunting knife and pressed the point into Shaun's ample stomach. He held the moment: red faced, eyes closed, slowing his breathing. He opened his eyes, and leaned in close, face to face. Shaun looked up to the ceiling, denying Fletcher the satisfaction of eye contact.

Fletcher raised his voice, but kept it clear and steady. 'If you ever tell me to fuck off again, I will cut out your intestines. Now. *Money*.'

48

Eva Gregory climbed into the Corsa. She was dressed down —old jeans, walking boots, violet quilted jacket—and only lightly made up.

She tossed a compact backpack onto the rear seat and pivoted to regard Sawyer for a second. He leaned forward, hoping for a kiss. Eva smiled and fitted her seatbelt. She turned away, and yanked open the glovebox. 'Have you got any chewing gum?'

Sawyer moved off, onto the Monyash road. 'There's eclairs. Chocolate.'

She gave him a look. 'You really are such a boy. I bet you've got a catapult in here somewhere.'

He smiled. 'Peashooter.'

Eva sat back and swept her glossy black hair over one shoulder. 'Is this technically a date, then? A trip to a cave?'

'I think so. We could sit in a touristy café and have jacket potatoes and beans, or we could eat artisan sandwiches in the shelter of a limestone crag.'

She gazed out of the window. Foggy grey sky, backlit by sun glow. 'Might be a nice day.' Sawyer paused at a red light, turned on the music. Arpeggiated piano sequence, mournful synth. Eva turned her head. 'What's this?'

'Moby. *Everything Is Wrong*.'

'You do like your nineties music.'

The light turned green; he sped away. 'I'm a bit stuck there, I suppose. Formative teenage years.'

She nodded. 'So, we've got some catching up to do. You've been arrested on suspicion of murder.'

'I didn't do it. I'm on bail.'

'Trying to find who did do it?'

Weak smile. 'Amongst other things, yes.'

'And you think my husband is trying to kill you?'

'I shouldn't have told you that. I need to investigate more.'

She turned and stared at him, shaking her head. 'I won't say anything to him. I'm clever like that.'

He nodded. 'Your "husband"? Are you still separating or going for his idea of taking a break?'

'We had a talk. He wants to change. Swears he *is* changing. I don't think it'll work.'

'People don't change. They just get better at showing what they want to show and hiding what they want to hide.'

'That is so cynical. And what exactly is Dale hiding?' Sawyer started to speak; she interrupted. 'Oh, wait. You're investigating, yes?'

He glanced at her. 'Do you like the car?'

'No. Should have brought my Mazda. Where's the other one?'

'Garage.'

Eva took out her phone, scrolled through Instagram. 'You drive too fast.'

'I'm just keen to get you into the dark cave.'

'So, what else are you investigating?'

He had a sudden ache to talk to Maggie. He'd tried to call, left messages. No replies. 'Not on active duty. I'm not allowed to officially work. Until they lift the suspension.'

'"Officially"?'

He grinned. 'I'm keeping my hand in. Bit of freelance.'

'And when will they lift the suspension?'

'Soon. They don't have much. Circumstantial.'

He turned off, passing through Hartington. A large sign had been tethered to a post in the town square.

HARTINGTON CHRISTMAS MARKET
CHRISTMAS LIGHT SWITCH ON AND LANTERN
PARADE
FREE FESTIVE FUN FOR ALL THE FAMILY
2PM TILL LATE

Eva nodded at the sign. 'That's tomorrow. It's nowhere near Christmas yet. Seems to come earlier every year.'

'The event, or the complaints about it coming earlier every year?'

———

He parked at the Tea Junction tea room, at Hulme End, and they joined the walking trail that led south to Waterhouses.

Eva led the way. 'So this is your old childhood hangout?'

'One of them. I used to come down from Wardlow on weekend trips with my brother. He's a bit older.'

She pushed through a snarl of bracken. 'Do you see him now?'

211

'Sometimes. He's not well.' His burner phone rang. Jensen. 'Sorry, I need to take this. We won't have any service further up.'

Eva gave him a mock sigh. 'Investigate away. I'll take some pictures.'

Sawyer stepped back a few paces and took the call. 'Rich.'

'Jake. How are you getting on with the camera?'

'Good. Just... experimenting with something.'

Jensen laughed. 'You do have a remarkable way with shifty euphemisms. Listen, that image you showed me. The eye. I knew it looked familiar. I haven't checked any deeper yet, but I'm pretty sure it's from a game I used to play on the PC. I would have been fifteen, sixteen, so it would be late nineties. I can see it sketched out, as you showed me, but animated as a line drawing. A recurring symbol. Maybe a company logo. Something in-game, perhaps. It's the lines around the centre of the iris. Like a sun. I'm sure that's what's pinging my memory.'

Sawyer looked out at the stripped-back farmland off one side of the track. 'How do we even begin to check that out?'

'I'm sure your colleagues have done this, but I tried a reverse image search. It looks too much like an eye, though, so the algorithm wasn't picking anything out. Computers aren't our infallible overlords yet.'

'Thanks, Rich.' He looked up. Eva hovered at the edge of the path, head angled to the side, watching him. 'Got to go. I'm wanted.'

'Alive, I hope?'

———

The track opened out, criss-crossed by quiet connecting roads near Wetton and the disused Swainsley Tunnel. Sawyer realised they were close to Ecton Mine, where he had rescued Luka from Dennis Crawley back in the autumn.

As they approached a road sign for Ecton, he distracted Eva. 'You ever been here before?'

'We came to the Dovedale stepping stones a couple of summers ago, with Luka. That's near here, right?'

He caught her eye, smiled. 'No. This is Wetton. That's Dovedale. Clue's in the title.'

She shoved him. 'How far is this cave, anyway?'

'Ten minutes.' He trudged past her, taking the lead. 'What does the name "Holden" mean to you?'

Eva frowned. 'I don't know anyone called Holden, if that's what you mean? Is this part of your investigation?'

'Something I'm looking into, yes.'

They walked in silence for a few seconds.

Eva looked up. 'The only thing that comes to mind is Holden Caulfield, from *The Catcher In The Rye*.'

Sawyer nodded. 'Oh, yeah. Haven't read that for a while. We had to do it at school, so it felt too much like work to actually enjoy it.'

'Yeah. I did it at GCSE. I liked it, but it does kill the joy, having to study something, second-guess the essay questions. Holden is the main character and the book is written in his voice. Cynical, teenage.'

'Didn't Mark Chapman, John Lennon's killer, use it to inspire him?'

Eva nodded. 'He complained that Lennon was a "phoney". That's a word Holden uses a lot in the book.'

'Tell me more about it.'

She laughed, a little breathless from Sawyer's walking pace. 'Is this a test?'

'Yeah. *Outline the main themes in JD Salinger's* The Catcher In The Rye.'

She waved a hand. 'It's just... Holden's brother dies, doesn't he? Before the start of the novel. I think that kicks off his alienation, the way he separates himself as special, and sees everyone else, particularly adults, as phonies.'

'Using alienation as a kind of self-protection.'

'If you like. It's about the fear of change. He knows he will become an adult one day, and so he's terrified of becoming a phoney himself. I remember that feeling when I was a teenager, going through puberty. The way everything is so overwhelming and complicated and you just want things to be easy and fixed.'

'It sounds a bit like autism, Asperger's.'

Eva shrugged. 'It's probably just a typical teenager. Terrified of the adult world and what it represents. Turning it into this big, cynical place where everything is fake. It's more complicated than that, of course.'

'And Holden wanted to stop children becoming phoney and cynical, didn't he?'

'Yeah. "Catch" them before they fall out of the rye field, over the cliff into adulthood. Preserve their innocence. It's a metaphor, Jake.'

Sawyer looked at her. 'No. It's womansplaining.' He turned ahead, and pointed up. 'There. That's where we're going.'

Further ahead, the crag jutted out, high above the track. The entrance to Thor's Cave loomed down: a ten-metre-high circular hole, bored into the rock.

'How are we getting up there?'

Sawyer smiled. 'Steps.'

———

They climbed the rugged stairs carved into the crag and ate sandwiches in the cave, at Sawyer's favourite spot: perched at the top of the sloping entrance, looking out over the Manifold Valley. Eva grumbled about the climb and the sludgy rock, but she relaxed when she saw the view, and moved in closer, swinging her long legs over and resting them across Sawyer's knees.

Sawyer gulped back a lungful of chilly air. 'We should have bought a flask. Hot tea. Coffee.'

Eva shook her head. 'I bet you'd have a Teasmade if it wasn't so sad.'

He smiled. 'So, was *The Catcher In The Rye* a big teenage book for you?'

'Sort of. And *The Bell Jar*.'

'Of course.'

She leaned forward, studying him. 'I bet you were an *Outsiders* type. Or Bukowski.'

'*American Psycho* was my guiding light.'

'That's reassuring.'

Sawyer and Eva clambered back down to the track, and bought tea and cake at the Wetton Mill Tea Room. They sat on a bench overlooking the River Hamps: tea mugs on the floor, cake plates balanced on their knees. A group of middle-aged bikers roared in and parked their bikes in the courtyard outside the tea room.

Sawyer turned and watched for a while, then took out his phone. 'Do you recognise this guy?'

Eva finished a mouthful of Victoria sponge and peered at the picture of Fletcher. 'I've seen him before, yeah. I take it he's not your new hairdresser?'

Sawyer looked down into the river, swollen by the recent rain. 'No. I think he's the one who tried to kill me. And he's clearly not giving up.'

'Why do you say that?'

Sawyer gave a subtle tip of his head, gesturing behind him; Eva looked over his shoulder. The man in the image sat alone at one of the wooden picnic benches, with a mug on the table in front of him. He tugged at his baseball cap and raised his head. He held eye contact with Eva for a few seconds, then turned back to his book.

49

Sawyer dropped Eva at home, and called in at the High Peak Bookstore on the way back to Edale, where he bought a new paperback edition of *The Catcher In The Rye*. Fletcher hadn't followed them back along the track, and there was no sign of his hired silver Ford Fiesta.

At the cottage, he kicked off his walking boots and sprawled out on the bed, dipping in and out of the book. The connection with the profile name could be irrelevant. The killer might simply be called Holden himself. '82' could be his year of birth, or something else. A random number, the number of his house.

The burner phone buzzed. Message from Walker.

Briefing in an hour.

3:30pm. Sawyer browsed the book for a while, with Bruce curled into a ball at the corner of the bed, then made coffee and logged in to the listening device app at 3:45pm, to check the signal. He screwed in his earphones and winced at the pure crackle of static. No office noise.

He fiddled with the settings, reset the app, reinstalled it.

Nothing. Just static.

'*Fuck.*'

Bruce leapt off the bed and stalked into the sitting room.

A knock at the front door. Sawyer sighed; he knew the rhythm.

He padded to the door and opened it wide, greeting Shepherd with a big smile. 'Coffee?'

'I'm fine.'

Sawyer beckoned him inside. 'Last time you paid me a surprise visit, you slapped me in handcuffs.'

Shepherd stepped in and closed the door behind him. 'Just me this time.'

Sawyer took a box of Ritz crackers from a kitchen cupboard. He popped a couple into his mouth, shook the box at Shepherd, who held up a hand. 'Can I have my listening device back, then?'

Shepherd glared at him. He took the small block of grey metal from his pocket and set it down on the coffee table.

Sawyer nodded, offered a sheepish smile. 'Walker?'

'He was using his phone in briefings. And his contributions were too random, too leftfield. This is way off the map, sir. You're lucky I found it, and not Moran. Or Keating.'

'Like I said, I can help. I *am* helping.'

'You're not helping Walker.'

Sawyer tossed the cracker box into the recycle bin. 'Keep him out of it.'

'I'm saying nothing. But you have to let this play out. Has to be airtight.'

Sawyer shrugged. 'How's Maggie? She's ignoring me.'

Shepherd lingered at the back of the sofa. 'She's not ignoring you. She's been warned about contact. So have I.'

'And this is "airtight"? Popping in for a chat?'

He pointed at the device. 'I'm not stopping. I'm doing you a favour.'

'Maggie's my friend, Shepherd. I'd like to talk to her.'

'She's in pieces. You're not...' He gathered himself. 'You're not a superhero. Sir, we've got good people working on this. We're doing everything we can.'

Sawyer slurped at his coffee. 'Any joy with house to house? Near where Holly was found?'

Shepherd sighed. 'No. Keating still doesn't buy the idea that Holly Chilton escaped and died accidentally. He thinks it was staged, and she was dumped that way to put us off the scent. He's relying on Drummond to find something with DNA, toxicology.'

'He thinks. But he's wrong. The stabbing in the third crossbow killing. It tells us something. There's anger. Either new, or renewed. Maybe in reaction to Holly. A message?'

'Resources are all focused on the children for now. On finding Mia.'

Sawyer scoffed. 'Nobody cares about dead paedophiles, right?'

'We're just prioritising. You know how it works.'

Sawyer moved to him, around the sofa. 'You're being too black and white. The two inquiries might be linked. A paedophile abducting children. A killer taking out paedophiles.'

Shepherd smiled. 'Go on, then. While I'm here. What else do you know?'

'I think there might be a gaming connection in the crossbow cases. And as for the children, I spoke to a paedophile hunter group. Since you're forcing me to operate out on the edges, I thought I might as well hang out with the freaks.'

'What do you mean by "a gaming connection"?'

'The symbol on the bolts. The eye, with the sun rays

around the iris. Look for a computer game from the late nineties. Maybe an independently published game with a similar logo. It might be the company insignia, or a logo related to something in the game. It could mean that the killer has a connection to gaming. Maybe retro gaming.'

Shepherd cast an eye down to Sawyer's PlayStation.

Sawyer laughed. 'I'm bored, but not that bored.'

'I need to get back for the briefing. There's a press conference, about Mia. So, hypothetically speaking... If, say, you were still an active serving officer, what would you be tasking me with?'

'I'd be telling you to investigate the child abductions and crossbow killings as connected enquiries.'

Shepherd shook his head. 'So, as Walker said, via yourself, it's a tit for tat thing? A child gets taken, and our man kills a paedophile in response. He uses the social networks to source targets, lures them to remote locations.'

'So, what's the motive?'

Shepherd's eyes searched the room. 'Someone from one of the hunter groups gone rogue? He doesn't think it's good enough, handing them over to the police. He thinks they all deserve to die. There are plenty of them who feel that way. Have you seen the comments on the Facebook pages?'

Sawyer shook his head. 'They're already rogue. There's something deeper. Much more than your typical grandstanding fury about "nonces". Check the timings. The times of death, the abductions.'

'How do you mean?'

'Maybe it's the other way round. Maybe one of them is abducting children in response to the other's killings.'

50

Ash sat back on the PVC sofa. He selected his character for the practice lap of *Mario Kart 64* on the Nintendo 64 and took a sip from a can of Monster. The retro gaming section in the Fairfield branch of Players was well stocked with refurbished consoles plugged into a row of cheap flat screen TVs. The patrons were mostly teenage boys, with a few twenty and thirtysomethings hogging the older machines.

'You're a Yoshi man, eh? I prefer Toad.'

Ash tossed his dreadlocks and turned his head to the man standing behind. He shifted his backpack away from the side of the sofa and wedged it between his legs. 'Same difference. Yoshi ain't called "Toad", though. That's slimy, you get me?'

Sawyer stepped round the sofa and sat down next to Ash. He angled his body to face him.

Ash eyed him as he played. 'Multiplayer, yeah? Be with you after this.'

Sawyer watched the screen. 'You're not hopping. Makes all the difference. You need to hop over the gaps at corners. It'll improve your times.'

Ash looked at him. 'I know that. Just getting a fix on

this new course, innit?' He smiled. 'I'm not playing you, bruv. You was probably around when this came out.'

Sawyer nodded. 'I was thirteen. Used to play it with my brother. He was always Donkey Kong. He only beat me once, when I had flu. Is there anyone here who knows about older games? PC?'

Ash grinned. 'Looking to revisit your youth, eh?'

'Yeah. Sold my gaming PC ages ago. It got tedious, trying to keep up with all the graphic and sound cards.'

Ash nodded towards the row of nineties arcade cabinets and pinball tables at the far side of the room. 'That guy there. Mayhem. He's in here a lot. Pretty sharp on the older stuff. Couple of gaming PCs back there, too.'

Sawyer nodded, kept his eyes on Ash. 'Cheers, mate. One more thing.' He lowered his voice. 'Do you know where I could get some gear?'

'How the fuck should I know?'

Sawyer raised a small paper pouch, tightly wrapped around a white powder. 'Well. This was in your backpack. Looks too grainy for coke. And that's probably outside your pay grade, anyway. So I'd say... bath salts? Monkey dust, that is.'

'I know what it is, bruv. That's not mine, though.'

Sawyer smiled. 'It's okay. You can have it back.' He tossed the pouch onto the sofa next to Ash and nodded to the backpack. 'Plenty more in there, though. Easily enough to bring you in for dealing.'

Ash finished the lap and turned his piggy eyes on Sawyer. 'You a copper?'

Sawyer stood up. 'Nothing gets past you, eh?' He strolled over to the wall of retro cabs. A thickset man in a sheepskin collar jacket was hunched over a *Track & Field* machine, hammering at the buttons. On-screen, a pixelated athlete sprinted across a scrolling playfield, leaping over hurdles. 'You should use the finger drumming technique.'

The man kept his eyes on the screen. 'Yeah. Hard to get the rhythm on the hurdles, though. It's alright on the hundred metres.' He finished the race and stood upright. 'Third time round. Didn't qualify.'

'Are you Mayhem?'

The man turned to face Sawyer. He was late thirties: jowly, with a prominent overbite. He wore old, oval-rimmed glasses that were barely big enough to cover the width of his face. Dark hair, waxy. He wrinkled his nose. 'That's not my real name.'

'Really?'

Mayhem nodded, sage-like. 'Sort of a gamer thing. What can I do for you?'

'Apparently, you're the man for the older games?'

He laughed. 'Not sure if that's a good thing or not.'

'I've been trying to find this game I used to play on the PC.' Sawyer took out his phone and navigated to the eye symbol. 'Driving me mad. It had this logo. Do you recognise it?'

Mayhem wrinkled his nose again and peered into the screen. 'Yeah. That's an easy one. Looks like Raysoft. They did a few shareware games in the late nineties. Shooters. Quite idiosyncratic. And by that, I mean quirky, culty. Not shit. Just different.'

'Do you remember any of the game names?'

Mayhem grimaced as he pondered. 'No, sorry. I'm pretty sure that's the Raysoft logo, though.' He smiled. 'JFGI.'

———

Sawyer left the Corsa in a side street by the club and walked over to The Source coffee shop. Dean Logan was installed at the table beneath the TV.

He waved Sawyer over. 'Got you a coffee. The cake's finished, though.'

Sawyer sat down. 'I'll cope. Got something you can take a swing at. Charles Kelly. He's our old family GP. He used to own a burgundy BMW. 2008 X5.' Logan made a note. 'Klein told me he'd seen it following him. I saw it, too. Last time I was with Klein. I want to know who has this car now. Somebody acquired it, and has been keeping it legit with MOTs. It's fallen through the admin cracks.'

'You got this Kelly's address?'

Sawyer nodded. 'I'll send it to you. Use your wily ways. Find out where the car might be now. Ask anyone still living there.' He blew on his coffee. 'I mean, I'd do it myself. But I'm too famous now. Thanks to your colleagues in the fourth estate.'

'I'm annoyed about your arrest story getting out, too. Didn't come from me.'

'I'm so sorry you didn't get the opportunity to take the credit for something.' Sawyer took another sip of coffee, drifted off for a second. 'Careful with this car thing. The driver might have had something to do with Klein's death, and setting me up.'

Logan raised his eyebrows. 'I appreciate the concern.'

'How was the press conference?'

'Pretty desperate. They wheeled out Mia's father. Looked like a fucking ghost. No sign of the mother. I don't think they've got much. They put out the standard appeal for Mia's safe return, took a few questions about the new dead guy, Abbott. I had another go about your case. Nothing. I know more than they do.'

'About what?'

'Mia.' Logan snorted. 'I have a source who claims he saw Mia with someone at the Christmas market, being pulled along quite roughly.'

'Man? She was with her dad.'

Logan shook his head. 'Woman. Older.'

51

The tall man walked down the hall and crouched by the two-seater sofa. He picked up the crossbow and pointed it down, resting it vertically on the floor. The older woman emerged from an adjoining corridor and stood behind the sofa, watching, as he primed the bow and flicked on the dry fire safety switch.

The man glanced over his shoulder. 'Are they ready?'

'We've been outside. Chilly, though. Nights are really drawing in. They're eating now. Joshua has a bit of a cold.'

He nodded. 'Have you got a permission slip from his parents? About paracetamol?'

The woman forced a laugh. 'Are you going out again?'

The man pressed a button on a remote and the hall was flooded by the sound of simmering ambient guitar. He lowered the volume. 'They need company.' When the woman didn't reply, he looked over his shoulder, searching her with his eyes. He put on his silver-rimmed glasses. 'This is far greater than the sum of an individual parent's grief.' His voice was quiet, whispered: almost inaudible. 'You know this. You've felt it.'

The woman frowned. 'I'm not doubting anything. There's just... A lot of risk.'

He took a bolt from a box on the sofa, and passed his skinny fingers over the eye symbol etched into the centre. 'We need to step it up. This way is quicker.' He dropped his head and winced, as if struck by a sudden pain. 'What's happening out there? After Holly?'

'As you'd expect. Police press conference.'

He nodded. 'Witnesses?'

'No mention. Just an appeal for help.'

He loaded the bolt into the bow. 'Yes. I am going out again tonight.' He aimed the bow at the target on the easel. 'I'll be with the children in half an hour.' He fired. The bolt thunked into the bullseye, just off centre.

The woman stepped forward and rested a hand on the man's shoulder. 'Love, how long?'

He stood up, primed the bow again. 'How long for what?'

She closed her eyes, bracing. 'When do we *stop*?'

The man dropped the bow onto the sofa and walked around to her. He leaned down, inches from her face, and bared his jagged teeth. 'This is the start. We stop when we are finished. When we agreed.'

She opened her eyes. 'Five?'

He nodded. 'And then, the glory.'

52

Sawyer sat low in the Corsa, parked across the road, watching the Fairfield Players club. Ash emerged and sauntered up towards town, and Sawyer crawled the car behind at a safe distance.

Ash stopped to light a cigarette, then turned into Pavilion Gardens. Sawyer parked, and followed on foot. He drew his collar up around his neck and kept his eyes down, tracking Ash along a parallel side path.

At the other side of the park, Ash crossed the road and headed into a low grade estate of boxy flat blocks. He approached the main door of the largest building—five storeys—and swiped a card on a reader. He disappeared inside, cigarette still burning.

It was dusk, but only the top two floors of the block were lit. Sawyer waited. The second floor light came on. He sat on a bench at a bus stop across the road, watching the building.

A few minutes later, two skinny teenagers shambled down the path towards the main door, laughing and shoving each other. Sawyer crossed the road and reached the door just as they were entering. He fumbled in his pocket for show, and as he reached the door, the second of the teenagers held it open for him.

'Cheers.'

The boy nodded, and caught up with his friend, who was waiting by the rusty doors of the building's only lift. Sawyer turned away and started up the littered staircase. As he reached the first floor, he heard voices from above, getting closer. Ash, and maybe two others. He slipped through the windowed connecting door and waited in the first floor corridor as the group came down the stairs, shouting and swearing. He looked out of the window, down at the path. The main door slammed shut, and Ash and three other boys careered away, towards the park.

Sawyer took the stairs up to the second floor and its identical corridor: windows looking down on the courtyard, three flat doors on each side. He paced down to the end, listening at each door. Music and conversation from the first two flats, TV noise from the second two. At the end of the corridor, Sawyer's nose wrinkled at the odour of weed.

He listened at the door of both flats. Kitchen noise from the first. Cutlery, a kettle boiling, a woman humming. The second was quiet, and he tapped at the door.

No answer. He took out the oblong black case and got to work on the lock with the kirby grips: twisting one pin into a kinked wrench to feel out the tension, using the other as a pick. The lock was an old Yale, and he had the door open in a couple of minutes.

Inside, the place reeked of smoke, and the sickly sweet tang of supermarket deodorant. The main living room was overrun with clutter: tea-streaked mugs, empty beer bottles, pizza boxes, drug paraphernalia. Sawyer crept through, listening for movement. At the far side of the room, through an ajar door, he could see the bottom end of a bed.

He put on a pair of latex gloves and sifted through the drug detritus. Needles, crumpled foil, a rubber tie-off hose, scorched spoons, candles.

A thud from the bedroom.

Sawyer backed away and ducked into a small side kitchen. He waited for a while, then emerged, and crossed to the bedroom, staying low and quiet.

He nudged open the door. A man in his twenties lay on the bed, fully clothed, mouth gagged with a strip of gaffer tape. His arms had been forced wide and his wrists tied to the headboard with thick rope, secured by multiple knots. He startled at the sight of Sawyer, and widened his eyes, bucking against the rope.

Sawyer raised a calming hand and looked around the room. A small portable TV sat on a dresser opposite the bed. The TV was off, but the remote lay near the pillows, within the man's reach. Sawyer pinched the side of the gaffer tape and raised his eyebrows at the man, who nodded back. He ripped the tape off in a swift, single yank, and the man stifled a scream of pain.

Sawyer stepped around the bed. More drug paraphernalia on the floor. Empty cans, foil takeaway boxes. 'It's alright. I want to help. This your place?'

The man nodded, and tossed his long, greasy hair over his shoulder. 'Yeah. It's mine. I rent it.'

'What's your name?'

'Robbie Carling. They won't let me go. Can you untie me, please?'

Sawyer pulled over a chair and sat down by the bed. 'Who won't let you go?'

Robbie looked around the room, avoiding Sawyer's gaze. He was flushed, sweating. 'They said it would be bad for me if I said anything. They said they know my mum. She's in hospital. It might be bad for her, too.'

'Are they selling drugs from here, Robbie?'

He snapped his head round to face Sawyer. '*Drugs*? Can you... Please...'

'Do you need a fix?'

Robbie nodded, eyes wide.

'You've got to hold on for a while longer. I'm going to help you, but you've got to be strong. And you can't say that I've been here. Can you promise me that?'

He grimaced, nodded again.

'Sorry about this. We have to put things back the way they left them. Or they'll be suspicious. Yes?'

Robbie closed his eyes, nodded again. Sawyer carefully reapplied the gaffer tape to his mouth and walked back into the sitting room, leaving the door ajar.

Shrill laughter from the courtyard below. He stood to the side of the main window and looked out, staying hidden. Ash and friends were heading back up the path, towards the flat block. Sawyer looked around the room, then up at the thin, pale-blue curtains. He took out the listening device, reached up to the metal rail, and snapped the magnetic plate into place, securing the small cube out of sight. He exited back into the corridor, closing the door behind him. At the staircase, he climbed the next flight up to the third floor, waited for the voices to pass below, then took the lift down.

Back at the car, he took out the burner and made a call. It connected immediately.

'Sawyer. I was hoping you could stay out of trouble for a day at least.'

'Not in my nature, Max. You need to get on to your Manchester vice boys. Keep them away from Strickland's place up there for now. Whatever you need to do. Anonymous tip-off, whatever. I think he's using a trap house in Buxton.'

'County lines?'

'Yeah. Recruiting local dealers through the clubs. I'll get some more detail, then feed you an address. They've got to hold off for a while, though. If they go into his Manchester place now, they'll alert him and the house here won't be useful to them any more.'

53

Back at the cottage, Sawyer flopped onto the sofa with his phone and laptop. He tuned in to the listening device but heard only silence from the sitting room, and a distant TV, probably from the bedroom. Ash and his pals must have gone out again. He needed to be patient. If he could catch some loose talk, it might help him pinpoint where the drug supply had been hidden. Hopefully, he would be reinstated by then, and could trace everything back through the Players clubs, and rub Dale out of the picture.

He set up some music—an old Depeche Mode deep cuts playlist—and Googled 'Raysoft'. He switched to the Images tab. The results showed mostly videogame screenshots: clearly older titles, with rudimentary graphics. Halfway down, he spotted the eye symbol: a basic sketch, identical to the image on the crossbow bolts.

He followed the link to a retro PC games website, where three Raysoft titles were available to download and play from inside an emulator program. He studied the accompanying images. One of the games, *Wormhole*, looked like a standard 3D space shooter. He installed the emulator, downloaded the ROM file, and ran the game.

Black screen. The eye image faded up: white outline, hand drawn. The word *Raysoft* scrolled up beneath the image. Music: melodramatic, strident. The screen cleared to reveal a large, pixelated title logo, rendered in orange and yellow: *WORMHOLE*. Across the bottom, in small type: *CODE BY H. BRIGGS*. Beneath, in smaller type: *DEDICATED TO SAM*.

The game was scrappy but compulsive. Blocky enemy ships emerged from a black starfield, forcing the player to move a small crosshair around and pick them off with flashing laser fire from gun barrels mounted in the four corners. Sawyer played for a while, then quit the emulator and returned to the Google home page.

He typed, 'H. Briggs', but the results were too random: a nineteenth-century tennis player, a US physicist, some ancient report on cost minimisation. He tried, 'Holden Briggs'. Nothing jumped out. Then, 'Sam Briggs'. This led to hundreds of results for a UK-born CrossFit athlete. He modified to, 'Sam Briggs 1982'. This clarified that the athlete had been born in 1982, but there was no obvious connection to either the crossbow murders or the child abductions.

He advanced through the search results. His eye fell on a link at the bottom of page two.

SIDNEY BLACK: THE TIDY CHILD KILLER

The supporting copy contained the name, 'Samantha Briggs'. Sawyer followed the link. It led to an article on a lurid website which had clearly set out to emulate Wikipedia, with entries dedicated to true crime cases. The content on Black was summarised at the top of the page, with a smudgy photo of a middle-aged man scowling into the camera.

Sidney Black (17th April 1937 – 12th December 1995) was a British convicted paedophile serving two life sentences for a string of rapes against young boys, and for the murder of three young girls: Rachel Hogan (8), Lydia May (10), and Samantha Briggs (10).

Black was notable for his penchant for abandoning his victims' bodies naked, next to their neatly folded clothing and shoes. In the case of his third victim, Samantha Briggs, her decomposed body was found in undergrowth. She had been tied up, gagged, and her underwear had been placed beneath her head, suggesting sexual assault.

Black was apprehended in July 1993, but died in HMP Strangeways in December 1995, following an attack from two other inmates.

Sawyer searched around the Samantha Briggs case. Her body had been discovered at Hollingworth Lake near Rochdale, after being reported missing for four months. According to a cutting from the *Daily Mirror* at the time, her father, Isaac, was a wealthy 'technology tycoon' who had patented software to IBM. He had put up a hefty reward for Samantha's return, but there had been no takers.

He dug deeper, typing, 'Briggs Samantha Isaac Raysoft'. The top result was a 1999 article from *PC Gaming* magazine.

RAYSOFT: BRIGHT FUTURE, DARK PAST

The link led to a site that archived old computer and videogame magazines. The *PC Gaming* feature was a double-page spread, which told of a new wave of 'back bedroom coders' making money by producing simple games that players could get for free and then choose to support with optional financial contributions. The tone warned of an unsustainable model, but with hindsight, it was a glimpse of the future.

The main thrust of the piece was the background of the Briggs family, and how they had coped following the death of Samantha, seven years earlier, and father Isaac, who had succumbed to a heart attack the previous year.

There were two accompanying photographs: a late teenage boy, posed at the keyboard of his PC. He was turned side-on to camera, struggling to hold an awkward smile. He was tall and thin and gawky: stonewashed jeans, silver-framed glasses, spindly fingers poised above the keyboard. The room around him was messy: consoles, TVs, piles of books, sci-fi movie posters and memorabilia. The caption read: *HARRISON BRIGGS, BOY WONDER.*

Harrison was interviewed in the piece. At one point, he explained how the company logo had come about.

'It was when we were kids. Me and my sister Sam were in my room and she drew this brilliant little picture. It was an eye with a sun in the centre, with rays around it. I've always kept the picture and thought it would be a nice tribute to her memory if we used it as the logo.'

The second photograph was taken outside, on the front lawn of a handsome detached house. The sky behind the house was white, and the grass yellowed and patchy. The caption read: *SOFTWARE HOUSE: Harrison Briggs, at home with mother Lynette.*

The teenage boy stood at the edge of the lawn, with an older woman at his side. She had one arm around his waist and looked up at him, with a curious smile. The size difference was comical: he was tall and thin; she was short and rounded. The boy was buried beneath a khaki parka, furry hood almost concealing his face; she wore a brown duffel coat, black woollen hat and bright yellow gloves.

54

Dale Strickland leaned forward, both palms planted on the windowsill. He looked at his watch: 2:30am. Down below, the city glistened behind a steady drizzle, powered down for the night. He had retreated to his plush, carpeted top-floor office, away from the last-minute snooker players. It gave him extra distance from the street, and dirty work required clean surroundings.

Shaun Brooks entered, in signature black blazer and polo neck sweater. He balked at the sight of Austin Fletcher, poised in the far corner. 'Boss. Is this about the other day, in Buxton?'

Dale didn't turn. 'I told you. Don't call me Boss.'

Shaun glanced at Fletcher. No cigarette; eyes down, fixed on the mock Persian at Shaun's feet. 'Having a late one, then?'

Dale shrugged. 'No rest for the wicked.' He turned, and eased into his revolving chair.

Fletcher looked up. 'Problems.'

Shaun checked Dale; his head was lowered, eyes fixed on the desk surface. Shaun moved closer and spoke to the bald patch on Dale's scalp. 'I count one problem.' He nodded towards Fletcher. 'We've got a fucking psycho on the loose, threatening people, when we're trying to set things up without attracting attention.'

'How's the club down there? Can your associates keep it moving without you yet?'

Shaun brightened. 'Clem's pretty sharp, yeah. Ash can handle distribution, with a bit of micro management. I don't need to be there to do that, though.'

'And how is Mr Sawyer?' Dale raised his eyes. 'Has he been to see you again?'

'He was fishing. I didn't bite.'

Dale smiled. 'He's been to the club twice since then. The second time, he followed you. To the flat.'

Shaun's gaze shifted to the window. 'I didn't know that.'

'No. I don't expect he wanted you to know.'

A noise in the street below. Fletcher moved to the window. 'They're here.'

Shaun raised his head. 'We expecting visitors?'

Dale opened the desk drawer. 'I want to thank you, Shaun. For all the effort. It's been mostly effective. You've certainly given us momentum, and I did promise you a reward. It's such a shame you couldn't resist rewarding yourself first.'

A crashing noise from outside, at street level.

'How do you mean?'

Dale took out a boxy black handgun with a long cylindrical attachment at the end of the barrel.

Shaun eyed it. 'What's that for?'

Dale looked up, surprised. 'Shooting people. It's a Glock G17. Semi-automatic.' He wobbled the gun in his hand. 'Nine millimetre. Short recoil. Favoured by law enforcement agencies the world over. This is a silenced version. Bit of a faff, because you have to replace the barrel before you fit the suppressor. Shoots the same ammo, though.' He released the magazine and let it fall into his hand. 'Three bullets left in the clip.' He slotted it back in, smiled. 'Plenty.'

Fletcher pushed away from the window. He moved around Shaun and opened the door, looked out along the corridor. He listened for a while, closed the door. 'AFOs.'

Dale cocked the weapon. 'You've been stealing from me. You've compromised a key location, and God only knows what you've been feeding our good friend, Detective Sawyer.'

A shout from the floor below. 'Armed police!'

Shaun took a step forward; Dale held up the gun, pointing it at his head. He was suddenly pale, wide-eyed. He held his hands out in front, palms up. 'Dale. For fuck's sake. I've said *nothing*. And... it's just a bit of pocket money. I fucked up, yeah? You'll get it back. Double.'

Dale smiled and squeezed the trigger. The gunshot was no more than a loud 'click'. There was a wet crack, as the bullet thudded into Shaun's forehead. He dropped to the floor, in an awkward heap.

Fletcher stepped around him and held out a hand to Dale, beckoning with his fingers.

Dale gave him the gun. 'We reset. Move again when things have died down. Go and clean up.'

55

Sawyer woke to the buzzing of the burner phone on his bedside table. He reached over and connected the call, from Max Reeves.

'Morning. Now, I've always wanted to do this. Turn on the TV. BBC News.'

Sawyer sighed. 'I'm still in bed. Give me the gist.'

'Raid on Dale's place in Manchester last night.'

Sawyer hopped out of bed and hurried into the sitting room. 'What happened?' He squatted down and fiddled with the TV. No terrestrial, so he had to navigate to the live section of iPlayer.

'Looks like they brought him in.'

Sawyer caught Reeves' pause. 'What?'

'I'm not hearing good things.'

'...*shots were heard in the vicinity of the top floor here.*' A female reporter spoke into camera. She turned and waved a hand towards a three-storey building on the corner of a busy street. The pavement had been cordoned off, and two officers in high-viz jackets stood by the main doors, as detectives and FSIs entered and exited. A sign above the door showed icons of a number eight Pool ball and a console joypad, beneath the word *PLAYERS*, rendered in joined-up, right-leaning script.

'*We understand that the club owner was on the premises at the time, and has been taken into custody.*'

The picture cut to reveal a brightly lit breakfast TV studio, with the reporter's live feed relayed on an inset screen. A male presenter nodded. '*Are there any reports of injuries, Caroline?*'

'*We're hearing from police that there has been a casualty, yes. But this is a developing story, and the circumstances aren't yet clear.*'

Sawyer pitched back onto the sofa. 'Did you get my message across?'

Reeves bristled. 'Yes, I did. And since I'm not the Chief Constable, there wasn't a lot more I could do.'

'*Caroline, we're just going over to Pendleton Police Station in Greater Manchester, where I believe the club owner's legal representative is making a statement.*'

The image shifted to the front of a redbrick building with blue window frames. A scrum of reporters surrounded an elegant, middle-aged man in an expensive suit. Dale stood behind him, head down.

The man fitted a pair of dark-rimmed spectacles to his face and addressed the crowd. '*Ladies and gentlemen, I have a short statement to read on behalf of my client, Mr Strickland, who has now been released on bail, pending inquiry.*'

Reeves snorted. 'That can't have been cheap.'

'*My client is shocked and appalled at the heavy-handed actions of Greater Manchester Police, and he will be aggressively contesting any charges which may arise from this morning's intrusion onto his property. He is a hard-working entrepreneur who has been building up a legitimate business since his release from prison, several months ago. Not only has this illegal police action compromised my client's business, but it has resulted in the tragic death of one of his most trusted employees, Mr Shaun Christopher Brooks.'*

Sawyer closed his eyes. 'Fuck.'

'Mr Strickland acknowledges that he has made mistakes in the past, but this does not entitle the police to hound him in this way. He has already been the subject of unwarranted harassment from a detective who is now himself under suspicion of criminal activity.'

Sawyer sighed. 'We almost had him. He'll milk this hard. And he'll freeze everything and regroup, be more careful.'

'He must have been expecting the raid,' said Reeves.

The phone buzzed.

'I'll call you back, Max.'

Text message from Dean Logan.

Another paedo down. Near Lud's Church. Convicted SO. Recently released.

Sawyer gathered his thoughts. Was Shaun's death his fault? Had he been seen with him at the Fairfield club? If Dale was planning to cover his tracks and counterattack, who else might be in the firing line? He remembered their recent conversation about Sun Tzu and *The Art of War.*

'Avoid what is strong and strike at what is weak.'

He scrambled into his clothes, threw some water on his face, and stepped out onto the porch.

The familiar tobacco smell lingered outside. Pungent, fresh.

He looked down. The micro listening device had been placed in the centre of the doorstep.

56

Sawyer sped down to Buxton and drove through the town centre, skirting the edge of Pavilion Gardens. He turned into the estate of social housing, and his stomach dropped at the sight of an ambulance parked outside the flat block with the trap house.

A small crowd had gathered on the pavement opposite, by the bus stop. Sawyer parked up and approached the group. Mostly teenagers: surly boys in sportswear with raised hoods; a couple of pale, worried-looking girls.

'What happened?'

One of the boys looked over his shoulder. 'Some guy OD'd.'

Another one shook his head. 'Bet they've taken his gear, too. It's not like he needs it now.'

Robbie.

A squad car entered the road from the other side and parked by the ambulance. Sawyer turned and ducked back into the Corsa.

Lud's Church was the local name for a natural ravine, not far from Maggie's home near the Roaches. It was an imposing, eighteen-metre-deep crack in the gritstone, opened by a landslip and coated top to bottom in pea-green moss.

Sawyer followed a walking track through the sparse woodland of Back Forest, and slowed as he reached the top of the ridge. The Scientific Services Unit van was parked off an adjoining road, surrounded by officers and FSIs. An outer cordon had been set up at the top of the worn rock steps that led down to the base of the chasm.

One of the FSIs wore a turquoise Tyvek suit, in contrast to the white coveralls of her charges. She looked over in Sawyer's direction and stumbled towards him, down a steep, gritty slope.

At the bottom, she flipped back her hood. 'Detective Inspector Sawyer. How in the actual fuck does a suspended officer get so close to a major investigation while the scene is still open? Or is that not something I want in my head?' Principal SOCO Sally O'Callaghan was tall, mid-fifties, with cropped peroxide hair. She was high born but earthbound; a newsreader with a sailor's tongue.

Sawyer dug his hands into his jacket pockets. 'Just felt the call. The lure of pagan worship.'

Sally smiled. 'Ah! That's a common myth about this place. No Satanists round these parts. It was mainly Christians who worshipped here, in the fifteenth century. They had to do their God-bothering in private because of state persecution. Where better than a big fuck-off hole in the ground like this?'

'You should campaign for a change in the tourist signs. "Lud's Church" is mysterious, but you'd get more footfall for "Big Fuck-Off Hole In The Ground."'

'Well. It's a major tit pain, scurrying up and down here.

Why can't this character leave his mess in easily accessible areas?'

Sawyer peered down past the cordon officer. The cascading moss sparkled with condensation. 'Another nonce?' Sally looked at him in surprise. 'Channelling DC Moran.'

She sighed. 'I'm not at liberty to discuss that, but yes. Apparently so. I'm sick of sneaking around, second-guessing who's supposed to know what.'

He waved a hand at the van, and personnel. 'Lot of effort for the lowest tier on the victim scale.'

'Remind me of the entries on this list?'

Sawyer angled his head. 'Top to bottom, I'd say child, pregnant woman, woman, man, middle-aged man, paedophile, Piers Morgan.'

She barked a laugh. 'No tears for paedos.'

'It's a sexuality. Wired in. Socially judged as transgressive.'

'Well. We don't live by Ancient Roman values any more, Jake.'

He nodded. 'Or Victorian. Did you know that in Victorian times, children had a *low* status? Because of the high rate of infant mortality. That's why they were sent out to workhouses, stuck up chimneys. Now, it's the other way round. We nurture them, save them. We value their innocence, vilify those who don't.'

Sally frowned. 'It's called progress. We don't see children as fair game for sexual exploitation any more.' She looked back up at the van. 'Shepherd thinks the killings and abductions are linked.'

Sawyer smiled. 'I agree. I have an idea about who might be doing this, or at least funding it. But I think someone is abducting children as a response to the paedophiles being killed. The guy down there. We might not value him too highly, but he could be the signal for another child to be taken. This is all theatre. Our real problem is to find whoever is abducting the children.'

'Abducting and *killing* the children.'

Sawyer stepped towards her. 'Sally. What does Drummond have from Holly Chilton's body? He must have been able to do some work now, following the body thaw.'

Sally stared past him, to the chasm. 'Nothing unusual in her system. A bit undernourished.'

'No traces? DNA?'

She shook her head. 'A few fibres. Generic. Wool.'

'Colour?'

She seemed to catch herself, but then her shoulders slumped, resigned. 'Yellow.'

57

Sawyer jinked his ship through the shower of glowing bullets. A phalanx of support craft materialised from the sides of the screen and discharged a kaleidoscopic barrage of hot-pink laser fire. He slipped in between the bolts, holding his position until the screen cleared and he could slip across and blast the enemies.

His thumbs twitched and rolled across the PlayStation controller, conducting the action with an efficient grace. Nothing unnecessary, nothing extraneous.

Inside, his mind whirled. He thought of Robbie Carling, Shaun Brooks. Would they still be alive without his actions? He recalled a previous session with Alex, where she had questioned his faulty fear response, and wondered if it clouded his judgement, put others in danger.

He played on, in a daze, as the weak daylight drained away, shrouding him.

A little later in the day than his previous viewing, he opened his laptop and logged in to the micro camera viewer, switching the image to full screen. His father was a meticulous man; ritual and repetition had been part of his coping strategy in the wake of his wife's murder. In the centre of an unfathomable chaos, he found a sense of order, by focusing only on the things he could control: honing his patterns, refining his routines. The same things at the same time in the same place.

And there he was: at the same time in the same place, moving from his studio into the adjoining outbuilding, turning on the light. The flicker from the small, high window; the shadow passing over it.

Sawyer minimised the app window and opened a web browser. He searched for the Sheffield art festival Harold had mentioned on his last visit. He'd said he was exhibiting and taking part in a panel discussion on analogue versus digital media. The event began tomorrow, and ran over three days. He found Harold's entry on the artist listings page, and checked the timings on the panel discussion, which recurred each day from 5pm to 6pm.

He closed the laptop and sat there in the dark for a while, basking in the nothingness. He called Maggie—it went straight to voicemail—then tried Walker, who answered immediately.

'Sir.'

'Can you talk?'

'One second.' Movement, a door closing. 'I've been checking out the HOLDEN82 thing. A total blank. No links to relevant convictions or crossbow sales. Tried narrowing it down to 1982 births. Still nothing.'

'I'm ahead of you. I found an article from an old PC gaming magazine, about the family of a local tech entrepreneur, Isaac Briggs. His son Harrison wrote some shareware games in the nineties. He called the company Raysoft, and used the symbol as the logo.'

Walker typed something on a keyboard: slow and noisy. 'So, do you know what the symbol is all about?'

'I know where it came from. Briggs's sister, Samantha,

drew the image. Samantha was murdered by a paedophile, Sidney Black, in 1992. She was ten years old.'

'Born in 1982.' More typing from Walker. 'So, what about the Holden part?'

'Still fuzzy on that. But if Briggs is funding the reverse grooming of paedophiles and the "82" is a reference to Samantha, then maybe the "HOLDEN" is a link to whoever's doing the killings.'

A moment of silence from Walker. 'Could it be Briggs himself?'

'It doesn't feel right. In the pictures from the magazine, he looks like he'd struggle to squash a fly, let alone kill another human being.'

'Might have filled out by now. And all but one of the killings are hands-off.'

Sawyer pressed on. 'It's more likely that he's using the MEETUPZ network to select victims for somebody else. This Holden figure? Or maybe that's a red herring.' He got up off the sofa and grabbed his jacket. 'Either way, we're nowhere on the child abductions. But if they're linked to the killings, then stopping them might buy us some time with the children.'

'Shall I track down this Briggs?'

'Not yet. Do some digging. We need to find out more before we have any grounds to arrest or risk alerting him with an interview. The symbol on the crossbow bolts might still be nothing to do with him directly.'

Walker coughed. 'And how are you, sir?'

Sawyer paused at the front door. 'Me?'

'Yes. How are you feeling?'

'Festive.'

58

Hartington Christmas Market was an annual community festival with all the standard trimmings: craft and food shops, traditional game stalls, brass band in the village square, Santa tent. Despite the small scale, it was always popular and well organised, and Sawyer had vague memories of being brought along as a young child.

The Christmas lights were up by the time he arrived, casting the stone-built houses in an amber glow. He shuffled through the crowds, past the pop-up stalls and LED window displays: animated reindeer, grinning snowmen, twinkling trees. Stewards funnelled the stragglers behind a rope cordon, set up for the centrepiece: a grand parade, where children from local schools snaked through the surrounding streets and into the square, brandishing custom-designed paper lanterns. If Sawyer's father had been there, he would be lecturing him on the religious significance of all this light: as a metaphor for Christ's love, a symbol of hope at the darkest time of the year. For most, though, the spiritual gave way to the practical: the market was a decorative top-up for local businesses before the out-of-season hibernation.

Sawyer bought a paper cup of mulled wine and took a sip. It was cloying, medicinal, and he abandoned the cup to a bin at the earliest opportunity. He reached the square, and the crowds thinned out as people jostled at the street corners, securing viewing spots for the imminent parade.

Live music from the Charles Cotton Hotel clashed with the brass band, and Sawyer ducked into a busy café, where the noise was muted to the babble and shouts from passers-by. He ordered coffee, and hitched up on a tall bar stool facing the window and looking out onto the street. He took out his phone and swiped through the recent images: a few shots from his day out with Eva, Fletcher at the Castleton café, screenshots from the *PC Gaming* feature, the eye symbol from the crossbow bolt. If his theory was correct, then the score was uneven: three dead paedophiles, two missing children. If he were the abductor, and he wanted to take a third child, as quickly and as recklessly as he had taken Mia, he would see the market as a prime opportunity.

The stabbing of the third man, Abbott, bothered him. The *anger*. He had missed his shot with the second victim, but finished him with a distance weapon: a spade. With Abbott, there was no evidence that the crossbow had missed, and yet the killer had still attacked him with a knife, in the back, and the back of the head. Still not connecting eye to eye, but closer. More intimate. As if he was lashing out. An impotent rage. Frustration at lack of control, at losing control. But of what?

Shouts went up from outside; the lantern parade had begun. Groups of children filed past, waving their school's signature lanterns. Many of the groups included drummers and trumpet players. Sawyer edged outside and moved in the opposite direction, tracking the procession back through the narrow streets, cramped with cheering onlookers. Not all of the children were taking part in the parade; siblings and friends milled around the fringes, watching and shouting.

Sawyer tracked the parade back to the broad main road that passed through the centre and scanned the end of the adjoining streets, searching for single adults who seemed out of place. There could be a false sense of security in busy, vibrant gatherings; the sense that the mood was infectious, and anything malevolent would be noticed and naturally warned off or policed. But the opposite was true. The shifting chaos allowed predators to hide in the open, to easily attract, redirect attention, take advantage of momentary lapses.

He was drawn to a man, sitting alone, in shadow, on a low wall outside a detached house. The garden at his back had been laden with flashing lights and animated models, and the cycling colours passed over his hunched form, picking out little detail in the dark. He seemed to be slumped: head forward, elbows on knees. But as a flare of bright green light washed over him, Sawyer could see that his eyes were up and fixed on the parade.

Sawyer waited for a while, smiling and applauding the passing children, keeping the figure in sight. The man stayed still, maintaining the same posture: slumped forward, his shoulders rising and falling.

There was no sign of the parade thinning out, as the school parties were joined by children and teenagers from youth groups, outdoor centres, sports clubs. Sawyer waited for a gap, and crossed the road, a couple of streets down from the man. As he reached the other side, the man stood up and stretched his arms back, as if limbering up.

Sawyer approached him. He was mid-twenties: sturdy build; just shy of Sawyer's height; maroon outdoor jacket with a flipped back, fur-lined hood. 'You alright there?'

The man puffed out his cheeks. 'Thanks, yeah. Just not feeling too well.' His speech was slurred; he'd clearly been drinking.

Sawyer forced a smile, as he stumbled past, towards the square. 'Take it easy.'

'*Stella*!'

A woman's shout, from the other side of the road. Sawyer followed the sound. Piercing, frantic. The woman was crouched before a young girl of around eight or nine, gripping her shoulders, imploring her. A fresh wave of lantern groups approached, flooding the road, and Sawyer had to run to get back across in time to avoid the horde.

'*You never, ever go off on your own like that. Do you understand*?'

The girl's face crumpled; she was on the edge of tears. 'There was a *lady*. She had coloured sparklers like on Bonfire Night.'

'Excuse me.' Sawyer slowed as he reached the woman and girl, careful not to get too close. 'I'm a police officer. Is everything okay?'

The woman looked up over her shoulder. 'Yes, thank you.' She turned back to the girl. 'Stella. Where's Amelie?'

Stella looked up at Sawyer, suspicious. 'She went with the lady.'

Sawyer crouched. 'Stella, I'm a policeman. Can you tell me where you saw the lady?'

Stella glanced at her mother, then back at Sawyer. She waved a hand, pointing across the road. 'Down there. By the post box.'

Sawyer stood up and craned his neck, trying to see past the bobbing lanterns as the dense crowd marched past. He caught a movement at the end of a side street, further back up the main road. A short figure in a black woollen hat—adult—and a child, hurrying away, along the street. Were the two holding hands? Was the adult forcing the child to go?

He sprang up and hurried along the pavement, pushing past the onlookers. The main road was a mass of revellers, most waving glowing paper lanterns above their heads, blocking his view. He ran sideways, jinking between the people on the pavement, straining to get a view across the road.

As Sawyer reached a point across from the side street where he had seen the figures, he plunged into a band of drummers, scattering them. Some stumbled to the floor, dropping their beaters, cursing. He barged through a group of lantern bearers and took a shove from a burly steward in a high-viz vest.

He lurched to the side, corrected himself, and pushed forward, onto the opposite pavement.

At the bottom end of the side street, he saw the short figure in the hat closing the back door of a car. The figure's head lifted, looking up to his position, face in silhouette. He couldn't tell for sure in the darkness, but the gait and movement seemed female. As the woman opened the driver's door and fell into the car, he caught a flash of colour from her gloves.

The engine started. Sawyer broke into a run, dazzled by the headlights. The car moved off, screeching its tyres, and turned left, into a narrow connecting road that led away from the town.

59

Sawyer paced the sitting room, shielding his eyes from the early morning light. He had slept in short, fidgety bursts— half an hour, fifteen minutes—and he had been close to driving down to the station and demanding the temporary lifting of his suspension, for the greater good.

Walker's phone rang for a long time before he picked up.

Sawyer caught his breath. 'Anything?'

'No sightings. Nothing from the road blocks.' He sounded distant, ghostly. Amelie Clark. Eleven. She was there with her schoolmate's mum and little sister. Schoolmate was ill, stayed at home with her father. Are you a hundred per cent on the car reg?'

'Didn't see anything. It was too dark. I was too far away. I got straight back to the mother. She'd already called it in. I gave a statement, description. Looked like a woman, but hard to tell.'

Walker sighed. Muffled office noise in the background; he was probably in one of the victimology rooms on the MIT floor. 'I have to go. Briefing.'

'Response was quick. The blocks would have caught

something. She must have been taken somewhere local.'

But Walker had already hung up.

———

Sawyer changed into his running gear and drove down to the Manifold Valley. He parked at the foot of Ecton Hill and hauled himself out into the icy air. His limbs ached from lack of sleep, and as he jogged down onto the Manifold Way trail, his foot caught on a protruding tree root, and he almost fell forward, into a tangle of bracken.

He screwed in his earphones and moved off at a slow pace, shaking his head, trying to reboot his thoughts. He played his favourite album, *Loveless* by My Bloody Valentine: a bewitching brew of drone guitar and off-kilter melodies. It was his staple regrounding soundtrack, for when he needed to settle the blizzard of connections and compulsions.

It was early, and he only passed a couple of runners on the way up to Thor's Cave. The slope at the entrance was slippery with dew and melted frost, and he had to push back against the wall, and sidestep up to the flat outcrop of rock where he had sat with Eva.

He looked out through the mouth of the cave, across the valley. Three men murdered, three children taken. A settled score, or an endless tit for tat? A brother, taking out his grief on the type of men who might have murdered his sister. Was Harrison Briggs a benefactor, an inspiration, or was his involvement in the murders more direct?

Three children: one now missing for four months; one —the daughter of his best friend—gone for close to a week; and now, Amelie Clark, stolen away before his eyes.

And Holly Chilton: cast out, or downed during a failed escape? Was her death a trigger for the abductor's change of method? From online grooming and secret meeting to high-risk public abduction. Why the change? Was it urgency? Some need to fill the gap left by Holly?

Water trickled down from the cave ceiling, splashing onto the floor in the central chamber behind. Rhythmic patterns. Uniform. Soporific.

Sawyer's eyes were suddenly heavy, and his head sank forward. He forced himself awake, and stared out at the restless treetops. He laid it out line by line, image by image: the eye symbol; the teenage Briggs in his room, turned to camera; Mia in the back seat of Maggie's car; Holly's defiant stare into the camera; Joshua's toothy grin.

He heard Stella's voice.

'There was a lady. She had coloured sparklers like on Bonfire Night.'

Sawyer hadn't seen anyone else in the car before the woman had driven away. Were they really looking for a female abductor? It was unthinkable, almost unprecedented. The FLOs would need to speak to Stella, try to coax more detail about the woman who had lured her and Amelie.

He had only seen the figure in silhouette. He closed his eyes and pictured the scene from the previous night, using the "reliving" technique he had been taught by Alex. He spoke out loud.

'I can hear a cry. "Stella!" I'm crossing the road, avoiding a group of children holding glowing lanterns. I'm looking back across the road. I can see a figure with a child.' The images replayed in his mind. 'She is holding the child. They are walking off down a side street. I am running across the road. I bump into people carrying lanterns and drums. I am running to the top of the side street. The figures are near to a car. The child is not there any more. The woman is wearing a black woollen hat. She looks up at me.'

He flexed at his memory, but saw no detail in the face.

'The woman is getting into the car, into the driver's seat. The interior light is on her. I see her gloves. Yellow.'

Sawyer opened his eyes and took out his phone. He opened his photo app and found the screenshots of the PC magazine. He swiped away the shot of Harrison in his bedroom and zoomed in on the image taken outside on the front lawn. Caption: *SOFTWARE HOUSE: Harrison Briggs, at home with mother, Lynette.*

He zoomed in on the image of Harrison, standing at his mother's side. It was a little grainy and washed out, but the colours were clear enough: the khaki of Harrison's parka, Lynette's brown duffel coat, black hat, yellow gloves.

Sawyer gazed out across the valley, his breathing quickening.

He sprang up and slid down the rock slope on his backside, almost tumbling off the drop at the end. He scrambled out of the cave and descended the steps to the Manifold Way track. The nearest spot for phone service would be just outside Waterhouses, to the south. He ran hard, with his phone in hand, checking it every couple of minutes. As he crossed a rickety wooden bridge over the River Hamps, the phone showed a bar of signal.

He stopped, and called Sally O'Callaghan. When she answered, he was panting, struggling to catch his breath.

'Jake. I didn't know you felt this way.'

'The fibres.'

'Good morning to you, too.'

Sawyer steadied himself. 'From Holly Chilton's body.'

'What about them?'

'Are you sure they were yellow?'

She lowered her voice. 'Positive. Natural wool, dyed yellow. Why?'

He hung up, and ran.

60

Sawyer drove into Buxton and parked near the golf course. He headed for the Fairfield branch of Players, sticking to the narrow side streets, hanging back and waiting under shop awnings, scanning for signs of followers. He knew that professional surveillance was co-ordinated work: several operatives stationed at strategic points, in constant communication. But Fletcher was a lone threat, and he could see no sign of him, and no questionable behaviour in any of the other few people in the area.

The club was busy with an early lunch crowd, and he paid a half-day all-access fee to the new face on the reception desk and settled in by the wall of arcade cabinets, selecting a game—*Juno First*—which gave him an eyeline on the main door. It was a simplistic but moreish top-down shooter, and Sawyer found himself relaxing into the gameplay, blasting the swooping aliens with rapid bolts of elongated laser fire.

After half an hour, Ash shambled in, flanked by a couple of chubby teenage associates. His body language was surly, downbeat. He paid his entry fee and broke away from the others, stopping at a *Bride of Pin-Bot* pinball machine near to the retro arcade section. Sawyer continued his game, watching Ash between waves. He hammered at the flippers, swore loudly at lost balls, gesticulated at missed bonuses.

When Sawyer had lost his final life, he sidled up behind Ash, a little too close, and watched him play.

Ash sensed his presence. 'Never seen a pinball before, yeah?'

Sawyer smiled. 'Not really my game. Too random. Not enough control.'

Ash turned his head, irritated. He clocked Sawyer and held his gaze for a moment. He had pitted circles under his eyes, and he'd grown out a layer of uneven stubble. He turned back to the game.

Sawyer stepped closer. 'Pretending you don't recognise me. That hurts.'

Ash shrugged. 'Just playing my game, bruv.'

'So, are you the big man?'

'You what?'

Sawyer moved around and entered his eyeline. 'Now the bigger man has gone?' Ash ignored him, tried to focus on the game. 'I imagine you're at a bit of a loose end? No line manager, and nobody with learning difficulties to boss around?' He nodded at Ash's two colleagues. 'Although it looks like you're not far off with those two.'

Ash cursed, and pinged in a fresh ball; he was working hard to keep up the pretence of not being bothered by Sawyer.

'I've got a proposition for you. Let me tell you my side of it first. I solemnly swear that I won't arrest you for participation in a county lines drug trafficking operation. PWIS: Possession With Intent To Supply. And if you're really good, I might even forget to investigate the offence of kidnap and false imprisonment with a possible bonus of manslaughter for Robbie Carling's unfortunate but inconvenient overdose.'

Ash pushed away from the game and turned to face Sawyer, glaring at him through hazy eyes. 'Yeah? And what do I do for you?'

61

Harrison Briggs looked up from the bottle-green sofa, as Lynette entered the old sitting room. He set down his book and inspected her with his shining eyes. He had opened the blind at the top of the window, letting more light into the room. He had also changed his clothes: fresh blue hoodie, a new pair of skinny jeans, a different pair of bright red trainers. But the room still sang with his necrotic musk.

'Love.' Lynette stepped inside and turned down the music: softer, more ambient than usual. 'You should take a shower. Before the lessons.'

Harrison smiled. 'You should be quiet.'

She stood by the speakers. 'The quiet woman.'

He glared at her. 'There's dignity in silence.' He rose to his full height: rakish, stringy; long, long bones with a heavy, misshapen head. He was a vision from the Hall of Mirrors: unnaturally elongated, as if gravity had toyed with him, raising him high then stretching him back down, for its own amusement.

Lynette recoiled as he approached. 'We could get some Christmas decorations up in the children's rooms? Might help to keep them settled.'

He stood over her. 'You won't go out again.'

'What?'

'I'll take the final two.'

'You?'

'Me. And then, the glory. The *learning*.'

Lynette turned away, braced for his rotten breath. 'What do I do then, love?'

'You'll assist me.' She dropped her head. They stood there for a moment. 'I slept yesterday.' He dropped his voice to the watery whisper. 'Sam was there. It was now, but she was still a child. Trapped in time. Her innocence defiled. A life interrupted.' He turned away. 'It's such a pity. Those idiots who killed Black, in prison. I would trade the rest of my life to be able to take his life. To take my time taking his life.' He closed his eyes, crumpled his face in agony. 'His kind should suffer.'

Lynette turned back to him. 'This is better. That would be over so quickly. Now, you're... bringing good to the world.'

He shook his head. 'The world doesn't know what's good for it. That's the problem. That's what we're going to start. That's what we're going to fix.'

Three loud raps, from the front door knocker.

Harrison strode back to the sofa. 'Deal with that, then I'll meet the new girl.'

Lynette walked out of the sitting room and closed the door. She walked around the perimeter hallway, past the central staircase that led up to the children's rooms.

Three raps again, just as she reached the front door. She raised on tiptoes and peered through the one-way peephole.

It was a man, seemingly alone. Young, pale, excess weight hidden behind baggy sportswear. He had his head bowed, face covered in a tangle of dreadlocks.

Lynette called to him. 'Who is it?'

He looked up, swept away the dreadlocks with a chubby hand. 'Oh! Hello. Sorry to bother you, like. I wanted to talk to Harrison. I'm a big fan of the Raysoft games.' He stumbled. 'Like... *Wormhole*. And the others. I was wondering if he'd sign something for me.'

Lynette opened the door a few inches; it was restricted by two sturdy chains at the top and bottom. 'How did you get this address?'

'Oh. My friend has got an internet site, all about UK game developers, innit? He's got lots of info and cuttings. I live in London but I'm on a trip near here with my folks.'

She studied him. 'Harrison isn't available, but if you give me an email address then I'll get him to drop you a message, maybe send a signed picture later.'

Ash widened his eyes. 'Thank you! That would be awesome.' He took out a notepad, scribbled something, and handed the paper through the gap in the door. The woman looked at it, nodded, and closed the door.

———

Ash headed back down the path, alongside the broad driveway. He side-stepped through the narrow foot entrance by the wrought-iron gates and sauntered down the main road. He turned off into a side lane, and climbed into Sawyer's Corsa, parked on a verge behind a tall hedge.

He slumped into the passenger seat, turned to look at Sawyer, who had his eyes fixed on his phone. 'Mission accomplished. Whatever the fuck it was.'

Sawyer took out his earphones and looked up. He held out an open palm, and Ash took the listening device out of his inside pocket and handed it back. Sawyer smiled. 'Must be a strange feeling. Bringing some good to the world. What did the woman look like?'

Ash shrugged. 'Bog standard. Like, old. Whatever.'

'Tall? Short?'

Ash squinted at him, incredulous. 'Short. But not like a little old lady type, you get me? Not bad for her age, like.' Sawyer raised his eyebrows. 'Fuck off, man. Not like that.' He sat back in the seat. 'Why can't you do this shit yourself, anyway? You get off on scaring old ladies?'

Sawyer looked out at the lane. Sparse flurries of snow fell on the farmland at the outskirts of Hartington. 'I had to be sure he was at this address. And I showed you the newspaper report. I can't be seen here.'

Ash sighed. 'Listen. I don't want your dirty secrets. Was the email address real?'

Sawyer nodded. 'Couldn't risk them checking and finding a fake.'

'Listen, man. I've had a rough week, yeah? Can we get out of here now?' He stared at Sawyer. 'Are we cool?'

Sawyer started the engine. 'For now. But you need to find some better friends.' He glanced at Ash, as he drove away. 'Or we'll be seeing each other again soon.'

62

Sawyer stood before the bedroom mirror, shirtless. He switched to Wing Chun horse stance and flashed out a few limbering punches. He stood still, eyes closed, and took a deep breath in through his nostrils. He slipped into horse stance again, and executed the precise disciplines of the third Wing Chun form, *biu gee*. Darting fingers.

Elbow strikes, finger strikes, rapid changes of direction to avoid attack and prepare for counterattack. He measured out each motion and transition. Nothing for exhibition, nothing unnecessary.

He showered, and layered up for the weather. Outside, the snowfall was thickening; he sat on the bed and stared out at the flakes, fluttering through the dark.

He took out the burner phone and called Walker. Again, it rang for a long time before he answered. 'I thought you were screening me for a second.'

'Lot going on, sir. As you can imagine.'

Sawyer headed out of the front door and stepped onto the porch. 'Shame you're still a man down.'

'Well...'

He climbed into the Corsa. 'Matt. Here's what's going to happen. You're going to finish this.' He propped the phone in the dashboard mount and switched it to speaker, then took a pair of leather gloves out of his pocket and put them on.

A pause from Walker as he moved into a different room. 'What do you mean?'

Sawyer started the engine and moved off, taking the road down through Castleton. 'The children, the dead men. It's the same perpetrator. Harrison Briggs.'

'The son of the tech entrepreneur?'

'Yes. Like I said, he's using the MEETUPZ network to support the paedophile hunter group, Justice For Kids. Probably others, too. I think he's also used it to reverse-groom the men into the meetings at the stations and Lud's Church. The disgust for them, the use of a long-range and silent weapon. Clinical, surgical. He sees them as parasites, invaders. Similar to medical anomalies. Aberrations, to be removed, taken out of the system.'

'But what's this got to do with the children? If he's culling paedophiles for the greater good, in the name of his murdered sister, then what's he doing with the children?'

Sawyer slowed for traffic near the Sparrowpit turn-off. 'I'm not sure. But I know he's behind the abductions. When Holly was found, there was new anger in the killings. I'm certain that her death wasn't intentional. She escaped. Probably underestimated the conditions and the cold.'

'You'd have to be pretty desperate to do that.'

'Or determined. Remember her parents' comments about her being "wilful" and "pushing boundaries"? I don't think Holly Chilton was the type to sit and take whatever Briggs was doing, or planning.'

Walker took a moment to absorb it all. 'So, how do you connect him with the abductions?'

'The anger of Holly's death changed something, made him less patient. There's a mission, a project. The pace of the abductions has accelerated. He might even have taken enough children to see it through now.'

'But how do you know he *is* taking the children?'

'He's not. His mother is. Lynette. She would have taken Mia from the first Christmas market in Bakewell, and I was there when she took Amelie from Hartington. There's a picture in the old gaming magazine. She's standing outside with Harrison. Cold day. She's wearing yellow gloves. I'm sure the woman who took Amelie wore yellow gloves. And I take it you know about the fibres found on Holly's body?'

'Uhuh.'

Sawyer squeezed the accelerator and pushed on, through the snow. 'I'll send you the links to all this. Remember: You're going to finish it. You're going to finish it *tonight*. Tell Keating and Shepherd you put it together. Might not be the best idea to say you had help from me. The mention of yellow gloves is in the statement I gave at Hartington. Pitch it to them as soon as you get my links, and the address. It's a big house, about twenty minutes on foot from where Holly was found.'

'How do you know the address?'

'Complex subterfuge.' A pause. 'Googled it. Cross-checked with the electoral register. You can see the place on Google Street View, set back from one of the adjoining roads. I think the children are there, and the logic supports a Section 17. There's threat to life and limb, grounds to question both the mother and son. Dive on this now, Matt. Get it under Shepherd's nose. And bring a decent-sized team. We've no idea what's inside that house.'

Sawyer turned into the lane where he had waited for Ash, and parked on the verge.

'Where are you now?'

He reached over to the passenger seat and pulled on his chestnut-brown balaclava. 'Text me when you're near. I thought I'd have a quick look around.'

63

Sawyer crunched through the snow, across an open field. He stayed low, close to a line of withered trees, and aimed for a perimeter hedge at the back of the three-storey building. Lights were on: a faint red glow from a room on the ground floor, bright yellow from the third floor.

He tracked the hedge from its furthest corner, along the back and down the side of the house. There were three weak points where the vegetation had thinned out enough to accommodate a person. But the branches were still dense and gnarled, and he would be risking injury, perhaps leaving blood or fibre traces. Sawyer pulled the balaclava tight over his face, and selected the gap that looked like it would offer the least resistance. He shouldered into the hedge and picked his way through the clawing bramble until he could prise it apart and squeeze through to the other side.

He was at the bottom of a double-level garden: plants and flower borders below, with a shallow stone staircase leading up to the moonlit back wall of the house. The windows were all closed and covered, but he could just make out a narrow path at the top of the staircase, leading round to a gap between house wall and hedge. He listened. Distant cars, the odd night bird, and a vague rumble of running machinery, somewhere around the front of the building.

Sawyer crouch-walked up the staircase, peered around the wall, and edged into the gap. He reached a wooden door: old, but sturdy, with an outmoded cylinder lock. He took out his kirby grips and prepared the kinked wrench and pick combination. The lock was basic, but the internal plug had grown rigid with age, and it took him a tense ten minutes to twist and feel his way through and get the door unlocked.

He eased down the handle and pushed open the door, wary of immediate threat, particularly dogs. He waited, and listened for a while, then moved inside and closed the door behind him.

A short passage with a stone floor connected to a laundry room on the right and a cluttered storage area off to the left. The house smelt damp and sour, with a deep-set chill that made him shudder. He brushed away the snow and inched forward, taking slow, silent steps.

Sawyer turned on his phone light at a low brightness, and pointed it at the floor; it gave just enough glow for him to see a few feet ahead. He turned a corner and passed through a long galley kitchen, towards an internal door with a large glass panel. Weak light filtered through from a corridor beyond the door. He squatted and shuffled forward, pushed up against the kitchen units, in case someone walked past the door and glanced through the glass.

He reached the door and edged it open. The machinery sound increased in volume: a low, steady rumble, punctuated by rhythmic bumps and thuds. Was it *music*?

As he crept along the corridor, the sound grew richer, more complex: a relentless pulse of bass feedback; a cycling three-note guitar figure; vocal howls and groans which rolled in and melded with the fuzz, then splintered and faded. The sounds pitched and swelled like a dark liquid, flowing through the corridors.

Sawyer reached a corner, and pressed up against the wall. He raised his phone light higher to pick out an object which faced into the next corridor. It was a shooting target, mounted on an easel before a backstop net, which hung down from the ceiling. An unlit picture lamp sat above the target. He edged his head around the wall, to get a view around the corner. The corridor facing the target was more like a long hall: broad and gloomy, with several closed doors. He could just make out furniture and cupboards at the far end. Wall cabinets, chairs, a sofa.

He stayed close to the wall, and edged around the corner. Now, it was clear that the music was coming from somewhere near the far end of the hall; it was vast and pervasive, but still oddly muffled. Halfway down the hall, a carpeted staircase led up. He climbed the steps, moving faster, keeping his eyes on the landing above, knowing that any sound of movement would be swallowed in the storm of the music.

At the landing, Sawyer turned and pushed up to the first floor. Another long, hall-like corridor led both ways, into darkness. The steps carried on up to the top floor. He covered his phone and looked up the stairs, squinting. There was definitely light up there.

He pressed on, relieved to get some distance from the devilish soundtrack. He was used to drone guitar, ambience, repetition, but this was more extreme: monolithic, designed to disturb, drained of melody.

The top-floor corridor was shorter, lit by bright light from a glass-panelled door near the far end. Up here, the music was vague and muted, but still simmered away below, unbroken.

Sawyer pushed up against the wall and moved towards the door. If someone walked out into the corridor, his position would at least buy him a few seconds before he would be spotted: enough to spring away and dash into cover, behind the wall at the top of the staircase.

Voices. Soft and low, from the lit room. Children.

He reached the door and checked along both sides of the corridor, then peeked through the glass panel, into the room.

The walls were bare, but the room was decorated in loud, friendly colours: yellows, purples, bright blues. A large side window looked out across the snow-covered fields behind the house, with a closed skylight above. On the far wall, a grid of gym lockers sat behind a long wooden bench. In the centre of the room, individual tables and chairs had been arranged in rows of three, facing a portable whiteboard and large desk and chair.

It was a classroom.

Three young children sat at the desks, sullen and distant. Sawyer recognised two: Mia, and Joshua Maitland. The third, a redhead, he assumed was Amelie Clark. All three wore black blazers and matching V-neck sweaters. The girls wore skirts; Joshua, in black shorts, sat nearest the door. Sawyer ducked under the window, crawled to the other side of the door, and peered in again. From the new perspective, he could see that each child had a thick metal collar visible above the sock on their right leg.

There was a side door, ajar, at the front of the room, behind the whiteboard. Sawyer adjusted the balaclava, eased the main door open and stepped inside.

Amelie and Joshua were angled away from the door, talking to each other, but Mia spotted Sawyer and gasped. The other two turned to him, and he held his finger to his lips with one hand, and his other hand out in front, palm down, bobbing it up and down to suggest quiet.

In the time it had taken Sawyer to acknowledge the children, Lynette Briggs had emerged from the side room. She froze, stared at him. Her shoulders slumped and she felt her way across to the desk chair and sat down, eyes fixed on Sawyer's masked face.

Sawyer glanced at the children, and took a step closer to the desk. 'Where's Harrison?' He kept his voice low, almost whispered.

'Who are you?' Her voice was solid, unwavering.

Sawyer raised his head. 'I asked first.'

Lynette drew the chair up to the desk. 'Harrison is in his study. He's going out soon.'

'In this weather?'

Lynette forced a smile. 'He's a hardy soul.'

'What are the ankle collars?'

Lynette stayed still, at the desk, glaring at him.

'You can't save us!' It was Joshua, on his feet. 'We're not allowed to leave.'

'Joshua!' Lynette scolded him, but he continued.

'We have to wear them. He's got a bracelet, and if we go too far he gives us a shock. Holly told me—'

'*Joshua!*' Lynette sprang up from the chair. '*Sit down and be quiet.*'

He lowered himself back down. The two girls kept their eyes fixed on the floor.

A moment of silence. The distant thrum of the music.

Sawyer angled his head, gesturing to the corridor. 'Is that Harrison's choice? Good job you don't have neighbours.'

275

Lynette dropped her eyes to the desk. 'As I say, he's going out tonight.'

Sawyer nodded. 'And that's his psych-up music?' He stepped closer to the desk, around the side, where he could see Lynette's hands down by the drawers. 'What's going on here?'

She didn't look up. 'You'll have to talk to Harrison about that.'

Sawyer glanced at the children; they were all watching now. 'Whatever this is, it's finished. Derbyshire's finest are on their way.' He leaned around the desk, only a few feet from Lynette now. He took out a pair of handcuffs and stepped closer.

Amelie had started to sob. 'Are you the police?'

Lynette smiled. 'No. You heard him, dear. They're on their way.'

Sawyer pounced forward and grabbed Lynette's left arm. He fixed one end of the handcuffs to her wrist and tightened the ratchet. She bowed her head, offering no resistance. He pulled her chair to the back of the room and fixed the other end to a sturdy radiator pipe that ran across the bottom of the far wall, holding her firmly in place.

He patted her down for phones or weapons. Nothing.

Lynette kept her gaze on the floor, holding that strange little smile. She was mid-sixties, but Sawyer was struck by how much older she looked up close, and how easily she had wilted. She seemed more relieved than resigned.

Sawyer checked the desk drawers. Folders, papers. Nothing practical or threatening. 'Now, are you going to tell me what is going on here?'

He froze.

The rumbling two floors below had fallen silent; the music had stopped.

Lynette had left the top drawer on the right side of the

desk open. Sawyer moved around her and pushed it shut, revealing a small white button built under the rim of the desk.

Lynette sneered at him. 'As I say, you'll need to talk to Harrison. He's expecting you.'

64

Sawyer told the children to stay in the classroom, and moved out into the corridor. He aimed his phone light at the floor, and crept down the first staircase, pausing every few steps to listen.

No sight or sound of movement below.

As he reached the first floor landing, the music reared up again, startling him. It seemed louder this time: booming bass, rasping guitar, guttural growls and bellows. He continued down to the ground floor hall and approached a large door at the near end: the source of the music. When he had first entered the house, the door had been closed; now, it was open a few inches, and leaked a deep red light that cast the corridor in a fiery haze.

Sawyer pressed against the wall at the foot of the stairs, and looked down the hall, towards the sofa and the crossbow target, scanning for movement. He reached the door and eased it open, staying out of sight at the edge of the frame. Luminous red flooded the hall, and the music ramped up. He moved around, through the frame, and inched forward into the room.

Red light blazed down from a vast, shadeless bulb in the

tall ceiling. The room was cavernous, with fat candles flickering in shallow metal dishes, spaced out across the dark-wood floorboards. There was no furniture, apart from a minimalist music system with stacked speakers, a wall of bookcases, and a bottle-green sofa on the far side, beneath a huge window covered by a Venetian blind.

Sawyer squinted, adjusting to the change of light. As he edged further into the room, he saw movement from the sofa. A long, slim figure had been reclining across its length, but now it shifted and rose up to its full height, dappled in shadow from the blind. The figure was at least a foot taller than Sawyer. At this distance, the features were vague, in almost total silhouette, but there were flashes of colour at the top and bottom of the body: silver from large-framed spectacles; red and white from the shoes. Harrison Briggs took a small step forward, measuring the distance with his stalk-like legs. He held his hands down at his sides, clenching and unclenching his spindly fingers into fists.

The movement shifted him into the light, painting a little more detail over his gaunt features. He tipped his head back and regarded Sawyer for a few seconds, then reached back to a remote control on the arm of the sofa. The music faded to a low murmur.

Sawyer stayed still, just inside the door. He checked around the room; no sign of anyone else. 'I need the control.' Harrison said nothing. 'For the ankle collars. And a key to get them off would be nice.'

'Who *are* you?' Sawyer recoiled at his watery hiss. 'You're not the police. Are you a hunter? Which group? I haven't seen you before.'

Sawyer shrugged. 'Just a concerned citizen.'

Harrison smiled. Even from this distance, Sawyer could see his stained teeth, premature wrinkles. 'None of this is your *concern*.'

Sawyer glanced at the sound system. 'Nice music. Is this how you stir yourself up to kill?'

Harrison dropped his head. 'It's a band called Sunn. Experimental. Not your verse, chorus, verse type.' He raised his voice. 'You need to leave my house.' He looked up again. 'Will you leave my house?'

Sawyer shook his head. 'I can't. Not yet.'

Harrison turned his back, retrieving something from the sofa. He faced Sawyer and raised the Nexgen crossbow. Sawyer dropped to the floor, as the bolt swished over his head and crunched into the plaster of the wall behind. He scrambled to his feet and charged, as Harrison reloaded, holding the crossbow vertically against the floor and drawing back the cable. As Sawyer reached him, Harrison let the crossbow fall forward; he drew back an arm and swung it around in a wide arc. His extended reach caught Sawyer by surprise, and the swipe connected with the side of his head, sending him back to the floor, sprawling onto his right shoulder. By the time he had righted himself and spun back, facing the sofa, Harrison had reloaded the bow.

He pointed it at Sawyer, looking down the sight. 'Stay where you are, on the floor. Put your hands on your head.'

Sawyer shuffled upright, knees bent. He rested both hands on his head and clasped his fingers together.

Harrison kept the crossbow trained on Sawyer's forehead. 'From this range, the bolt would crack through your skull, enter your brain. You may not even see or hear anything.' Sawyer remained impassive. Harrison narrowed his eyes. 'You are a trigger squeeze away from oblivion. You should say, "Please". And, "Don't do this". You should beg for your life. And yet, there you sit, like an obedient dog.' He sighed. 'Have you harmed my mother?'

Sawyer shook his head. 'Lynette is fine. I cuffed her to the pipe, away from the children.'

'You know who I am. You know what happened to me.'

'Not just you.'

Harrison nodded. 'No. My mother and father, too.'

'But you were twelve. Innocent. Like Samantha.'

Harrison shuddered at the word, closed his eyes briefly. 'I never called her that.' He forced a weak smile.

Sawyer sat up. 'Sidney Black took Sam's life, and he ended your childhood.'

'This is what the deviants do. They prey on purity. The children... They're like these candles. And the predators snuff out their flames.' Harrison backed off and sat down on the sofa, keeping the bow trained on Sawyer. The candlelight fluttered across his pallid skin, and he lowered his voice again: a strangled whisper. 'Think of the moment you're born. All that sound and fury, as you're torn from your mother's shelter. And then your own inner light starts to burn. But, nothing gold can stay. That glorious light of life is destined to fade and die. For some, the fading happens too early, because of trauma or premature responsibility. Others get to bask in it for longer. But now... The *internet*.' He spat out the word. 'The online world. A glorious achievement of human communication, now just a conspiracy to kill that light as soon as possible. It wants children to hurry up and be adults, with spending power. And it also gives predators access to them, to dim their light in a different way.'

'That's what Black did to Sam.' Sawyer kept his eyes on the crossbow, as it wilted in Harrison's grip.

Harrison glanced at him. 'This thing they call "the dark web". They named it well. The images they share there. The depravity. The children in those pictures have already lost their light, and those moments of defilement are passed around for the pleasure of predators. Technology has built them a playground. If it were terrorism, we would have

281

declared war on it. But instead, we look the other way. We don't want to see. We don't want to know.'

Sawyer nodded. 'Because there's no money at stake.' He shuffled in place; Harrison caught the movement and raised the bow again. 'There's no bigger picture. No politics.'

Harrison sighed. 'Someone once said, "The creative adult is the child who survived." Today, children aren't allowed to grow into creative adults. Their colour, their light, it's muted by the way the technology gives them infinite access to all these layers of distraction and degradation. They deserve a chance to flourish. To grow and play, without all that noise, all those phoney influences.'

Sawyer sat up. 'Phoney. HOLDEN82. So it *was The Catcher In The Rye*. You want to put Holden Caulfield's ideas into practice. Protect children from the corruption of the adult world. Preserve their light. And you're doing it in Sam's name.'

'In the book, Holden wants to catch the children as they fall out of the rye field, over the cliff, losing their innocence. I know I can't catch every child.'

'How many, then? Is three enough?'

Harrison bowed his head. 'I will take five. We can manage five.'

'What happened with Holly Chilton?'

'She wouldn't rest. She ran. I couldn't save her.'

Sawyer kept his focus on the crossbow; Harrison had let it drop again. 'And were you going to keep the children for good?'

Harrison's head jerked up. 'No! They will be released, when their education is complete.'

'Back into the wild?'

'Yes. But fortified. Better equipped. Uncorrupted. And after that, the glory.'

'*Glory*? You think you'll be heroes?' Harrison didn't answer. 'And meanwhile, you take direct action against the predators, the paedophiles who steal other children's innocence, and light?'

Harrison ran his fingers along the side of the crossbow. 'The ones we love, they never really leave. They merge with us. They walk beside us. My sister doesn't have a voice any more, and so my actions speak for her. I'm her vessel. The crossbow bolts are her rebukes to the deviants. She was shown no mercy, and so she gives none. She reaches out, from beyond death, and takes her vengeance through me.'

Sawyer's phone buzzed in his pocket, making an audible vibration against the wooden floor.

Harrison raised an eyebrow. 'So, who are you, if you're not the police? I take it they're coming?'

Sawyer steadied himself; Harrison still hadn't raised the crossbow again. 'It sounds like you've admitted defeat.'

'Against what?'

'Technology. The online world. You see it as the enemy. But all the big companies... They only know about your habits based on what you do and say and buy. They can't own what's inside your head.' He moved his leg around, slowly, bracing his foot against the floor. 'Humans have a wonderful thing that computers will never replicate. We can improvise, find lateral ways to solve problems. They want us to accept ourselves as malleable and easy to manipulate, with their clickbait and algorithms. But we're not conditioned animals. We're better than that. We're extraordinary, and we can do extraordinary things. You've done an extraordinary thing here. Your intentions are good, but the consequences would be catastrophic. You can't reprogramme people, retro-fit them for a world that no longer exists. You have to give them power, not take it away. Show them that they have it in themselves to be more than just slaves to technology. In your own way, Harrison, you're also stealing their light, by depriving them of parental love.'

Harrison raised the crossbow. 'Take off the mask.'

A shout from upstairs. Lynette.

Harrison startled, and raised his eyes to the door. Sawyer sprang forward. Harrison shot back across the sofa and lifted the crossbow. Sawyer anticipated it and lurched to the right, ducking down by the sofa's near side. The bolt skimmed across the sofa's arm and wedged in the floor behind Sawyer. Harrison rose up and gripped the end of the bow with both hands, wielding it like a club. Sawyer scrambled to his feet and drove at him. Harrison swung the frame of the bow into Sawyer's left shoulder, sending him back down to the floor, sliding away from the sofa, beneath the window. He pulled himself back to his feet, and caught a glimpse through the blinds: light, out at the front of the house. Car headlights.

Harrison held the bow vertically against the floor, pulling back the cable, priming it for reloading. Sawyer pushed forward and sprinted for the door.

He made it outside, to the end of the hallway. It would take too long to get to the door that led back to the kitchen, and Harrison's line of sight would be too straight. He bounded up the staircase.

Harrison reached the door of the sitting room as Sawyer made it to the first landing. He ducked under the frame and stood in the hall, silhouetted against the red light. He aimed the crossbow up and Sawyer darted around the corner. Harrison fired again, and the bolt tore into the landing wall.

Another shout from Lynette. Children's voices, too. Mia and Amelie, crying out.

Sawyer raced up to the next landing. He took a breath and checked his phone. Walker.

Sawyer pushed on, up to the top floor. He ran to the classroom door and peered around the edge. The desk had been upended. All three children were crowded around the captive Lynette. She had curled into a ball, and Joshua was beating her, pounding at her back and head with both fists. Amelie and Mia struggled with him, trying to pull him away.

Sawyer rushed over and eased Joshua back, to the desks. He was sobbing, wild, desperate to get to Lynette. Sawyer moved in front of her, and crouched in front of the boy, eye to eye. 'Joshua. Let the police deal with this. You're safe now. You'll see your mum and dad soon, back in Youlgreave.' Joshua backed into one of the desk chairs and sat down. 'You'll be okay. This will all soon be just a bad memory. It won't be able to hurt you any more.'

Joshua wiped his eyes and focused on Sawyer, behind the balaclava. 'You *know* about us. He... they kept us here. Holly got away, but... Why didn't you come *quicker*?'

A shout from below, outside, at the front of the house. 'Armed police!'

Sawyer glanced at Amelie and Mia, and ran out through the door, into the corridor. He froze. Harrison had reached the top of the stairs. He spotted Sawyer and raised the bow. Sawyer slammed the classroom door shut behind him, casting the corridor in darkness. Harrison was barely a shadow, rendered in the distant light from below.

Sawyer ducked low and ran at him, bending his movement laterally, sticking to the far edge of the corridor. Harrison tracked him with the bow, and as Sawyer lunged for him, he fired. The bolt planted into the wall behind, and Sawyer barrelled into him, head down. Harrison dropped the crossbow, and rolled his arms, trying to stay upright.

But the impact was too strong, and he toppled backwards. His gangly frame tumbled down the stairs and crumpled into an angular heap on the landing, where he lay still.

A crash downstairs. The AFO team would enter and run through a precise, room-by-room securing process. There was no telling how long it would take them to reach the back corridor and sitting room. If he was spotted, he would be detained.

He charged down the stairs and checked on Harrison. Unconscious, still breathing. At the first-floor landing, he could hear the shouts of the entry team, as they covered the rooms at the front of the house. He made it to the ground floor and sprinted past the sofa, towards the crossbow target and the route through the kitchen into the back garden. He eased open the glass-panelled door and ran through the galley kitchen to the short passage with the stone floor.

Voices echoed from behind the side door that led outside. Sawyer ducked down and threw himself into the messy storage area, opposite the tidy and open laundry room. He tucked himself behind a protruding wall unit and crouched in the darkness.

The side door slammed open, and the AFO support team broke into the passage. Three officers, probably four. He heard one enter the laundry room, and the heavy boots of a second tramped into the storage area, a few feet away from his hiding place. It all depended on the officer's competence, and diligence. If he poked around, checked for concealed threats, he would surely spot Sawyer, hold him at gunpoint, and detain him. Game over.

Sawyer crouched there, next to a pile of discarded plasterboard, breathing steadily, listening to himself.

Nothing. Just a higher breathing rate from the exertion. No racing heart. No symptoms of stress or panic. No fear. It was almost the opposite. He was seconds away from discovery and detention. All was in danger of being revealed: his illicit surveillance and correspondence; the contact with Shepherd, Walker, Sally O'Callaghan; the entanglement with Shaun and Dale. On top of the murder investigation, it would surely be the end of him as a serving officer.

And yet, there was nothing. Apart from a curious sense of irritation; something close to boredom.

The officer's colleague called, "Clear!" and he repeated, loud enough and close enough to make Sawyer wince. They both moved out into the passage, through to the kitchen. Sawyer had no way of telling if there were more officers in the grounds of the house, but he didn't wait; he pushed out of the storage room and peered around the side door, down to the gap in the hedge. The snow fell thick and fast now, but there were only footprints off to the left; nothing in the back garden. The AFO team must have entered around the side, from the front of the house.

He dived out of the side door and ran along the wall, crunching through the fresh snow. At the hedge, he dropped onto his belly and scrambled through the gap, crawling out the other side, into the field where he could break for the trees and disappear.

As he prepared to emerge, he stopped, and listened.

Footsteps in the snow. One person, approaching from around the other side, walking towards the hedge, only feet away. Low voices, further off.

A light shone down and caught Sawyer as he pulled himself upright. The barrel-mounted torch of an automatic weapon?

He raised his hands to his head slowly, and squinted into the light.

It was a standard torch, and the holder lowered it, revealing his face.

DC Walker. Suited up, with a bullet-proof vest under a thick overcoat.

'*Sir*?'

Sawyer lowered his hands. 'One adult male, unconscious but armed with a crossbow. Still a possible threat. Last position on the staircase, second floor. One adult female, secured. The three children are with her in a room on the top floor. No evidence of anyone else in the house.'

Walker's walkie-talkie crackled; he spoke into it. 'Rear of house secure. Be advised. Two adults inside, one possibly armed with crossbow. Three children in room on third floor.'

Sawyer caught his breath. 'He wanted to save them, keep them pure. Protect them. Stop them having to grow up before their time, like he had to.'

Walker nodded. 'It's kidnap. Murder.'

'I suppose for him, the end justified the means.' Sawyer gazed out at the snow-covered fields, shining through the dark. 'I need to go.'

'You were never here.'

Sawyer locked eyes with him. Walker smiled, opened his mouth to speak again. Sawyer held up a hand. 'I'll say it.'

'What?'

'Good work.'

Sawyer moved off, away from the house, up the field towards the trees. Running. Not looking back.

65

In the morning, Sawyer trundled the Corsa through the minor roads outside Thornhill village. The temperature had risen overnight, and turned the lighter snowfalls into slush, but the track down to Shepherd's cul de sac was treacherous, and his wheels spun as he parked the Corsa near the farm gate.

He sat there, staring down at the stone-built semis, listening to 'Chill Out' by The KLF: a dreamy, drifting, ambient collage, evoking a rail journey across America's Deep South. It was music he often used to carry himself off to sleep. But here and now, with the world outside in stasis, on ice, he wallowed in the chirping cicadas, gospel choirs, clanging freight train. He craved the heat, the aliveness, the sense of motion.

Shepherd emerged from his house, blowing into his hands. He trudged out to the Range Rover and scraped the snow from the windows. Sawyer opened the Corsa passenger door and gave a slight toot of the horn. Shepherd looked up and approached, measuring his steps across the thinner patches of snow.

He climbed in and closed the door.

Sawyer lowered the music volume, kept his gaze on the street ahead. 'It's not a style choice.'

Shepherd looked at him. 'What?'

'The car. The Mini's still indisposed.'

Shepherd nodded. 'The children are safe. It was a guy whose sister was murdered by a paedophile when they were kids. His dear old mum was helping.'

Sawyer feigned shock. 'His mum?'

'Yeah. Keeping it in the family. Revenge for his sister, her daughter. Looks like the fella was driving it all. We think he used social networks to groom Holly and Joshua, but then the woman took over after Holly's death. Luring the kids, taking them. Easier to trust a woman, I suppose. Quicker, too.'

'And no sexual assault?'

Shepherd gave a pained smile. 'No. According to the children, they were just... conducting lessons. Maths, English, History. Acting like a proxy school, but denying the kids access to technology. They said the woman gave the lessons. Probably helped convince her that the end justified the means. And Rhodes pulled some pretty strange things off the computers. Some of it looks like notes on targets. Government agencies, ministerial departments, public bodies.'

'Terrorism?'

'Could be. Lots of references to "the glory".'

Sawyer did his best to look confused. 'And what about the crossbow killings?'

'The guy was doing those himself. Computer history shows he was reverse-grooming the predators, using the same social networks he first used to groom the kids. Tempting them to meeting spots, taking them out. There was a symbol on the crossbow bolts that linked back to his murdered sister.' He sucked in a breath, puffed it out;

the vapour swirled around the car. 'Walker put it together.'

'The press will be all over him. Back from the dead to save the innocents.'

'Might take some of the attention away from you.'

Sawyer snorted. 'You were his boss. You know how it works. The praise trickles upwards. You might get DI.'

'Too soon.'

'How's Maggie?'

Shepherd shrugged. 'Born-again happy. It was Keating who told her not to contact you.'

'It was a good decision. Too much emotion.'

'No history between her and Walker.'

Sawyer raised his eyebrows. He took an open packet of chocolate limes out of the glovebox and waggled it at Shepherd. He grimaced and shook his head.

Sawyer unwrapped a sweet and slid it into his mouth. 'Signing in today. I was hoping it would all be over by Christmas.'

Shepherd took a breath, hesitated, let it out. 'I haven't heard anything. Not sure if that's good or bad.' He looked away. 'Be nice to have you back soon, sir.'

Sawyer laughed. 'Doesn't look like you need me. You want to be careful. The brass might see it as an excuse for a budget cut.'

'I've got to move. Lots of wrap-up stuff.'

'You interviewed the guy yet? The mother?'

Shepherd shook his head. 'Later today. Sally's team have been at the house overnight. The guy was submissive, but the mother had to be restrained. Ranting and raving about the intrusion. At the moment, she looks like the crazy one. He's said nothing.'

'You'll get the charge. He'll probably confess.'

Shepherd opened the door. He lingered, nodding.

'Walker definitely smashed it. For a junior detective recovering from a life-threatening assault, it was incredible solo work. Although...' He paused. 'The woman's insisting there was someone else in the house, before Walker's team got there. Some bloke with a mask who restrained her, fought with the guy. None of the team recognise the description or saw anyone.'

'As you say, ranting and raving. Any hard evidence of the mystery man?'

'Not yet. Snow will have covered any prints around the house. Might get a few impressions, but I doubt it.'

Sawyer nodded, chewed his lip. 'Those community support officers can get pretty zealous.'

Shepherd got out, glanced over his shoulder, shot Sawyer a wry smile. He picked his way back down to the Range Rover, climbed inside, and pulled away, not looking over as he drove past.

Sawyer sat there for a while. He turned up the music, switched on the engine and heating.

As he pulled away, his phone vibrated in his pocket. And again.

He checked the screen. Call from Dean Logan.

He killed the music, mounted the phone in the dashboard dock and connected the call.

'Paedo killer in custody!' Logan spluttered, took a sip of something. 'The county's sex offenders are free to walk the lanes. You must be delighted, DI Sawyer. And the children back, too. Was this guy responsible for both?'

Sawyer turned onto the Hope Road, towards Buxton. 'Are you seriously trying to pump *me* for information?'

Logan laughed. 'It's fine. There's a conference later today. It's a good win. Justice for all. In other news...' He paused, teasing. 'The burgundy BMW. I went to see Dr

Kelly's widow. Turns out...' Another pause. 'Your dear old dad was at his place a lot.'

Sawyer sighed. 'He was our family GP. They were friends.'

'Yeah, but she said he was there *a lot*, four or five years ago, not too long before Kelly died. She's sure she saw Harold drive away in the BMW, and she doesn't remember seeing it again. Like I said, Sawyer, it sounds to me like your old man was a few steps ahead of you. And I'm wondering why he was using a car with dodgy paperwork, handed on by his dear old mate, to keep a close eye on Klein after his release. And you.'

Sawyer crossed the car park at Buxton station; head low, hands dug deep into his pockets. The snow had been shovelled into grubby mounds up on the verges, but he had to take short, cautious steps around the patches of black ice that had gathered by the walkway.

As he headed for the main entrance, a silver Ford Fiesta parked at the roadside across from the station.

Sawyer strode down the corridor, past the yellow-panelled doors. Uniforms and detectives milled around, smiling and laughing. The air crackled with triumph and relief.

Sergeant Gerry Sherman clocked Sawyer's approach and made a phone call, stern faced. Sawyer waited at the custody and charge desk as Sherman finished the call.

His mind wandered. He would see his father later: confront him about the car, demand to see inside the locked garage by the studio. Better still, he could check the camera and cross reference the timings with the Sheffield art festival that evening.

Sherman turned, forced a smile. 'DI Sawyer.'

'Gerry.'

Sawyer moved around to the privacy barrier. Sherman hesitated for a second, then produced the bail document. Sawyer eyed Sherman as he countersigned. He was normally chatty and welcoming, but he'd kept his eyes down, at odds with the mood along the corridor.

At the far end of reception, the lift doors opened. DCI Ivan Keating stepped out, fitting his cap over his cropped white hair. Two taller male uniforms followed him out of the lift. The group made straight for Sawyer. Keating moved in close, while the two detectives dropped off, blocking the corridor back to the entrance.

Sherman typed at his keyboard. 'Mr Sawyer. The decision has been made to charge you on one count of murder. You have the right to inform someone that you're here, the right to a copy of the police code of practice, and the right to speak to a solicitor free of charge.' He looked up from the screen, glanced at Keating. 'Umm... A few welfare questions. We've got these on the system from before, but since this is effectively a re-arrest... Do you have any known allergies?'

Sawyer let his head tip back. He gazed up at the ceiling. Off-white, a dark patch in the far corner. 'No to all the welfares, Gerry.' He turned to Keating. 'Congratulations.'

Keating fixed him with an icy stare. 'Is that sarcasm?'

Sawyer smiled. 'On solving the child abduction and crossbow murder cases.'

Keating nodded. 'Jake Sawyer. You are charged that on the 6th of November 2018, in Castleton, in the county of Derbyshire, you murdered Marcus James Klein, contrary to common law. In answer to this charge, you do not have to say anything, but it may harm your defence if you do not mention now something which you later rely on in court, and anything you do say may be given in evidence. Do you understand the charge as it has been read to you?'

'I do.'

'Is there anything you wish to say in reply?'

Sawyer shook his head, turned to the uniforms. 'Guards. Take me away.'

'It's early. So you'll be detained for the day and taken to South Sheffield Magistrate's Court later this afternoon.'

'Not keeping me overnight?'

Keating shook his head. 'No room.'

One of the uniforms stepped around Sawyer and opened the side door that led to the back of the station.

Sawyer turned to Sherman. 'I'd love a lasagne for lunch, Gerry. If that's okay.'

He walked through the door, down to the cells.

67

Sawyer lay on his side, eyes open, facing the scratch-marked wall by his cell bed. They would probably build a case around his mental state. Point to the bare-knuckle fight, the clash with Viktor Beck's bodyguard, the reckless solo journey into the old mine to apprehend Dennis Crawley. Maybe they knew more about his covert involvement in the Briggs case. Surely Shepherd hadn't reported his discovery of the listening device? The multiple examples of insubordination would support the case that he was unstable enough to force the transfer from London, befriend his mother's killer, then finish him off in the same way he had murdered her.

He refused breakfast, but got his lasagne: Tesco own brand, but at least fully defrosted. They had taken his phones, tactical pen, wallet and belt. He was allowed to keep his jacket, and since his boots were slip-on, he was spared the indignity of having his shoelaces confiscated.

A couple of hours later, the uniforms escorted him back to the custody desk and Sherman booked him out for the journey to Sheffield. Keating appeared, and followed

Sawyer and the uniforms back down the corridor past the cells.

The uniforms paused at the door leading out to the private car park. Sawyer turned and held out his hands, wrists a few inches apart.

Keating sighed. 'I'm sorry.' He clicked the handcuffs into place. 'It's just for the journey to the transport.'

Sawyer nodded, smiled. 'No comment.'

Another prisoner stepped into the corridor near the external door, escorted by a burly uniformed officer. He was young, maybe teenage, black, and wore baggy tracksuit trousers and a shabby hoodie with a stain near the collar. The uniform cuffed him and he shuffled into the space behind Sawyer, bringing a reek of sour sweat and cheap deodorant.

The burly officer opened the door, and led Sawyer and the other prisoner outside. It was a freezing afternoon, close to dusk, and Sawyer hunched his shoulders as he walked across the car park and climbed into the side door of a tall, white G4S secure transport van. The vehicle was effectively a portable prison: a detachable semi-trailer of individual containment cages bolted to the tractor unit. Another large man, an escort officer in a black G4S gilet with shirt and tie, waited by an open side door at the centre of the semi-trailer. The station uniform and escort officer signed the handover, and the escort officer took the other prisoner inside, then climbed back out and nodded to Sawyer.

He ducked inside, and the officer followed. There were six cages, all empty, apart from the one on the left near the back, which contained the other prisoner, slumped forward on the narrow flip-down seat. It smelt dank and metallic.

The officer put a hand on Sawyer's shoulder. 'First on the right.' Sawyer sidestepped into the cell. 'Face me.' He turned and squeezed out a smile. The officer closed and locked the finely meshed metal door. He opened a square, letterbox-style flap in the centre. Sawyer fed his hands through. The officer unlocked and removed his cuffs, then closed and secured the flap.

Sawyer lowered himself onto the flip-down seat. The officer closed the van side door and stepped into the cab, alongside the driver, who was just out of Sawyer's sight. Both men sat in front of a transparent security screen. The officer looked back and checked on the two prisoners. He nodded, and the van moved off.

They made slow, steady progress. There were no side windows, and Sawyer could only navigate by the view from the windscreen. He guessed they would stick to the gritted roads, but would need to pass through a few minor routes to take the most direct path out of the National Park, up near Hollow Meadows. He closed his eyes, and dropped his head, resting his elbows on his knees.

Around half an hour into the journey, the other prisoner made a grunting noise and Sawyer raised his eyes. He was standing, stretching, puffing out his chest.

He saw Sawyer watching and narrowed his eyes. 'What you do?'

Sawyer smiled. 'I didn't do it.'

The man guffawed and pointed at him. 'You'll fit right in. In prison. That's where all the innocent men go. All the guilty ones are still out there, getting away with it.'

The van lurched to the side, aquaplaning on a patch of ice. The driver corrected it, spinning the wheels.

'These fuckers!' The prisoner raised his voice. The man in the passenger seat looked over his shoulder. 'They're as bad as the coppers, innit? Fucking *worse*.' He smiled, making sure the driver and assistant heard every word. 'At least the coppers are doing proper work. These fuckers are their *little bitches*.' His shoulders heaved as he chugged out a baritone burst of laughter. 'They do this cos they can't get a job on the bins.'

The assistant rapped on the screen. 'Keep it down back there.'

'Fuck you, man. You can't silence me. I know my rights. I'm not under caution here. I'm "in transit", innit? I can say what I want.'

Sawyer sighed and tipped his head back against the van wall. 'Take it easy. Your behaviour will be noted. The judge will take it into account.'

The prisoner sneered at him. 'The fuck do you know so much about it?'

The van picked up speed. Sawyer guessed they would have reached the A57 and turned up into the single-track roads that twisted through the Bradfield dales.

Sawyer smiled. 'I know so much about it because I'm a copper. A Detective Inspector. As for you, you're what we call a "toerag".'

'You *what*?' The prisoner barged forward into the mesh of the cage, gripping it with both hands. The clattering sound alerted the assistant driver, who turned his head again and raised off his seat. 'Sit down back there.'

The van slowed, and the driver said something to the assistant. They turned off, taking a left, and picked up speed again.

'Hey!' The prisoner shouted. 'I object to my fellow prisoner. I do not wish to be transported with a copper. You are under breach of my human rights, innit.'

The assistant driver laughed. 'You can get out and walk if you like, mate. Take you a while, though, in this weather.'

The snow had started again, and the van's wipers swept across the windscreen at double time. Sawyer leaned into the right wall of his cage as they crawled up an incline, then hopped over the brow of a hill and picked up speed again.

The van drifted slightly on a slippery patch, and the driver corrected it.

He heard the driver's voice. 'Pretty bad.'

The assistant looked at him. 'Don't brake too hard.'

Sawyer's stomach lurched as the van fishtailed, and the driver overcorrected, tilting it to the right.

The other prisoner banged on the cage with his fists. 'Did you *hear* me? I demand alternative—'

'Shut the fuck up back there!' Driver's voice.

The assistant turned again, and checked on the two prisoners. Sawyer clocked the emotion in his eyes: irritation, fear?

He turned back to the driver and leaned forward, squinting through the heavy snow. 'Take the next right. Get back down to the main A-road. None of these are gritted.'

'There's a bridge.'

'It's high enough.'

The van jolted to the right, fishtailing again. They were still going too fast.

The assistant looked across to the driver, raised his voice. 'Steer *into* the turn.'

'I know what—'

'We won't get under. It's too low.'

'Easy.'

The brakes squealed.

'Fucking wheels are locked.'

A couple of seconds' silence, as the car aquaplaned again, then jolted, as the right front wheels bumped up onto something rough.

Sawyer dropped to the floor, instinctively staying low.

The other prisoner was thrown against the back of his cage. 'What the fuck?'

Sawyer caught a glimpse through the windscreen: the van headlights shone off the yellow-and-black reinforced rim of a low footbridge, smothered in snow. The van had tilted to the left, on the right kerb. The front-right corner crunched into the rim of the bridge, peeling away the cab roof and tearing into the right side of the semi-trailer. The impact spun Sawyer round, bouncing his left shoulder off the front side of the cage. He tumbled to the floor.

Shouts from the driver. The assistant, ducking down. An almighty roar of splintering glass and collapsing metal.

The brakes unlocked and the tyres screeched as the driver tried to steer away from the point of impact.

And in a second, they were still, and silent. No engine. No headlights. Just the feeble glow of a streetlamp at the near side of the bridge.

Sawyer looked up, checked himself. His shoulder blared with pain, but there were no obvious external injuries.

He looked over at the other prisoner: he was sprawled at the base of his cage, groaning. The assistant driver lolled forward, breathing hard, forehead sunk into the pillow of a dirty-white airbag. Sawyer couldn't see the driver, but he would have caught the worst of the collision from the front-right corner.

Again, he listened to himself. And again, the irritation. The boredom.

He bowed his head, steadying his breathing, wincing at the pain in his shoulder.

Something cold prickled at the back of his neck. He looked up.

The impact had hacked through the corner of the van and semi-trailer, and peeled back the bodywork like a sardine can. Almost half of the right side of the trailer's roof had been scalped, and Sawyer gazed up through the ragged hole to the night sky above, snow falling onto his face.

68

Sawyer got to his feet and felt for a hand-grip in the lateral supports at the side of the cage. He shunted himself up, pushing one foot against the door and the other into the near side wall. The rip in the bodywork had caught a few chunks of concrete from the bridge; he pushed them out and raised his elbow through the hole and planted it out onto the roof. He steeled himself and pushed off his leg, reaching up and out with his other arm. The snow had eased, and he puffed away a few eddying flakes as he hauled himself up, out of the van.

He had to squeeze through a tight gap between the peeled metal and the bridge's reinforced rim, but he managed to crawl out, flat onto the cold. He slid over to the back of the roof and dropped down onto the road behind.

The van had mounted the kerb and rolled up a roadside verge, by a low footbridge that spanned the road. Sawyer scrambled to the top of the verge and looked down on the scene. The van's front-right corner had caught the bridge rim and the bodywork had been torn away, above the cab and partway through the trailer roof. The snow on the road and lower verge sparkled with broken glass.

He slid down to the right side of the van and looked into the smashed driver-side window. Both the driver and assistant were slumped forward into their airbags. The driver lolled back and looked around. No obvious injuries. He squinted at Sawyer, confused, then reached down to his door handle. The van shook as the driver tried to open the buckled door.

Sawyer moved to the back of the van and looked down the road. It was difficult to tell in the dark, but from the featureless sweep of the farmland, and the intended destination in the northern part of Sheffield, he guessed they were somewhere around High Bradfield, with Middlewood Ambulance Station ten minutes away.

Headlights on the road behind. The van crash had partly blocked the single track road beneath the bridge, leaving just enough room to squeeze past. Sawyer stepped out into the road and waved his arms up high, flagging down the car. It slowed and stopped, at a cautious distance from the van, and sat in the road for a few seconds, engine running. Sawyer walked over, and the driver—a middle-aged man in a chunky work jacket—opened the window a few inches.

A second car slowed, much further back along the road. It pulled up, keeping its headlights on.

The man looked up at Sawyer. 'What's happened?'

'Mounted the kerb and hit the bridge. We've got a couple of casualties. Could you help us out?'

The man studied Sawyer for a few seconds. He switched on his full beams to get a better look at the crash. 'Nasty. What's in the van?'

'Nothing. Secure transport. We've just dropped off some supplies down at Buxton. Heading back up to the depot in Worrall.'

The man nodded. 'Anyone hurt? I'm first-aid trained.'

He switched off the engine and stepped out, leaving the lights on. He stood in front of Sawyer and rolled his neck, cracking the muscles.

'I don't think there's anything serious, but we should get an ambulance here.' Sawyer held out a hand. 'I'm Lloyd. The driver.'

The man shook. 'Phil. I'm a mechanic.' He ducked his head and walked over to the van, studying the trailer, assessing the damage. 'You'll need more than an ambulance, mate. This is going nowhere.'

'Could you call the ambulance, though? My phone's out of charge.'

The man turned. 'Sure.' He took a phone out of his inside pocket. 'You're going to need a recovery truck with a winch, too. Hold on... is that G4S? Security?'

Sawyer slipped into the car and inserted the ignition key, lifted from the man's jacket pocket. He closed the door and started the engine. The man looked back, confused. Sawyer floored it, spinning the tyres on the wet road. The man made a move to block Sawyer's exit, but he was forced to jump back as Sawyer sped past, through the gap, under the bridge.

69

Sawyer stuck to the minor roads and farm tracks, taking care through the fresh snow, staying just inside the northeastern border of the National Park. He crossed over the Midhope Reservoir, approaching his father's house from the east. He concealed the car in a clump of trees outside the village and joined a steep walking route, which wound up above the banks of the Langsett Reservoir, into the open fields around the back of the house. It was clear that his father had some kind of security device to give warning of an approach from the dirt track at the front, and he might have installed something similar for visitors around the back. But Harold was scheduled to appear at the art festival that evening, and the car's clock told Sawyer he should have at least an hour's grace before he was due back home.

His jacket was light, and the cold gnawed through to his bones, making him shiver. At the top of the hill, he picked his way through the surrounding fields until he spotted the garage and outbuilding at the back of the house. As he moved closer, through the trees, he could see a light on, somewhere round the back. Sawyer moved closer to the outbuildings and matched his position with the view from the security camera. It was still in place: apparently undisturbed. He wrenched it away, and stuffed the device and cable ties into his pocket.

He moved in, keeping low, and tracked around the side of the house, at the back of the garage. His father's Volvo wasn't parked in its usual spot, but it was impossible to say when he might return.

Sawyer inched around the wall of the garage and peered into the small window on the far wall. It had been covered with something from inside: a tarpaulin or temporary curtain. He looked away, and drove his elbow into the glass, smashing it. He reached in and lifted up the tarpaulin, which hung a few inches below the frame. The burgundy BMW was parked in the centre, taking up most of the floor space.

He closed his eyes, ran through the explanations. His father had been looking out for him, keeping a check on Klein, both. Maybe he had secretly bought Sawyer's version, and wanted to confirm it by monitoring Klein's movements, which just so happened to include Sawyer? But why go to so much trouble to acquire the car from Dr Kelly, and keep it hidden, and hard to monitor?

He unlocked the latch, pushed the window open and wriggled inside. The interior was damp and smelt of rubber and car polish. The garage was tiny, maybe even purpose-built to house the BMW. He side-stepped around the car and looked along the single shelf bolted to the wall at the back: neatly lined-up bottles of oil, wax, screenwash, and a green plastic box, which folded open to reveal a set of hand tools: screwdrivers, wrenches, and a set of Allen keys held together by a coiled metal ring. Sawyer unhooked the keys and opened the ring out into a wavy length of wire. Digging a small pair of cutters out of the toolbox, he snipped the wire into two sections and stuffed them into his pocket. He pushed up off the car and wriggled back outside, through the window.

At the front of the house, the light he'd seen earlier filtered through from the passage connecting his father's reading room to the studio. No noise or movement from inside. If the dogs were in, they would hear him and recognise his scent, but he wanted to stay undetected for as long as possible.

He took out the pieces of wire and got to work on the front door lock. It was fiddly work, with little light, and the wire was thicker than his usual tools, and barely fit for purpose. But it only took a few minutes to feel out the tension and pick his way his way through the pins. He released the lock and opened the door. Rufus and Cain bounded through from the open door to Harold's reading room and greeted him, pawing and licking. He petted them and walked through into the reading room. The dogs followed, and when they were safely at the far side of the room, he slipped back out into the connecting passage and closed the door behind him, feeling guilty.

Sawyer walked through into the studio and turned on a small table lamp by the sofa. He took a breath and looked around. Harold's work in progress had been removed, probably for the festival, and the room seemed bare without the easel in the centre providing a splash of colour above the chevron pattern tiles. He checked the side door that led through to the outhouse. It was locked, by a new-looking mechanism with a small keyhole: too thin for the strips of wire he'd used on the front door.

He looked around: blank canvases stacked in the corner, colour-coded shelving, multi-drawered cabinet on the red shelf. As usual, everything was neatly arranged, in its rightful place. Nothing extraneous. A row of paint pots had been set along the yellow shelf, with their swatch labels ordered in colour intensity from left to right: oily black to gleaming white. Sawyer leaned in; the swatches on the right had been ordered into a perfect horizontal line, with the edges of the coloured strips all uniformly aligned. But the third pot along—a deep red, the slightest shade up from black—hadn't quite been turned to fit; the right-hand edge of the swatch strip was the only one that didn't connect to its neighbour.

Sawyer picked up the pot; it was surprisingly light. Something rattled inside as he shook it. He prised off the lid and took out a small key. He hurried over to the connecting door and tried the key in the slot; it fitted perfectly, and he unlocked the door and walked through into the outbuilding.

He turned on the overhead light. The building had a stone floor, and contained a single room, around twenty-feet square. The walls were lined with metal shelving units, full of marked boxes with various supplies and accessories. Sawyer browsed through a notepad on the top of a dresser in the corner. It contained a scrupulous audit of materials and household maintenance: groceries, electricals, large and small repairs, building work. The detail was extraordinary, and disturbing. Why would a man who lived alone bother to maintain such a meticulous record?

Next, Sawyer examined the steel door in the far wall. It had been fitted with a heavy duty lock connected to an electronic security system with a wall panel that showed a vivid red light. He tried the handle, but the door was so solidly fitted, it barely rattled in the frame as he tugged.

He looked back, and up, to the small, frosted glass window set high into the roof. From the mini camera footage, he had seen Harold enter and turn on the light. Then, after a pause, a shadow had passed over the high window. He pulled a short stepladder out from between the shelving and climbed up to the window. A slim, protective wallet had been wedged into a groove in the brickwork. He took it, and climbed back down.

The wallet contained a blank white card with a magnetic strip. Sawyer held it against the reader on the panel by the steel door. The red light turned to green. He tried the handle again, and eased the door open.

70

Stone steps, leading down. Pale light. Sawyer closed the heavy door behind him and crept forward, crouching, trying to get an early glimpse around the corner to the room below. He paused at the bottom and took in his surroundings.

The cellar had been converted into a clean, uncluttered basement: tiled floor, white walls. A dark-wood bookcase covered the far wall, below a tiny frosted skylight window in the corner. A television had been mounted to the facing wall, looking down on an armchair with a bed extension. A small table and chair sat in the second corner, before a compact kitchen: cupboard above, work surface with sink and kettle, mini fridge below.

The ceiling was dotted with dim spotlights. A fan with three slim wooden blades sat in the centre, spinning at a low speed, barely disturbing the mulchy air.

Sawyer looked around to the near side corner, next to the stairs. A compact treadmill had been pushed against the wall, beside a lidless steel toilet bowl and flushing handle. A ventilation grid was fitted high in the wall above the toilet bowl.

He moved away from the stairs and stepped around to the side of the sofa bed. An elderly man lay asleep in the chair, turned onto his right side, head resting against the back cushion. He was in his seventies, with a scruffy wisp of white hair and a thick moustache. A book lay flat over his hip, and his knees were raised up and pressed together, protruding from a thick blanket, which had gathered at the foot of the chair. Music played from the slim headphones around the man's neck: light and classical, low volume.

Sawyer reached down and eased the blanket away. The man's legs were restrained by sturdy ankle cuffs. The connecting links were clasped to a long, thin chain, which was locked to a thick, U-shaped anchor, riveted to a metal panel in the floor. Presumably, the length of chain would allow the man to walk around the room but would not reach the top of the staircase.

The man stirred in his sleep and shifted position, bringing his left arm up around his neck. He wore a chunky rotary wristwatch.

Sawyer leaned in, studying the man's face: thin lips; flat, pock-marked nose. His hair was completely white, but his eyebrows were still hirsute, with a faint tint of grey. The moustache hair was slightly darker, almost black in places.

He opened his eyes.

Deep-set. Dark irises, almost black.

Sawyer startled, and took a step backwards.

The man raised himself up on his elbow, clearly shocked by his visitor's presence, but too frail to move quickly. He squinted up at Sawyer, breathing heavily. His head dropped and he drew in a deep, shuddering sigh.

When he raised his head again, a darkness had seeped in behind his eyes. His stare stabbed into Sawyer. It was the man in his sketch; the man in his nightmare.

The man who had murdered his mother.

William Caldwell sat upright in the chair, keeping his black eyes on Sawyer. He reached a hand up to his forehead and wiped away a film of sweat. 'Hello.' The voice was cracked but resonant. 'And you are...?'

'Jake Sawyer. Detective Inspector.'

Caldwell reached down by the side of the chair and took a sip from a glass of water. 'How long have you been looking for me?'

Sawyer broke his gaze, eyes darting around the room. 'All my life.'

Caldwell sat forward, rattling his chains. 'I wish I could say I was sorry. But I'm not. The years have washed that out of me.'

A scalding rush in Sawyer's stomach; a swell of nausea. He took another step back from Caldwell and steadied himself on the bookcase.

When he looked up again, Caldwell had perched on the edge of the sofa, staring up at him, arms folded. Sawyer got a flash of the black-and-white photograph: Sheila, on the beach; the shorter man beside her, grinning.

'I saw your wife.'

'Oh, yes? Shacked up again, I expect. Probably days after I went missing. Is she still at the Padley house?'

Sawyer ignored him. He steadied the breathing, rode the nausea.

Caldwell rubbed at his eyes. 'You've done well. Not an easy thing, to dig up a dead man.' He angled his head. 'And you didn't follow Jess's advice, did you? You looked back.'

Sawyer shuddered at the sound of his mother's name. He walked to the sink by the toilet bowl, ran the tap, splashed water on his face. 'How long have you been here?'

Caldwell turned, watching him. 'As a guest of your

father? Many years. He doesn't let me see news or newspapers.' He nodded to the television. 'Just DVDs from time to time, as a treat. But I have my watch, and I mark the days.'

'Why not just kill yourself? Lots of ways to do it down here.'

Caldwell sneered. 'Like I said, I'm already dead, to the world. I stay alive for my captor's pleasure.' The sneer stretched into a foul little smile.

Sawyer nodded. 'He won't kill you, and you won't kill yourself.'

'As Plato said, "Life must be lived as play". And there's always hope. Hope that he'll keel over one day when he's down here, or when he takes me out for exercise. He thinks he's made my life a living hell. But he's also a prisoner, of his choice of revenge.'

Sawyer walked over to the kitchen and opened the cupboard. Bread. A few packets. He pulled open the drawer. White plastic knives, forks, spoons.

'Looking for a hammer, Jake?'

A clunking sound from above. Both Sawyer and Caldwell looked up and fell silent.

The heavy door at the top of the stairs squeaked as it opened.

Footsteps, descending the stairs.

Sawyer braced.

His father peered around the corner, from the bottom of the staircase. He turned his back, and reached up to a high shelf near the bookcase, setting down something heavy, then turned to face them both.

Harold Sawyer wore a fitted suit and red tie beneath a winter overcoat, and a neutral expression. Down here, Sawyer was struck by his father's size, his bulk. Caldwell was a waif in comparison.

Harold met his son's gaze. 'Chilly out there.' He moved into the light, with his back to the bookcase. 'I heard your voice, son.'

Caldwell sneered again. 'Shall we run a little debrief, Harold? All good coppers together.'

'Is this your "commensurate justice", Dad? He took a life, so you take his away?'

Harold dropped his head. 'There are fates worse than death.'

Sawyer nodded. 'I thought only God forgives, or condemns.'

Caldwell released a quiet laugh. 'That's how he's justified this. Don't you see? It's the ultimate God complex. Every villain is the hero in his own mind.'

Harold looked up, at Sawyer. 'He was my old boss at the station. They had an affair, Jake.'

Caldwell waved a hand, enjoying himself. 'I had *sex* with her. Your dead mum.'

Harold kept eye contact with Sawyer. 'He does this sometimes. Tries to goad me into finishing him off. Ignore him. Focus on me.'

'I wouldn't have sex with her now, obviously. I'm in a bad way, but I'm not that desperate.'

Harold continued. 'We had problems. They met at a function. I think Jess realised it was a mistake. She got close to Klein. *He* couldn't stand that.'

Sawyer moved nearer to Caldwell. 'He saw Klein put the number on his door. He offered Casey a way out of the burglary charge if he'd break in to Klein's, steal him the hammer.'

Caldwell stood up, chains clanking. 'And then I murdered the silly bitch,' he doubled over, laughing, 'and the teacher did my time.' He held out his arms, stepped closer to Sawyer. 'Come on, Jake. That was clever. You've got to *give it to me.*' He drew eye contact, and lingered there for a while, glaring at Sawyer, arms by his sides. 'Listen. If you're still angry at my hitting you and your brother, and killing your yappy little dog...' He dropped his head into a childlike pose of mock contrition: bottom lip pouting out. 'I'm truly *sorry*. But look at you now. Detective Inspector! I can't help but feel partially responsible for your success.'

Sawyer turned back to Harold; his voice was flat. 'And you've had him here, for over twenty years?'

Caldwell slumped back onto the chair.

Harold nodded, stepped forward. 'I kept him in the house for a while. Did all this work myself about ten years ago. The security door, soundproof cladding, air purifier. He's got the treadmill, but I exercise him outside from time to time, if he's been civil.'

Caldwell scoffed. 'Another treat. I go for a walk, on a lead. Like a fucking *dog*.' He leaned forward and buried himself beneath the blanket, holding it over his head.

'I fitted a motion sensor to the front gate that notifies me if anyone walks or drives in that way. Gives me plenty of time to get him back inside.'

Sawyer kept focus on Harold. 'And what about Dr Kelly?'

Harold dropped his gaze. 'He helped. Gave me faith.'

'He knew about all this?'

'There were a few medical issues over the years. Wear and tear. He helped with drugs, treatment. We spoke about justice, and how society's retribution for some crimes just isn't enough. The removal of freedom, but dignity retained. A dignity denied to the victims.'

Sawyer stepped towards his father. 'And you would have been happy to deny *me* that freedom? By framing me for Klein's death?'

Harold sighed, pushed his fingers through his lank grey hair. 'I had to do it. Because of this. To stop *this*.'

Caldwell edged the blanket away from his face. 'Klein's dead? That poor fucking bastard. Nothing but collateral. Framed once, thirty years inside, then killed by the man whose wife he was accused of murdering.'

A noise on the stairs.

Harold backpedalled to the bottom of the staircase, looked up to the door, and raised his arms in submission.

Austin Fletcher stepped down into the room, holding a Glock handgun with a silenced barrel in his right hand. He looked round, at Sawyer and Caldwell, and spoke to Harold. 'Corner.' He inclined the gun towards the far edge of the bookcase.

Harold backed away and stood beneath the skylight, arms up.

Caldwell sat up. 'And who's this?'

Fletcher stepped back, keeping his eyes on Sawyer and the gun trained on Harold.

Sawyer took a step away from Caldwell, towards Fletcher. 'This really isn't a good time.'

Fletcher aimed the gun at Sawyer. 'Upstairs.'

Caldwell looked from Harold to Sawyer. 'Are we all going?'

Fletcher swept a layer of melting snow from his bomber jacket, then pointed at Sawyer. 'One.'

Sawyer shook his head, and locked his steely green eyes into Fletcher's pinhole death stare. 'Do it here.'

Fletcher gave a barely perceptible shake of the head and nodded to the staircase. 'Now.'

Sawyer nodded. 'Too messy?'

Fletcher shifted the gun to the left, aiming at Harold again. He jerked it up to the ceiling. 'Now, or he's first.'

Sawyer smiled, glanced at Harold. 'This is Mr Fletcher.

Dale's action man. Dale doesn't like me.' He let his head sink down and leaned forward, towards Fletcher, keeping his eyes on him. The motion could have been mistaken for a bow. 'Mr Fletcher tried to kill me recently. Tried to make it look like suicide. Seems like he's gone to Plan B.'

Fletcher jabbed the gun towards Sawyer. His forehead seemed suddenly red, flushed. '*Up. Stairs.*'

Sawyer raised his arms slowly, fingertips in line with his neck, and walked towards the foot of the staircase.

Fletcher stepped back, making room. He levelled the gun at Sawyer's head. 'Turn.'

Sawyer pivoted, arms up, facing the bottom step.

Fletcher checked on Harold—still in the corner—and Caldwell, sitting in the chair, watching. He moved closer to Sawyer and aimed the gun at the back of his head. 'Move.'

Sawyer stood there, lowering his hands down to chest level.

Gun in right hand. Pointed at head. Too risky.

He glanced over at Harold.

Wait.

The room was quiet. A faint ticking from the ventilation grid. Fletcher's quickened breathing, close behind. He would be used to getting his way, used to being obeyed without question.

Sawyer turned his head to the side, then forward. Fletcher still had the gun pointed up at the back of his head. 'Your last kill was impressive. A guy with learning difficulties. A heroin addict. Tied to his bed. What do you do for an encore? Old ladies?'

No response from Fletcher.

Gun in right hand.

'So, is this your style with the able bodied? Doing it from behind? I think you're only in it for the view, following me up the stairs.'

Fletcher stepped in and prodded Sawyer in the back with the gun. '*Now.*'

Sawyer side-stepped to the left and spun, anticlockwise, facing Fletcher. The movement was instant, but flowing and natural, replicating the form on the wooden man dummy. As he turned, Sawyer hooked the crook of his left arm under Fletcher's outstretched forearm and trapped it at the elbow, locking Fletcher's wrist against Sawyer's left shoulder. The gun now pointed away from Sawyer, back at the stairs behind.

Sawyer held the trap firm. He lifted his right heel and pivoted his hip, planting an explosive hook punch into Fletcher's jaw. Fletcher's head snapped to the right and Sawyer drove his right knee up into his chest, keeping Fletcher's gun arm fixed and his wrist locked.

He braced for a desperate gunshot, hoped for the sound of the gun hitting the floor. But Fletcher held his ground, grappling and twisting to make an angle for a left hook. He pulled his gun arm, trying to get it free, but Sawyer held firm and headbutted him, square on the bridge of his nose.

Blood splashed into Sawyer's eyes. He blinked it away and drove a *biu jee* finger strike towards Fletcher's eyes. But his opponent jerked back his head, dodging the attack.

Fletcher was a beast: solid and strong, almost immovable. Sawyer turned his back on him, keeping his gun arm trapped. He chopped at the hand holding the gun —once, twice—then pivoted again, this time connecting an elbow into the side of Fletcher's head. At last, the blow staggered him, and Sawyer wrenched away the gun. He scrambled back from Fletcher and raised the weapon, but Fletcher's reaction was instant: he slapped at Sawyer's wrist with what looked like an open-handed *pak sao* block, firm enough to dislodge the gun and send it flying across the room, by the side of the treadmill.

Fletcher's face was now bright red with fury. He shoulder-charged Sawyer, and they crashed into the wall at the side of the stairs. Fletcher closed his hands around Sawyer's neck, finding the Adam's apple with his thumb. Sawyer pulled away, trying to roll him and regain the upper hand. But Fletcher was too strong, and pumped with rage. Up close, Sawyer caught his odour: sour and unwashed; pungent with the unmistakable scent of exotic tobacco. Fletcher pushed his face close to Sawyer's. He grimaced, and the blood from his broken nose streamed down over his bared teeth.

Sawyer spluttered as Fletcher tightened his grip. He was trying to finish the fight by choking Sawyer unconscious. Sawyer kicked out his legs, but Fletcher widened his stance, stabilising his grip. Sawyer wrenched left and right, and gained an inch of leverage, to pivot his right hip and deliver another elbow strike to the side of Fletcher's head. It didn't carry much power, but it was enough to force him back and break his hold.

Fletcher staggered into Caldwell's chair, just about staying upright. Caldwell fell to the floor and Fletcher gripped the backrest of the heavy armchair with both hands. He let out a primal roar, and spun the chair across the room towards Sawyer. But his aim was poor, and it skimmed off to the side, smashing into the table by the kitchen.

Harold ducked his head, wincing at the impact. He shifted over to the high shelf by the bookcase. Fletcher caught the movement, but turned to focus on Sawyer, who had made it to the gun on the floor by the treadmill. Fletcher rushed him, just as Sawyer turned and fired.

Muzzle flash, muted gunshot. The bullet buried itself in the ceiling, releasing a shower of plaster. Fletcher thundered forward, barrelling into Sawyer, and the two fell to the floor, by the metal toilet bowl.

Fletcher managed to get Sawyer onto his front. He closed his beefy fingers around the back of his neck and slammed his head down into the blunt edge of the toilet bowl. Sawyer grunted with the impact and wriggled free, blood flowing from a cut on his forehead.

He turned, fired another shot.

This time, the bullet skimmed close to Fletcher's head, tearing through his left ear, splashing Caldwell with blood. Fletcher roared again, and held his hand to the side of his face. He backed away from Sawyer and slowly raised his head. His eyes flared, feral and sightless. Blood dripped through his fingers, down into his panting mouth.

He took a step forward.

Sawyer raised the gun, aiming at Fletcher's head. He swiped the blood from his forehead, out of his eyes. 'Third time lucky.'

Fletcher smiled and bared his bloodied teeth. He took another step toward Sawyer. 'Empty.'

Sawyer backed away, into the wall. He glanced at the gun, aimed it up, ready to fire and check.

But from behind Fletcher: the deep double-chunk of a shotgun being cocked.

'Okay.' It was Harold, standing over by the high shelf, holding the double barrelled shotgun he'd set down on entering. He aimed the gun at Fletcher. 'Over to the stairs, hands up high.'

Fletcher sighed, and raised his arms. He edged over to the foot of the staircase.

Caldwell shifted across and sat with his back to the wall beneath the television. 'This is the best entertainment I've had in years.'

They stood there in silence: Harold with the shotgun trained on Fletcher, Sawyer with the Glock still raised.

A sharp buzzing sound from something in Harold's pocket. Three bursts, a pause, three bursts.

He wedged the shotgun handle into his shoulder and reached the other hand into his pocket, silencing the noise.

Fletcher bolted, up the stairs.

Sawyer twitched, ready to follow, but looked back at Caldwell, and his father. 'Is that the motion sensor?'

Harold nodded. 'How did you get here?'

'They charged me. Transport hit a bridge in the snow. I got out.'

'My God, Jake.'

Sawyer furrowed his brow. 'I took a car. They'll have tracked it.'

'*Charged* you?' Caldwell leaned forward.

Rufus and Cain from the house above, barking.

A crash from upstairs.

'Armed police!'

Harold backed into the corner, under the skylight. He lowered the shotgun. Sawyer stuffed the Glock into his back pocket.

Boots, thundering down the stairs. Two heavyset AFOs jumped down into the room. They wore armoured vests and carried semi-automatic carbines. One held his gun on Harold, while the other covered Caldwell and Sawyer.

DCI Ivan Keating ducked down behind them and stepped into the room. He was a lordly figure for such a lowly setting: full uniform, cap, polished insignia. Keating surveyed the scene: the blood, the shotgun. His eyes widened at the sight of the chained man, reeling in recognition. 'Put down the weapon, Harold. What's the situation here?'

Harold turned the shotgun towards Caldwell. Keating

raised a hand, placating the AFOs. 'Yes. This is your ex-DCI. William Caldwell.' Keating stared at the hunched figure, chained to the floor. 'He had an affair with my wife, thirty long years ago. And then he killed her because she wanted to end it.'

Sawyer caught Keating's eye. He dabbed at the blood on his forehead.

Harold continued. 'I looked into Jessica's murder, five years after Klein was convicted. The hammer, dropped too close to the murder site. I knew there must have been evidence manipulation, and when I discovered that Caldwell personally interviewed Owen Casey, I checked the burglary victim statement and saw Casey mentioned but the rest of the paperwork buried.'

Caldwell tipped back his head and screwed up his face, braced for the end.

Harold looked at Sawyer. 'I tried to visit Klein. I wanted to ask him about the hammer, where it was kept, if he saw anyone suspicious. But he wouldn't see me. So I started a freelance investigation into my commanding officer. Turns out he had a thing for spooking out sex workers. Driving them to remote locations, getting rough, laughing at their threats to call the police. He got wind of my snooping and threatened me, saying his rank would protect him, and that I'd never be able to prove anything. He said that you and Michael would be next if I didn't back off. And so I bought this place, and set up the garage. I lured him to a meeting here...'

Caldwell groaned. 'And the rest is history.'

'I tried so many things to numb the agony. And when I put it all together, it just wasn't enough. To end his life as payment for Jessica's. They just weren't *equivalent*.'

Sawyer dropped his head. 'And so you created this. A

living hell. A purgatory. A prison for a man both alive and legally dead.'

Harold closed his eyes, trying to hold off the tears. But they trickled down the lines in his cheeks, glinting in the light. 'And in the end, my desire for revenge took away my humanity, my soul. I was willing to sacrifice my son's freedom to keep his mother's killer captive.'

Keating took a couple of steps toward Harold. 'Did you kill Klein?'

Harold opened his eyes. 'Yes.' He focused on Sawyer again. 'I used a hammer to imply that it was retribution for Jessica's murder. I left Jake's sweet wrapper at Klein's flat, hoping it would be enough to stop his investigation. I just wanted it all to end.' He kept the shotgun aimed at Caldwell, and wiped away the tears with the inside of his arm. 'After Jess had gone, it almost broke me. But I kept going. I'd lost the love of my life, but I tried to find a new love, with my faith. I raised my boys. I shouldered the sympathy. I was a vision of upstanding masculinity, outward dignity. And all the while I splattered my pain onto those canvases, sold it to restaurants, hotels.'

Keating held out a hand. 'Harold. You still have plenty to offer, plenty to care about. Jake, Michael. You have a talent. The paintings aren't just pain. That's the love you had for Jess, guiding your hand. She left you in body, but she's still with you in spirit.' Harold stared at him, then back at Sawyer, Caldwell. Keating nodded. 'You're going to prison, Harold. But the judge will consider your age, the circumstances. I'll make sure your conditions are decent, and you can continue to paint, follow your faith. Isn't that what matters now?'

Sawyer raised his head. 'Then all shall be well, Dad. Like Mum used to say.'

Harold's face crumpled, the sobs overtaking him. He

lowered the shotgun a few inches, then raised it back up, keeping his aim on Caldwell. Keating raised his hand to the AFOs again.

Caldwell smiled. 'Do you know what Jess said to me on the day I killed her? She said, "*Why*?" What a stupid fucking question. She'd told me she wanted it all to stop, that I was too "controlling".' He raised his eyes to Sawyer, then back to Harold. 'I didn't kill her because I was humiliated that she wanted to end the affair. I was more angry with myself, believing that for once in my life I'd found a woman who knew what was good for her, who *wasn't* stupid.'

Sawyer stepped out, between Harold and Caldwell, in the line of fire. 'It's better that he lives, Dad. Better that he continues to suffer, rots away.' He took a step forward, towards Harold, towards the shotgun.

Harold fixed his reddened eyes on Sawyer; he was barely aware, deep in a dark trance. 'I'm sorry, son. I love you.' He glanced at Keating. 'Will you look after my lads, Ivan?'

'Harold. Of course. Give me the gun now. Let's all get out of here safe.'

Sawyer kept walking, blocking Harold's aim on Caldwell.

Harold raised the shotgun, aiming at Sawyer's head. Sawyer froze. 'Jake. That thing Mum used to say.' He caught himself, struggled to hold his voice steady. 'It was a kind of vision, from a Christian mystic, who said that there would always be sin, evil, but "all shall be well." You can't fall into despair at the state of the world. "There is nothing in darkness that will not be disclosed. Nothing concealed that will not be brought to light." Luke. 8:17. Take care of your brother, Jake.' He closed his eyes. 'I'm sorry.' He turned the shotgun and dug the end of the barrels into the flesh beneath his chin.

'*No!*' Sawyer dived forward.

Harold gripped the shotgun barrel with one hand, squeezed the trigger with the other.

The shot was a thunderclap; its echo rolled around the basement room. Sawyer's hearing cut out, replaced by a continuous shrill ringing.

Harold's body dropped to the floor. Sawyer looked up, to the skylight, plastered with blood and bone. A central smear of bright and dark red. Surrounding patches of white flesh, grey hair.

He stared at the spray, measuring his breathing, alone with the ringing in his ears.

He turned. Keating had lowered his gaze, but the AFOs both stared over at Harold's body.

Sawyer dived towards the nearest AFO, and delivered a sharp elbow strike to the side of his head. He fell awkwardly against the wall, and Sawyer wrenched the carbine out of his grip. He moved in on Caldwell, and dug the gun barrel deep into his cheek.

The second AFO raised his gun at Sawyer's back.

Keating held up a hand. '*Stand down*!'

Sawyer stood over Caldwell, breathing hard, eyes fixed. Caldwell raised his gaze and curled up the corner of his thin lips. 'Jess told you to run. She told you not to look back. But you've been brave. She'd be proud of you. That's *her* finger on the trigger, isn't it? What would she do now?'

Sawyer screwed his eyes closed. The blood from his forehead ran across his brow and trickled down his cheek.

The raised hammer. Metal on bone. The animal screams.

A hand on his shoulder. Keating.

He opened his eyes.

'William Caldwell.' Keating's voice, muffled. 'I'm arresting you for the murder of Jessica Mary Sawyer...'

Sawyer lowered the gun barrel. He turned and handed the carbine to the nearest AFO.

Keating. Still talking, from somewhere deep and dista.

'You do not have to say anything...'

Sawyer walked to the staircase.

'But, it may harm your defence...'

He pushed up onto the bottom step and started to climb, not looking back.

71

FOUR WEEKS LATER

Maggie Spark spooned two lumps of white sugar into Sawyer's mug. He lifted his eyes from their table in the centre of the Nut Tree.

Maggie paused. 'What?'

'You went for the white. Not the brown.'

She stirred the tea. 'There's no such thing as wholemeal sugar.'

He gave a weak smile, and dropped his eyes to the table again. 'How's Mia doing?'

Maggie sighed. 'Fewer nightmares. Still jumpy in public places. She's been writing to Joshua, the boy.'

Sawyer looked up. 'Writing?'

'Well, WhatsApping. Snapchatting. She wants to go and visit, but... I don't know.'

'I'll come and see you once it's settled, talk to her. I'm good with ex-abductees.' He daubed a hunk of jam over his teacake. 'My father left me the house in Midhope. It's too far out for me, though. I'm selling it to a rental agency. He had a decent estate, too. Half to me, half to Michael, with a percentage ringfenced for his speech therapy.'

'How was the funeral?'

'Low key. Tried to get him in with my mum but couldn't make it work with the church. He's up at another place in Sheffield, near to his old family home.' Sawyer used light caresses of his knife to spread the jam out to the edges of the teacake. 'Michael came. Some of Dad's family, a few colleagues, one or two arty types. It was like a weird dream. I wasn't really aware of much.'

She nodded, watching him. 'What about the dogs? Are you keeping them?'

'Couldn't do it. Not fair on Bruce. I took them to the Manchester Dog Trust centre. The handler sent me some pics last week. They went to a decent-looking family near Bury. Big house. I insisted they stay together.'

Maggie sat back. 'How about you?'

He shrugged. 'What about me?'

'Your defences are up.'

'Can you blame me?' He crunched into the teacake.

'Are you still seeing Alex?'

Sawyer nodded. 'Haven't been for a while. Appointment this afternoon.'

'You should take a holiday, Jake. Get away. Winter sun.'

He laughed. 'Canaries are nice this time of year.'

'I'm serious. Recharge. Get a bit of distance.'

'Maybe. I need to get back to work. Now I'm official again.'

She sipped at a herbal tea. 'Will you be involved in the case against Caldwell?'

'Don't think so. Guilty plea. The CCRC overturned Klein's conviction for my mother's murder. Caldwell pled guilty, but they're making it watertight in case he gets obstructive over my father's actions.'

Maggie dunked the teabag, pondering. She leaned forward and kept her voice low. 'Mia told me what happened, during the raid on the Briggs place.' Sawyer raised his eyebrows. 'She said that Joshua attacked the woman, the mother, and she had to fend him off, along with the other girl. And she said that someone in a mask came in, before the police, and handcuffed the mother.'

Sawyer shrugged. 'Special ops?'

She nodded. 'Mia's very sharp. Observant. She said this man had green eyes.'

'Lots of people have green eyes.'

'And that he sounded a bit like you.'

He angled his head. 'Lots of people sound like me.'

Maggie smiled. 'I liked the piece in *The Mirror*. The 'hero cop' who hunted down his mother's killer. Dean Logan must have been paid well for that. National exposure.'

He took a slurp of tea. 'I thought I might as well tell the story myself.'

'Have you sold the film rights?'

He laughed. 'I think it's more of a BBC thriller. Mini-series. Sunday evenings.'

'You might find things more difficult, now you're a celebrity.'

'Hardly a "celebrity".' He shrugged. 'I'll retreat to Lanzarote for a couple of weeks. If that doesn't work, I can always fake my own death.'

She reached over, rested a hand on his. 'I prefer you alive.'

72

Alex Goldman hobbled into the consulting room and flopped down in the mauve armchair, groaning and rubbing at her thigh. Sawyer tore his eyes away from the waterfall photograph. 'You okay?'

She winced. 'Just age. *Time.*' She looked up and straightened out her beige roll-neck. 'Or, to put it another way... Varicose veins. I'm not even *seventy*, Jake.'

'Is that only a seventy-plus condition, then?'

She poured the tea. 'Well, I thought it was somewhere around there, yes. I have to wear compression stockings for a few months.' She looked up, smiled. 'Anyway, I'll get an early night, since it's the shortest day.'

'Winter solstice. It gives me a rare sense of optimism.'

'Darkest before dawn, eh?'

'I like the feeling that it can't get any worse now. Can't get any darker.'

Alex handed Sawyer a cup of tea, with two Bourbon biscuits wedged into the saucer. 'Do you believe that?'

He scoffed. 'I'm working on it. The Stoics would say that there's no such thing as good or bad events. Dark or light. It's all about how you choose to respond. That's all you can control.'

'Events. Plenty of those in the last few weeks for you. Is this a change of outlook? Moving forward with a sense of hope? Optimism?'

Sawyer snapped one of the biscuits in two. 'I wouldn't go that far. Hope isn't necessarily a good thing. Optimism is unrealistic. I'm trying to scale everything down to the moment in hand, then build out from there. Have you seen the film *La Haine*?' She shook her head. 'French. Disaffected youth, police brutality in the Parisian suburbs. It opens with the lead character telling a story about a guy who falls off a skyscraper.' Sawyer munched on the biscuit. 'As he passes each floor, he keeps telling himself, "So far, so good".' He reached into his pocket and pulled out the *Memento Mori* medallion. 'My father gave me this.' He handed it to her.

Alex turned the medallion round in her fingers, read the inscription. 'You could leave life right now.'

'My father couldn't let go of the past, and live life in the present. In the end, his desire for revenge destroyed him.'

Alex handed back the medallion. 'In the recording we made, reliving the day of your mother's murder, you said that she told you to run, to not look back. Are you familiar with the myth of Orpheus and Eurydice?'

He nodded. 'Vaguely.'

Alex leaned forward. 'Eurydice was Orpheus's love, and when she died he was so stricken with grief, he travelled to the underworld to bring her back. He charmed the god of the underworld, Hades, who said he could reclaim Eurydice, but only if he didn't look at her on the way back to the overworld.'

Sawyer smiled. 'And Eurydice followed Orpheus out of the underworld, but she was behind him, and he couldn't resist looking back to check she was there. And so she was sent back to the underworld.'

'Yes. You see something similar in the Bible, where Lot's wife was told not to look back as she escaped the destruction of the city of Sodom. But she did, and was turned into a pillar of salt.'

Sawyer dunked the other half of the biscuit. 'I get it. Move forward. Don't live in the past. You can't go back, you can't change things there.'

'No, of course. But we have to push on with the reliving therapy. You lost two things on the day your mother was murdered. Your childhood innocence, and your mother herself, your protector. Try to see the therapy as going down into the underworld, to retrieve the pain of all that loss, and turn it into an adult memory. Something you can process and *live with*.'

'There's still unfinished business, from the past.'

'I know. You need to revisit the brain scans, look into the possibility that your issues with fear are physiological, not psychological.' She took a sip of tea. 'And you have to help your brother to get better. But, yes. Focus on moving forward, away from the pain that sits behind you. You can't retrieve your mother from the afterlife, but the reliving will help you to reframe her memory, and see her as a huge influence that you carry around with you. You can use that influence to build your own growth.'

Sawyer looked back up at the waterfall, suspended in time. 'Sounds like hard work.'

———

He left Alex's, and drove back up to Buxton, to Enterprise Rentals. Howard shook his hand and led him through to a desk near the entrance to the parking garage. They signed off the Corsa's return, and Sawyer completed the paperwork for a new orange-and-black Mini Convertible.

Howard handed over the keys and took a folder out of his top drawer. 'What would you say if I tried you on the extended cover again?'

'You mean as in, "I told you so"?'

'Obviously, I don't know what happened to the old vehicle. None of my business. But I don't get the feeling it was planned.'

Sawyer smiled at his cheek. 'I'll be more careful this time.'

———

He parked up outside Tideswell Church, in the shadow of the fourteenth-century 'cathedral of the Peak'. He took out the polaroid of his mother, smiling at the garden gate. For the first time in years, he felt a twinge of distance, as if the scene had lost some of its weight.

He held the photo up to the window. The image was fading, growing less distinct; the light that defined its outlines whiting out, draining away. It was not his mother; it was just her image. Just one moment in her brief, beautiful, complex time; a random capture of something unrepeatable, immutable. His mother was in bad shape in the present day, but she was eternally bright and alive, there by the gate on that morning. He slotted the photograph back into his wallet: a chunk of the past that had at last broken off and begun to drift away.

Sawyer trudged between the low stone pillars and stood at his mother's gravesite. He set down a bunch of white lilies and stared at the gravestone: a custom commission he'd installed to replace the previous dour default. A rose-

white oblong headstone, with plain black capital lettering
and a quote from his favourite poet, Philip Larkin.

JESSICA MARY SAWYER
1954-1988

WHAT WILL SURVIVE OF US IS LOVE

73

'*I'm pressing the button*. To tackle. It's not doing what I tell it to do.'

Sawyer held up the PlayStation controller and demonstrated by tapping his thumb against the X-button.

Luka sat back on the sofa and smiled. 'That's the pressure control. It's to contain the player with the ball. If you want to stop them going forward, you have to press the O-button.'

Sawyer shook his head. 'I'm doing that, as well.'

'Your timing is bad, then.' Luka turned back to the screen. 'Like real-life football. You have to judge the best time to try and take the ball.'

Eva poked her head around the sitting room door. 'Luka. Upstairs now. Too late for this.'

On cue, the final whistle blew on their game of FIFA. Luka sprang to his feet and strode to the door.

Sawyer slumped. 'I lost to the controls.'

Luka smiled. 'Like you said, nothing good is easy. Keep practising.' He slipped through the door and charged up the stairs.

'I'll be up in ten minutes,' Eva called after him and

joined Sawyer on the sofa. She was dressed for home: yellow-and-black hoodie, faded blue jeans, her long black hair loose. She set down a tumbler of Coke on the coffee table and draped her legs over Sawyer's knees, sipping from a glass of red wine. 'He's better. Good report from the counsellor. Teachers are happier.'

Sawyer powered off the PlayStation and took a slug of Coke. 'Dale?'

'Hasn't been around.'

'Probably explains why Luka is brighter.'

'I guess so. Spoke to him on the phone the other day. There's an investigation into what went wrong with the raid on his club. The guy who was killed.'

'Shaun.'

'Yeah. He's accusing the police. Says it was all botched and they shot him. There's an inquiry or something.'

Sawyer nodded. 'The operation will be reviewed internally. Chain of command. Orders given. Shots fired. It'll take time. And a parallel investigation into what happened to Shaun.'

'Will he be charged?'

'I doubt it. They'll look into ballistics. I'd guess that Shaun was killed with a sidearm similar to the ones issued to police.'

Eva frowned. 'Really? You think that Dale had someone kill Shaun so he can accuse the police of doing it?'

He nodded. 'A lot depends on how closely they can match the bullet to the actual murder weapon. They'll need a suspect gun to fire and make a match. It can be as accurate as fingerprints. If they can connect it to Dale, he'll be in a bad place.'

Eva gazed into the blank TV screen and sipped her wine. 'And how about you, Jake? What kind of a place are you in?'

'In what sense?'

'After what happened with your dad.'

He sloshed the Coke around the glass. 'Now all the admin has calmed down, it's beginning to sink in. He did so much for me and my brother. I have to help Mike more, now we're the only ones left.'

Eva leaned forward, rested a hand on his wrist. 'It's what your dad would want.'

He glanced at her. 'I know. He told me that himself.'

She set down her drink and took out her phone. 'Let me show you something. You'll like this.'

'Is it the meme of the guy getting run over by the ice-cream van?'

She looked up. 'What?'

He shook his head. 'You've taken off your wedding ring.'

Eva ignored him. She turned her phone horizontally. 'Dale did an interview for a local Manchester current affairs show. He was billed as an ex-con who had "turned his life around".'

She played a video. The footage showed Dale talking to an off-camera interviewer. He had scrubbed up: good suit; new, heavy-framed glasses.

'...we have a chronic drugs problem in this country, and it's too simplistic to tackle it by declaring a "war on drugs". That hasn't worked in the US, and it won't work here. It just drives the problem underground and brings more drugs into the system. We need to see it as more than just a crime. It's a social issue. The dealers, the kids, they're not being groomed by gang bosses. They've already been groomed, by society, austerity measures, denied opportunities...'* The interviewer tried to comment, but Dale waved a hand and continued. *Jason, some of these kids can earn up to five hundred quid a week. It's a social problem and we have to tackle the root* *causes at the highest level. It has to be overseen by someone who understands the system from both sides.'*

Sawyer sat back, waved the phone away. 'Jesus Christ. He's going to run for Manchester mayor next year, isn't he?'

'He's mentioned that before, yes.'

'That can't happen.'

Eva edged towards him on the sofa. He caught her perfume: rich, sensual.

'I have someone on the inside who might be able to help stop him. He's also got the problem of the enquiry.'

Eva ran her hand over Sawyer's arm, up onto his shoulder. She leaned in and kissed him. 'Let me get things settled with Luka. Then we are going to stop talking shop and start enjoying our evening.'

She got up and walked out. Sawyer listened to her footsteps fade as she climbed the stairs.

He took out his phone and browsed the BBC News app. The lead national story caught his eye.

NOTTINGHAM MURDER: WOMAN'S BODY FOUND IN PARK

The body of a missing West Bridgford woman has been found in woodland at Wollaton Park in Nottingham. Laura Bertrand, 34, was reported missing after she did not turn up for work on Monday.

He closed the app, took another sip of Coke, and launched a basic mobile game where he moved a cannon left and right to shoot bouncing balls that divided as they were destroyed. He settled himself, focusing on the game, blasting his virtual enemies, resisting the urge to re-open the news app.

In the street outside the house, a silver Ford Fiesta

pulled up on the corner and idled for a few seconds. A large male figure, dressed in black, climbed out of the driver's side and walked across the road, towards Eva's house. He crouched at the back of Sawyer's new orange-and-black Mini, and attached something to the inside of the rear wheel guard. He stood up, walked back to his car, and drove away.

BOOK FOUR IN THE JAKE SAWYER SERIES

JAKE SAWYER is feeling the heat. Returning to duty after an enforced psychological break, he's called in to investigate the murder of a young woman found near one of the Peak's key beauty spots.

Sawyer is intrigued by the unusual mix of extreme violence and decorative presentation, and when the death is connected to the earlier killings of three other local women, he joins a task force of regional detectives in a hunt for the man the media are calling The New Ripper.

As the UK sweats in a record-breaking heatwave, a fifth woman goes missing, and the killer contacts the police, personally challenging Sawyer to catch him before he claims her as his next victim.

https://books2read.com/prayforrain

JOIN MY MAILING LIST

I occasionally send an email newsletter with details on forthcoming releases and anything else I think my readers might care about.

Sign up and I'll send you **a Jake Sawyer prequel novella**.

THE LONG DARK is set in the summer before the events of CREEPY CRAWLY. It's FREE and totally exclusive to mailing list subscribers.

Go here to get the book:
http://andrewlowewriter.com/longdark

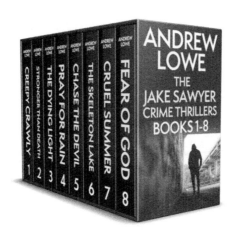

BOOKS 1-8 IN THE **JAKE SAWYER** SERIES

AVAILABLE IN EBOOK and PAPERBACK

READ NOW WITH **KINDLE UNLIMITED**

https://books2read.com/sawyerboxset4

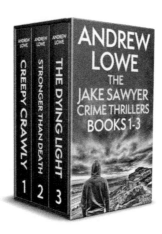

BOOKS 1-3 IN THE **JAKE SAWYER** SERIES

AVAILABLE IN EBOOK and PAPERBACK

READ NOW WITH **KINDLE UNLIMITED**

https://books2read.com/sawyerboxset1

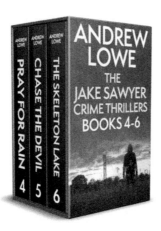

BOOKS 4-6 IN THE **JAKE SAWYER** SERIES

AVAILABLE IN EBOOK and PAPERBACK

READ NOW WITH **KINDLE UNLIMITED**

https://books2read.com/sawyerboxset2

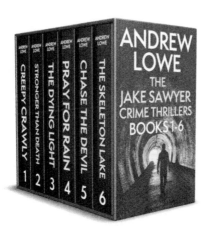

BOOKS 1-6 IN THE **JAKE SAWYER** SERIES

AVAILABLE IN EBOOK and PAPERBACK

READ NOW WITH **KINDLE UNLIMITED**

https://books2read.com/sawyerboxset3

ACKNOWLEDGMENTS

I couldn't have completed this book without the help of Detective Constable Ralph King, who consulted on UK police procedure and, with his advice on officers' legal constraints, helped to make Sawyer's outlaw predicament plausible and, I hope, compelling.

Thanks to the remarkable Bessel van der Kolk for his encyclopaedic book on trauma, *The Body Keeps The Score*; **Bryony Sutherland** for peerless editing and creative steerage; and **Book Cover Shop** for cover and website design.

Special thanks to **Julia**, for listening to me go on about it all.

Andrew Lowe. London, 2019

PLEASE LEAVE A REVIEW

If you enjoyed **THE DYING LIGHT**, please take a couple
of minutes to leave a review or rating on the book's
Amazon page.

Honest reviews of my books help bring them to the
attention of others, and connecting with readers is the
number one thing that keeps me writing.

Go here to leave your review:
https://books2read.com/thedyinglight

THE JAKE SAWYER SERIES

THE LONG DARK
CREEPY CRAWLY
STRONGER THAN DEATH
THE DYING LIGHT
PRAY FOR RAIN
CHASE THE DEVIL
THE SKELETON LAKE
CRUEL SUMMER
FEAR OF GOD
TENDER IS THE NORTH
BLOOD NEVER SLEEPS (2025)

BOOKS 1-3 BOX SET
BOOKS 4-6 BOX SET
BOOKS 1-6 BOX SET
BOOKS 1-8 BOX SET

GLOSSARY

ACT – Acceptance and Commitment Therapy. A form of psychotherapy that uses acceptance and mindfulness strategies along with commitment to behaviour change.

AFO – Authorised Firearms Officer. A UK police officer who has received training, and is authorised to carry and use firearms.

ALF – Animal Liberation Front. A political and social resistance movement that promotes non-violent direct action in protest against incidents of animal cruelty.

ANPR – Automatic Number Plate Recognition. A camera technology for automatically reading vehicle number plates.

AWOL – Absent without leave. Acronym.

BSE – Bovine Spongiform Encephalopahy. Colloquially known as 'mad cow disease'. A neurodegenerative condition in cattle.

CCRC – Criminal Cases Review Commission. Independent body which investigates suspected miscarriages of justice in England, Wales and NI.

CI – Confidential Informant. An individual who passes information to the police on guarantee of anonymity.

CBT – Cognitive Behaviour Therapy. A form of psychotherapy based on principles from behavioural and cognitive psychology.

CID – Criminal Investigation Department. The branch of the UK police whose officers operate in plainclothes and specialise in serious crime.

COD – Cause of Death. Police acronym.

CPS – Crown Prosecution Service. The principle public agency for conducting criminal prosecutions in England and Wales.

CROP – Covert Rural Observation Post. A camouflaged surveillance operation, mostly used to detect or monitor criminal activity in rural areas.

CSI – Crime Scene Investigator. A professional responsible for collecting, cataloguing and preserving physical evidence from crime scenes.

CSO – Community Support Officer. Uniformed but non-warranted member of police staff in England & Wales. The role has limited police powers. Also known as PCSO.

D&D – Drunk & Disorderly. Minor public order offence in the UK (revised to 'Drunk and disorderly in a public place' in 2017).

Dibble – Manchester/Northern English slang. Police.

EMDR – Eye Movement Desensitisation and Reprocessing. An interactive psychotherapy technique used to relieve psychological stress, particularly trauma and post-traumatic stress disorder.

ETD – Estimated Time of Death. Police acronym.

FLO – Family Liaison Officer. A specially trained officer or police employee who provides emotional support to the families of crime victims and gathers evidence and information to assist the police enquiry.

FOA – First Officer Attending. The first officer to arrive at a crime scene.

FSI – Forensic Science Investigator. An employee of the Scientific Services Unit, usually deployed at a crime scene to gather forensic evidence.

GIS – General Intelligence Service (Egypt). Government agency responsible for national security intelligence, both domestically and internationally.

GMCA – Greater Manchester Combined Authority. Local government institution serving the ten metropolitan boroughs of the Greater Manchester area of the UK.

GMP – Greater Manchester Police. Territorial police force responsible for law enforcement within the county of Greater Manchester in North West England.

GPR – Ground Penetrating Radar. A non-intrusive geophysical method of surveying the sub-surface. Often used by police to investigate suspected buried remains.

HOLMES – Home Office Large Major Enquiry System. An IT database system used by UK police forces for the investigation of major incidents.

H&C – Hostage & Crisis Negotiator. Specially trained law enforcement officer or professional skilled in negotiation techniques to resolve high-stress situations such as hostage crises.

IED – Improvised Explosive Device. A bomb constructed and deployed in ways outside of conventional military standards.

IDENT1 – The UK's central national database for holding, searching and comparing biometric information on those who come into contact with the police as detainees after arrest.

IMSI – International Mobile Subscriber Identity. A number sent by a mobile device that uniquely identifies the user of a cellular network.

IOPC – Independent Office for Police Conduct.

Oversees the police complaints system in England and Wales.

ISC – Intelligence and Security Committee of Parliament. The committee of the UK Parliament responsible for oversight of the UK Intelligence Community.

MCT – Metacognitive Therapy. A form of psychotherapy focused on modifying beliefs that perpetuate states of worry, rumination and attention fixation.

MIT – Murder/Major Investigation Team. A specialised squad of detectives who investigate cases of murder, manslaughter, and attempted murder.

Misper – missing person. Police slang.

NCA – National Crime Agency. A UK law enforcement organisation. Sometimes dubbed the 'British FBI', the NCA fights organised crime that spans regional and international borders.

NCB – National Central Bureau. An agency within an INTERPOL member country that links its national law enforcement with similar agencies in other countries.

NDNAD – National DNA Database. Administered by the Home Office in the UK.

NHS – National Health Service. Umbrella term for the three publicly funded healthcare systems of the UK (NHS England, NHS Scotland, NHS Wales).

NHSBT – NHS Blood and Transplant. A division of the UK National Health Service, dedicated to blood, organ and tissue donation.

OCG – Organised Crime Group. A structured group of individuals who work together to engage in illegal activities.

OP – Observation Point. The officer/observer locations in a surveillance operation.

Osman Warning – An alert of a death threat or high risk of murder issued by UK police, usually when there is intelligence of the threat but an arrest can't yet be carried out or justified.

PACE – Police and Criminal Evidence Act. An act of the UK Parliament which instituted a legislative framework for the powers of police officers in England and Wales.

PAVA – Pelargonic Acid Vanillylamide. Key component in an incapacitant spray dispensed from a handheld canister. Causes eye closure and severe pain.

PAYG – Pay As You Go. A mobile phone handset with no contract or commitment. Often referred to as a 'burner' due to its disposable nature.

PM – Post Mortem. Police acronym.

PNC – Police National Computer. A database which allows law enforcement organisations across the UK to share intelligence on criminals.

PPE – Personal Protective Equipment designed to protect users against health or safety risks at work.

Presser – Press conference or media event.

RIPA – Regulation of Investigatory Powers Act. UK Act of Parliament which regulates the powers of public bodies to carry out surveillance and investigation. Introduced to take account of technological change such as the grown of the internet and data encryption.

SAP scale. A five-point scale, devised by the Sentencing Advisory Panel in the UK, to rate the severity of indecent images of children.

SIO – Senior Investigating Officer. The detective who heads an enquiry and is ultimately responsible for personnel management and tactical decisions.

SOCO – Scene of Crime Officer. Specialist forensic investigator who works with law enforcement agencies to collect and analyse evidence from crime scenes.

SSU – Scientific Services Unit. A police support team which collects and examines forensic evidence at the scene of a crime.

Tac-Med – Tactical Medic. Specially trained medical professional who provides advanced medical care and support during high-risk law enforcement operations.

TOD – Time of Death. Police acronym.

TRiM – Trauma Risk Management. Trauma-focused peer support system designed to assess and support employees who have experienced a traumatic, or potentially traumatic, event.

Urbex – urban exploration. Enthusiasts share images of man-made structures, usually abandoned buildings or hidden components of the man-made environment.

VPU – Vulnerable Prisoner Unit. The section of a UK prison which houses inmates who would be at risk of attack if kept in the mainstream prison population.

A WOMAN TO DIE FOR

AN EX WHO WOULD KILL TO GET HER BACK

Sam Bartley is living well. He's running his own personal trainer business, making progress in therapy, and he's planning to propose to his girlfriend, Amy.

When he sees a strange message on Amy's phone, Sam copies the number and sends an anonymous threat. But the sender replies, and Sam is sucked into a dangerous confrontation that will expose his steady, reliable life as a horrifying lie.

https://books2read.com/dontyouwantme

**WHAT IF THE HOLIDAY OF YOUR DREAMS
TURNED INTO YOUR WORST NIGHTMARE?**

Joel Pearce is an average suburban family man looking to shake up his routine. With four close friends, he travels to a remote tropical paradise for a 'desert island survival experience': three weeks of indulgence and self-discovery.

But after their supplies disappear and they lose contact with the mainland, the rookie castaways start to suspect that the island is far from deserted.

https://books2read.com/savages

ABOUT THE AUTHOR

Andrew Lowe was born in the north of England. He has written for *The Guardian* and *Sunday Times*, and contributed to numerous books and magazines on films, music, TV, videogames, sex and shin splints.

He lives in the south of England, where he writes, edits other people's writing, and shepherds his two young sons down the path of righteousness.

His online home is andrewlowewriter.com

Follow him via the social media links below.

Email him at andrew@andrewlowewriter.com

For Andrew's editing and writing coach services, email him at andylowe99@gmail.com

facebook.com/andrewlowewriter

x.com/andylowe99

instagram.com/andylowe99

tiktok.com/@andrewlowewriter

bookbub.com/profile/andrew-lowe

amazon.com/stores/Andrew-Lowe/author/B00UAJGZZU

Printed in Great Britain
by Amazon

42475667R00219